The MYSTERY
of the BLACK
DIAMOND

A Jake Jezreel Adventure

DONALD CRAIG MILLER

WESTBOW
PRESS®
A DIVISION OF THOMAS NELSON
& ZONDERVAN

WestBow Press books may be ordered through booksellers or by contacting:

WestBow Press
A Division of Thomas Nelson & Zondervan
1663 Liberty Drive
Bloomington, IN 47403
www.westbowpress.com
844-714-3454

Scripture taken from the New King James Version®. Copyright © 1982 by Thomas Nelson. Used by permission. All rights reserved.

ISBN: 978-1-6642-3351-5 (sc)
ISBN: 978-1-6642-3352-2 (hc)
ISBN: 978-1-6642-3350-8 (e)

Library of Congress Control Number: 2021909244

Print information available on the last page.

WestBow Press rev. date: 05/11/2021

Dedicated to
my dad
John "Shorty" Miller

And to
my mother
Eleanor Elizabeth Miller
for leading me gently
into the presence
of the Lord

CONTENTS

INTRODUCTION

In my first book, in 2018, I introduced the world to a unique, one-of-a-kind first century individual. His name is Jake Jezreel. Why is Jake Jezreel unique? Jake has a one-of-a-kind profession. Jake is a first century private detective. There is no one like him during those Bible times. And like all private detectives after him, he makes his living by having clients hire him and then investigate their various dilemmas. In the first century, there is lots to investigate. Sometimes, it's the political winds that blow the worst trouble in Jake's direction.

My 2018 book was titled, <u>Trailing the Bloody Footprints</u>. In the book, Jake takes on a case of overwhelming magnitude. Jake is hired by a group of Pharisees to investigate a dangerous radical in Galilee, name Jesus of Nazareth. The Pharisees fear Jesus and his power. They demand that their detective dig up any kind of dirt they can use to accuse Jesus, so they can destroy the Nazarene. In the course of his investigation, Jake is swept up into the swirling onslaught by the religious leaders to crush Jesus. The investigation comes to an explosive pinnacle when a major conflict erupts between Jesus and the Pharisees when the Nazarene heals a man on the Sabbath. From that point on, the enraged Pharisees immediately begin plotting how they can murder Jesus. Jake realizes he has been dragged into this vicious vendetta against Jesus. The detective now faces a life and death quandary. How can Jake proceed with his investigation, knowing that Jesus is innocent of any crimes? What can he do to protect this good and godly man he has been hired to destroy? Will the relationship that Jake has developed with Jesus alter anything in the detective's life? In the end, events pivot in a way Jake could never have imagined.

In 2020, Jake Jezreel's adventures continued when I told his story during the great Christian persecution of the first century church. The 2020 book is titled, <u>Terror Outside the Door (The Persecution of</u>

Jesus Christ). The early church enjoyed wonderful joy and peace until the religious leaders brought down the hammer of persecution upon Christians. Jake finds himself caught in the onslaught and on the run. The heavy persecution was crashing in all around him. Jake tries to keep one jump ahead of the devouring enemy. But how long could he avoid the clutches of the vicious mob chasing after him? Terror Outside the Door (The Persecution of Jesus Christ) is a dramatization of the early chapters of the Book of Acts. During this ordeal, Jake has to deal with Pontius Pilate, imprisonment for his faith, and the snarling Saul of Tarsus. All throughout these troubles the presence of Christ never leaves. The assurance of Jesus' guiding love lingers close by in Jake's heart.

In this present book, The Mystery of the Black Diamond, Jake Jezreel again is drawn into a mysterious first century case involving a rare black jewel. The case rather simply begins with a request by James, the head of the Jerusalem church, to locate a missing fellow minister in the church. Soon, the investigation diverts Jake into a more elaborate course, that of trailing after a jewel known as The Black Diamond. Detective Jake Jezreel had never heard of The Black Diamond. And yet this mysterious object will plunge him into an adventurous investigation like he had never experienced before. What kind of power did this lustrous, gorgeous diamond have over men? How could it make men hate and attack each other to own it? Will Jake be drawn into the powerful, magnetic influence this black beauty possesses?

I've introduced Jake Jezreel to help us all come to know Jesus Christ in a more intimate way. Jake's experience mirrors every one of us who believe. He is someone, like each of us, who is trying to live for the Lord every day of his life. Hopefully, as you read this adventure that Jake experiences, you will gain an affinity with the detective. By putting yourself in his place, you will experience the new life that Jesus gives to each and every one of us who have surrendered our lives to Christ. Knowing and loving Jesus is the great endeavor of life. May God bless you as you read this book in helping you know and love Jesus Christ more and more affectionately.

Donald Craig Miller

1
THE DISTINGUISHED CLIENT

The private detective business can be a tough racket. It's like hot and cold. Night and day. There are some days when clients' paperwork is so scarce you can hear the wind whistling through the empty "IN" and "OUT" baskets. Some days a detective wishes there were three of him.

Private detective Jake Jezreel was in one of those empty lulls in client activity. He hadn't had a living, breathing prospect in several weeks. Cash flow was dwindling. Rock bottom was fast approaching. The bank account empty warning light had begun to blink on and off. Jake expected it to illuminate in a steady red glare any day now. The detective would be thrilled just to get any warm body to cross his office threshold.

From the time he was a little kid, Jake knew he wanted to be a private detective. His dad, Jedidiah Jezreel, had been a famous private eye back in the days of King Herod the Great. Jed Jezreel could solve a case, even when everybody else had given up. He had pioneered the art of investigative work. He was the original hardboiled detective. "It is simple, my dear son," he would often remind Jake. "You know my methods. Data. You must have data. Always look for the details in a case. The smallest, inconsequential details often will be the most significant. Always be honest, if you want to be a good detective. And always have integrity." And Jake had always tried to live up to this high standard which his famous dad had instilled in him. It wasn't always easy.

Times were rough for all Christians in first century Jerusalem. The Jewish religious leaders had "blackballed" any person who named the name of Jesus Christ as their Savior and Lord. Christians were labeled as a cult and ostracized from Jewish society. No Jewish citizen would hire a person who claimed to be a Christian. And since Jake was a Christian, well, it's easy to see why the bills weren't getting paid.

So, Jake sat here in his brown leather chair behind his brown oak desk wondering if he should do some in-person soliciting of his church friends. Or just do some advertising around town. Or place an ad in the Jerusalem Times newspaper. Something.

Jake's pretty wife, Hannah, had been very understanding about their situation. She knew what she was getting into when she married the detective four years earlier. Hannah had been Jake's secretary for three years before their marriage. She knew the tough times. The detective business is a tough business. Still yet, Jake longed to be able to provide a more stable life for her. She deserved it. More financial security. Nicer home. Nicer clothes. Even so, she never complained.

Jake heaved a heavy sigh and stood up. His five foot nine frame stretched out into a slender, erect individual. His jet black hair, parted on the left side, hung in a closely cropped cut. Stroking his carefully trimmed black beard, Jake gazed out his second story office window over the beautiful yellow topaz-tinged capital city of Jerusalem. "Surely in this great city there is some poor soul who frantically needs my help," he mused. "Someone in deep trouble, all confused and covered in desperation."

At that moment, Jake just happened to look down from his second story vantage point. He noticed one of the prominent leaders of the Christian movement in Jerusalem enter his office building at the main entrance from the street below. He thought for a moment. This church leader must have business in this building. And then again, maybe he is coming to see Jake. If that was the case, Jake decided to make himself look official … and busy. Especially busy.

Jake sat down in his brown leather chair behind his brown oak desk and straightened the name placard across from him. It read, "Jake Jezreel Private Detective". He took the few yellowed parchment papers on his desktop and spread them out a little.

"There," the detective muttered to himself. "Even though I'm not that busy, maybe I can make it look like I am."

In a moment, Jake could hear a conversation arise in his secretary's outer office. After a short time and a quick discussion, the detective heard a knock on his office door. Jake's perky wife and secretary, Hannah Jezreel, opened the door slightly and poked her head in. Hannah was a petite suntanned young woman, whose beige tunic rippled as she slipped inside Jake's office. She closed the door and leaned back against it. There was something wrong. Her soft brown eyes seemed to project distress for some reason. Her normally breezy smile was replaced by tightened lips.

Hannah stood and just looked at the detective.

"Well?" Jake said, raising his thick black eyebrows in a questioning expression.

"Pastor James, the head of the Christian church here in Jerusalem is waiting in my office," Hannah stated with an unusual depth in her voice.

"Well, shoo him in, sweetheart. Pastor James doesn't come to this part of town much. His business must be rather important."

"It is," Hannah stated solemnly.

Jake frowned, as he stared at Hannah. He sensed the tone in her blunt declaration meant trouble.

Hannah turned and opened Jake's office door and announced, "Detective Jezreel will see you now, sir." She swept her hand through the air toward Jake. Pastor James, the stately gentleman, head of the Jerusalem church strode through the doorway. "Thank you, ma'am," he said pleasantly and then proceeded on into the office, with a fixed gaze at Jake.

Hannah retreated back into her office and closed Jake's office door.

The detective stood up and respectfully greeted the honored church leader, advancing toward him.

"Pleased to meet you, sir," Jake said in a gracious tone. He reached out his slim right hand and James returned the gesture with a firm handshake.

"Pleasure to meet you, too," James said. "I have seen you in church but there are usually so many people in attendance, I have not had the pleasure of meeting you before now."

"Well, I'm glad we could correct that situation. Please be seated." Jake motioned toward the wooden armchair beside his desk.

"Thank you," James said quietly, as he sat down.

Pastor James was a very distinguished looking gentleman with strong features. He was about 33 years old with a kind face yet firmness etched in his expression. His robes were not gaudy but rather simple and humble in appearance, a tannish-gray color. His brown hair and short beard were closely cropped and he carried himself with a confident integrity. As he sat in the chair, he looked around Jake's office and commented, "I've never been in your office before but it looks very nice."

"I have the persecution of the church to thank for the nice facilities that you see all around you," Jake smiled.

James looked a little puzzled. "I don't understand."

Jake smiled even bigger, as he sank down into his leather chair. "During the persecution of the church, Saul's thugs raided my office and tore it completely apart. Reduced it to shambles. Everything was ransacked and destroyed. You couldn't even recognize the place. Well, I fell into the good graces of Governor Pilate when I had previously performed some detective work for Him. Due to having Pilate's favor, the governor forced the religious leaders to pay for the repairs to my office out of their own pockets. And he demanded that the repairs be the best, top of the line. So, what you see here is the best of everything, at the expense of the religious leaders!"

"That is amazing," James laughed. "The Lord does provide for His children, even though sometimes it seems to be in very strange ways."

"Sir, I want you to know it is an honor to meet you," Jake beamed, as he leaned forward in his chair toward his visitor. "I know you are the half-brother of our Lord Jesus. It must be very humbling to be part of Jesus' earthly family and the earthly brother of our Lord."

"Yes, having grown up with Jesus, it took me some time to figure out my brother's true identity," James stated frankly. "I must admit I was a little slow. At one point I thought – actually our whole family thought Jesus had gone mad. In fact, our family was so convinced that Jesus was out of His mind, we even pursued Him to Capernaum to take charge of Him and bring Him home. We were just too close to Jesus to see His true divine nature. Sort of like not being able to see the forest due to being too close to the trees."

Jake smiled at James' confession. "I was fortunate enough to meet your brother in the middle of His earthly ministry. His every action, His every word displayed His divine personality."

James paused and smiled. "Yes, Jesus spoke about you as a trusted friend," he said. "And that is precisely why I am here today. It is upon my brother's recommendation of you that I have come today to ask for your help."

"Upon Jesus' recommendation!" Jake exclaimed in shock. "When did Jesus tell you about me?"

"It was after Jesus' resurrection, during the forty days before He ascended back into heaven," James said with a glow on his face. "Jesus spent much time with the twelve and with His disciples explaining the future of the Christian church. This is the time when Jesus mentioned you."

"Well, now I really am intrigued," the detective stated, as he stroked his chin with his thumb and forefinger. "How can I be of assistance?"

James took a deep breath and leaned forward. He placed his elbows on the arms of his chair, with his fingertips together. A grave expression swept over his face.

"One of my dearest and most trusted assistants has disappeared." James' words rolled out from the back of his throat in a note of bewilderment. He looked at Jake with a baffled stare. "He just disappeared a few days ago. Abruptly. He never said a word to anyone. And he never told me good-bye. That part hurt a little. He was a very trusted assistant. Actually, I depended on him a lot for helping me in ministry. You could say he was my right-hand man. A trustworthy fellow servant for Christ."

Jake cocked his head to be sure he heard James' words correctly. "Disappeared. Without a trace?"

"Yes, he left all his belongings behind in his dwelling and just vanished."

"Alright, let's get some facts down on paper." Jake pulled out a fresh piece of parchment from the desk drawer. "Okay, first of all, what is this assistant's name?"

"His name is Alexander. He became a believer in Christ about a year ago. He immediately caught on fire for the Lord. He couldn't get enough Bible study. He was always at our scripture studies, asking important questions. Probing questions. And he grew rapidly in his spiritual maturity. And along with his maturity, Alexander threw himself totally into the ministry of helping people. He truly enjoyed ministering to people, whether it was helping me administratively or searching out some needy soul to provide food or clothing to."

"How long ago did Alexander disappear?" Jake asked looking down as he scribbled some notes on the parchment.

"It was three days ago."

"Three days!" Jake looked up from his writing. "Excuse me, sir, but a lot can change in three days."

"Yes, I've been waiting – hoping for his return."

"How did Alexander become such an important part of your ministry? He has only been a Christian for a year. He must have risen quickly in your estimation to prove himself to be so trustworthy?"

"Yes, he was a ball of fire!" James stated with a glow of admiration on his face. "But Alexander matured quickly. He was radically saved. Jesus radically changed him almost in a moment's time. From one minute being a criminal to the next minute forsaking all of his former friends and activities to chase after Christ!" James stood up, bowed his head slightly and began rubbing his forehead with the fingertips of both hands. "I just can't imagine where he's gone."

"Maybe the more important question is 'why' he's gone."

James's head jerked up from his bowed posture. "What do you mean?"

"What kind of crowd did Alexander run with before he surrendered his life to Jesus?" Jake probed.

"I really don't know all the details," James said as he eased back down into the armchair. "I know he was saved from a life among criminals. He immediately gave up his life of crime and never looked back."

"I see," Jake stated, scribbling down more notes. "Do you think Alexander may be in any kind of danger?"

James looked at Jake blankly. Slowly, quietly the word, "Danger?" rolled off of his lips.

"Yes, it is possible some of his old buddies may have wormed their way back into his life," Jake stated, looking up from his note taking. "That's what I meant when I asked 'why' Alexander may have disappeared."

"Danger? Now, I'm starting to get concerned," James said. "I hadn't given it a thought that maybe some of Alexander's old, evil friends may have somehow entangled him in their snare of the old life. Do you think they could make him go back to a life of crime?" James laid his palms on the desk top and thoughtfully tapped his fingertips. "How could we ever find out if that's true?"

"That's where I come in," Jake smiled. "That is my job. And I've got an advantage over anyone else who might try to investigate this case. I've got the Holy Spirit to guide me in my work."

"That is very encouraging. So, you will try to find Alexander?" James asked with heightened hope in his voice.

"I shouldn't have any trouble with it. I'll make a few contacts here in Jerusalem and I can probably turn up his whereabouts in short order. If he's fallen in with his old evil crowd, I'll try to persuade him to leave them. If he doesn't want to leave them, well, I'll find a way to convince him. Can you describe Alexander to me?"

"Well, he is young, about twenty-one. Tall, about six feet tall, perhaps a little taller. Dark, suntanned features. Black hair. Very intelligent. He has a smooth, deep voice. And he speaks with a Galilean accent. He grew up in Capernaum in Galilee but has lived here in Jerusalem for several years."

Jake scribbled more notes. Without looking up he asked, "What type of build does he have?"

"Very muscular. Quite athletic. Broad shouldered. A very well put together man. Some might call him strikingly handsome."

"Okay, are there any other features that would help me identify Alexander?"

"No. I wish I could give you more information."

"Do you know where he lived in the city?"

"I know he lived down in the ghetto on Kidron Street at one time," James said. "But he has been living with me ever since he became a Christian."

"Tell me the details about how you discovered Alexander was missing."

James looked down at the floor and rubbed his chin whiskers thoughtfully. He heaved a sigh and began. "I had just gotten home from my day of ministry," James said looking back up at Jake. "Alexander lives in a second story upper room attached to my home. The upper room can be accessed by a set of stairs that lead up the side of our dwelling. I have allowed Alexander to live in this upper room to give him a place of safety from his old life. That was to help him break all his associations from his past. When he surrendered to Christ, Alexander was very enthusiastic in finding a place of service in the church. So new to the faith was Alexander, I decided to keep him close to me. So, I let him minister alongside me every day. I let him learn the different aspects of how to help people in need and how to present the Gospel to those people who did not know Jesus."

"Was Alexander ministering with you the day he disappeared?" Jake asked.

"He was in the morning. But during the day a little servant boy stopped him in the street and gave him a note. That was when Alexander's countenance changed."

"His countenance changed. How so?"

"He suddenly got a grim expression on his face and he asked if he could be excused for a few minutes to tend to some other business."

"Did you see the message in the note?"

"No, Alexander quickly folded the note back up and stuck it in the pouch on his belt."

"What happened then?"

"I gave him permission to tend to his business and he hurriedly left me and my other ministers and disappeared around a corner. He finally rejoined me at my home that evening. We had supper together. I asked him if there was a problem that had arisen from the note he had received. He said that there was no problem, he had just had to meet someone to straighten out a misunderstanding. We had a short prayer time after supper and then we bid each other good night. He ascended the stairs to his apartment on the second story and that was the last I have seen of Alexander. That was three days ago."

"Three days is a long time for a disappearance. Why haven't you come to me sooner. So much evidence can be lost in three days."

"I know I should have come to you sooner. I lived every day in the hope that Alexander would show up. When he didn't come back to my residence after three days, I finally decided that someone with a better eye than myself needed to take a look into this situation."

"Have you talked to anyone around the neighborhood where you live?

"Yes, I have. I have talked to all the neighbors. So, have a large number of the members of our church. We have turned up nothing. Alexander has just dropped out of sight."

"Can you tell me any more about Alexander's former life and old acquaintances?"

"I don't know much about his old life. Like I said, he used to live on Kidron Street. It's a very dangerous place and a treacherous hideout for outlaws."

"Yeah, I know about Kidron Street. So, we don't know if he was an outlaw or what kind of crimes he might have committed in the past?"

"No, I concerned myself more with helping him grow spiritually and learn how to better love the Lord Jesus. I didn't delve into his past. I mainly pointed him into the future."

"I'm going to need to see Alexander's room. Could you show it to me? Maybe there might be some clues still intact that will help in this investigation.

"Yes, I can do that. So, you will take the case?" James asked hopefully

"Yes, I will," the detective said with a grin. "This information will give me a good start and seeing Alexander's room will help me tie it all together."

"Thank you so very much. About your fee …" James started to say, when Jake interrupted.

"We can discuss my fee later, sir," the detective stated.

"No, Brother Jezreel, I insist," James stated firmly. "You've got to earn your living and I know times are tough for all Christians financially."

Jake smiled in resignation. "Alright, I charge one denarius a day plus expenses."

"Are you sure that is enough? James asked. "It seems like a rather low fee."

"That's my special rate for Christian brothers," the detective smiled.

"Fair enough"

"Now, let's go ahead and look at Alexander's room," Jake said, standing up. "Before we leave I need to talk with my secretary for a moment. If you'll just wait in the outer office, I'll be right with you."

Pastor James stood up, gratefully holding out his hand to Jake. "Thank you so very much for helping me. This visit with you has been greatly encouraging."

"I'm glad I could provide a ray of hope in this situation," Jake smiled. He followed James to his door to the outer office. "I'll only be a minute with my secretary and then we can be on our way," he told James as he opened the door.

Pastor James exited the office and Jake signaled for Hannah to come over to him so they could talk.

As Hannah approached her husband, her head was slightly bowed and her lips pressed tightly together.

"You already know what's going on, don't you" Jake stated in a low voice. That fact obviously reflected from the look on her face.

"Yes, when Pastor James first came into my office, he told me the problem he came to see you about."

Together they stepped back into Jake's office. "This one smells like trouble," Jake said quietly to his wife. He put his arms around her in a cuddling embrace. He tried to hide the hardness in his face but she could sense the stress in her husband's voice and the tightness in his body.

"What do you think might have happened to Alexander?" Hannah quizzed.

"Well, I don't believe for one minute that he just bolted and ran away," Jake stated matter-of-factly. "He sounds like a genuine believer in Christ who for the last year has been relishing in his newfound Christian life. No, I think we are dealing with something far more sinister then first meets the eye."

Hannah looked up at her husband. "I know you and I know you'll figure it out," she encouraged.

"This may be a tough nut to crack. Alexander has been missing for three days. The trail may have gone cold by now."

"And I know that nose of yours," she smiled. "The bloodhound in you can sniff out even cold, frozen trouble."

"You know, honey, there won't be much money in this case," Jake stated, looking into his wife's pretty brown eyes. "I just can't charge Pastor James our regular fee. I just wouldn't feel right about that. I charged him half price."

"I know," Hannah said. "You'll be helping our church. I get it. I'll just tighten our budget and simply stretch out our supper plans by adding more water to the soup."

2

EVIDENCE

Pastor James led Jake up the outside stairs of his home residence, leading to Alexander's upper room apartment. As they climbed the gray stone stairway, the detective noticed a small, red bloodstain on the side stone railing.

Jake stopped James by touching his arm. "Have you noticed this tiny bloodstain before, sir?"

"Mister Jezreel, I have not," James stated with surprise. "I must have overlooked it before when I came up to check on Alexander's whereabouts."

"It's very small but it looks like someone scraped themselves on the stones. Notice how the blood is smeared. Do you have any idea how that blood could have gotten there?"

"No, I have no idea. I hardly ever come up these steps. The only time recently that I have climbed these steps was when I came to check on Alexander."

"Interesting," Jake said and started climbing the stairs again.

When the pair reached the top landing, they started to enter the door to Alexander's room. Jake noticed several gouges in the wood of the door around the handle and lock.

"Does the lock on the door still work?

"Yes, it does. Here I'll show you." James pulled a key from his belt and turned it in the lock.

"That is very intriguing," Jake said. "The gouges in the door indicate that someone tried to jimmy the lock or pry open the door. Since the lock is still intact, it would appear that this person was unsuccessful in forcing the door open."

Jake pushed open the door. Alexander's room lay before them. As the two men stepped into the chamber, the detective's gaze swept over the entire apartment. The room was small. About twenty by twenty. The walls were covered in tan plaster. They were bare except for a single hook. A brown, broadcloth outer cloak hung on the hook. The apartment was dark with only one window over to the left. A chair next to the bed lay on its side.

"Have you touched anything in the room?"

"No, I actually haven't come into the room. I just stopped at the doorway and looked around."

"That's good. How did you happen to have a key?"

"When I checked on Alexander the first time, the door was open. After checking for three days, I decided to take the key out of the door and lock it from the outside."

Jake's eyes began to dart around the room gathering facts. "It looks like his bed was slept in," he said, "but the blankets are so twisted up it looks like he had a thrashing nightmare. His outer tunic, his day clothing, is still hanging on the hook in the corner. Notice that this chair by the bed is knocked over but none of the other furniture has been disturbed."

The detective noticed that the drape over the window hung askew. He stepped over to the window, pulled the drape to one side and peered out.

"Ah ha!" Jake exclaimed. "You have a fair sized sycamore tree growing right outside this window."

"Yes, that tree started out as a volunteer sprout years ago in that little patch of dirt," James fondly said. "By the time I realized it was getting any size, I had become rather attached to the little sprig, so I let it continue to grow."

"And now it is a full sized tree," Jake observed. "Many of the branches of the sycamore tree are substantial and are rubbing up against your home's outside wall." Jake pointed out the window. "And notice several of the branches extend very close to this second story window."

James scrutinized the sycamore. "I knew the tree was growing up fairly large. I guess I didn't realize it was so thick and touching the wall."

Jake stuck his head way out so he could assess the sycamore more clearly. "Humm, just as I thought," he said. "The bark on the branches right outside this window is skinned up, as if someone had scrambled up these thick limbs. I can see from here that there is evidence of broken branch twigs. And the leaves have been disturbed all the way to the ground."

"So, someone has climbed up this sycamore. Perhaps even in the middle of the night to get into Alexander's room," James stated. "But why? Why not just enter by the door?"

"I imagine, as the evidence indicates, this person or persons tried that first. The gouges in the wood of the door indicate that they tried to quietly force the door open without making any noise while Alexander was sleeping. When that failed, this person climbed the sycamore during the night and entered Alexander's room through the window. They must have gotten hung up on the window curtain. That's why the curtain is hanging so weirdly."

"This is hard to believe," James said, shaking his head. "I live directly below and I heard nothing in the night. No cries for help. No sound of a scuffle."

"These walls are pretty thick. That could be one reason you didn't hear anything," the detective remarked. "They must have pounced on Alexander before he could cry out. There must have been somewhat of a scuffle since the bed blankets are all twisted up and the chair by the bed has been knocked over. Once they overpowered him, they probably tied him up and gagged him. All they had to do then was open the door from the inside and carry their hostage silently down the outer steps. You would have never heard them. Footsteps on cold stone stairs would make very little noise. And I construe the blood smear on the stone railing on the stairs occurred when one of the abductors scraped his body against the railing."

"Abductors? Are you telling me that you think Alexander was kidnapped?" James exclaimed.

"Yes. He was kidnapped."

"But who would do such a thing!" James exclaimed.

"That is what I am going to figure out," the detective stated wistfully, scanning around the room.

"This is just incredible," a flabbergasted James said. "Right under my nose. I don't understand how I could have let this happen. I should have suspected there was something wrong when Alexander got that note. He acted so strangely after that."

"That's right! The note!" Jake stated loudly. "Let's see if we can find the note!"

The two men began to turn the apartment upside down trying to find the note. They finally found the parchment note wedged far back in a corner under the bed. The note read simply, "YOU OWE US."

Jake read the note several times. "It appears that Alexander must have been in debt to some group. Gamblers? Maybe. 'YOU OWE US.' It could be any kind of debt. But one thing is for sure. The people Alexander owed money to decided to be sure they could collect."

"How can the kidnappers collect their money if Alexander is locked away somewhere?" James quizzed.

Jake looked down and rubbed the back of his thumb across his chin. He was trying to think of all possibilities.

"There's a number of ways they could generate money," Jake finally stated. "They could force him to commit more crimes. They could blackmail him into thinking he had to resume his life of crime. But the most likely reason for snatching him is that the kidnappers evidently know how valuable Alexander is to your ministry. The most obvious explanation is that Alexander has been abducted for the purpose of a ransom. His kidnappers even now may be conjuring up a scheme to demand money for Alexander's release."

The two men walked down the stairs and stood at the base of the steps. Jake still stared at the note. "May I keep this note? It may prove to be a key piece of the puzzle."

"Yes, of course," James said. "Where do you go from here?"

"I'm going back to my office. I'm going to write down all the evidence we discovered. And then I'll start to try to piece together that evidence with other facts I'll find in my investigation. I'll be in touch with you as I make progress in my investigation."

Hannah greeted Jake as he walked into the office. "Well? How'd it go?"

"Oh, I learned a lot and found a little evidence."

"Well, I can tell you what I think happened," she remarked confidently."

"O-k-a-y," Jake stretched out the word in anticipation of Hannah's guess analysis.

"Someone from Alexander's old life has reappeared in his life and ensnared him somehow," Hannah stated, looking rather proud of herself.

"Is that the way you map it out?" he asked.

"Of course. That's the only way it seems to play out in reality," his wife said, squinting her eyes a bit to emphasize the firmness in her tone.

"Good girl," Jake stated, giving her a big hug. "You have dissected the problem correctly. Now comes the hard work of filling in the blanks of the rest of the story."

The couple walked into Jake's office. He sat down behind his desk and she took a seat in the armchair.

"Where is our next move?" Jake thought out loud. "How do we fill in those pesky blanks?"

"You've still got your snitches out on the street," Hannah said. "Maybe they could give you a lead."

Jake shook his head a little. "So many of the trustworthy snitches I know have come to Christ and no longer have the contacts I need."

Hannah smiled, then she looked at Jake. "What about Pudge? You know you can count on him. I know he is a Christian now, after you witnessed to him, but he may still have some live contacts in the underworld."

Jake thought for a moment. "I think you've got something there, sweetheart," he said, grinning. "Pudge has become an honest tradesman making pottery. I wonder if his fingers ever get itchy to take up his old enterprise of picking his customers' pockets."

They both laughed. "You know better than that," Hannah jokingly scolded. "Pudge would never do that now. You know Pudge was completely transformed by Jesus. When he surrendered to Christ, he became a changed man."

"Yeah, I know and I thank God for saving Pudge," the detective smiled. "He truly is a good friend. He's saved my hide several times in the past. I think I'll look him up and prod him a little bit. See if he's still got the old touch for jabber on the street."

3

PUDGE'S OMINOUS WARNING

Jake hadn't lost touch with his old friend, Pudge, the former pickpocket. Pudge worked for a pottery maker over across the city on Gennath Gate Street, next to the Royal Palace and the Praetorium. His life flipped from a life of squalor in darkness, to a life in the light after surrendering to Jesus. Every time Jake saw Pudge in a church service or in a prayer meeting, the former thief always radiated happiness.

So, on this particularly beautiful spring morning, Jake walked into Eli's Pottery Shop and found Pudge singing as he worked the potter's wheel. Eli, the proprietor, approached Jake as he stepped into the shop.

"Greetings, Jake Jezreel," Eli called out to the detective. "For what do I have the pleasure of seeing you today? May I sell you a nice vase or a fine set of earthen cookware? I know you're a married man, now, and I'm sure the lovely wife would be happy to receive a gorgeous, exquisitely painted set of dinnerware for your table. Choose anything you'd like. I even have some excellent earthenware on sale at rock bottom prices."

"Great to see you, again, Eli," Jake stated, smiling. "Maybe next time. I've actually come by your shop in hopes that I could talk to your master craftsman, Pudge the potter, for a minute."

"Pudge?" Eli said, swinging his eyes over toward his singing employee. Still looking in Pudge's direction, Eli stated, "Pudge is right in the middle of some very detailed work, right now." Eli glanced back at Jake. "Perhaps later in the morning, at lunchtime."

"It would only take a few minutes," Jake probed. "I know Pudge is so good at his work that he could even talk to me while he shapes the most intricate, meticulous designs. How 'bout it, Eli. What do you say?"

"I don't like my customers interrupting my employees while they work. My craftsman are on the clock. They are on my time."

Jake realized he was getting nowhere and it was time to barter. "Eli, show me one of Pudge's latest creations. I think I'm in the market to buy."

Eli's eyes lit up at the prospect of immediate cash crossing his palm. "Why, yes, this piece right here is one of Pudge's finest production items. Notice the smooth texture of the exterior lines of the vase. How perfectly the fluted mouth of the vase blends into the body of the ..."

"I'll take it!" Jake interrupted. "How much is it? And will you now let me speak to Pudge?"

Eli quickly finalized the purchase transaction and graciously allowed Jake to walk back into the shop and approach Pudge. As the detective moved closer, he could hear Pudge singing a spiritual song they had just sung on the last Lord's Day. Jake started singing along, as he drew near to the former pickpocket.

Pudge glanced up from his seat next to his potter's wheel. "Hey, Jake. I seed ya come over here ta the real high class part a town. Great ta see ya, my man." he laughed, looking back down at his work, never missing a beat.

"Beautiful work," Jake complimented his friend. "You really do make lovely items."

"Thanks," Pudge stated, not looking up. "Eli's bin really good ta me, helpin' me learn da pottery trade. He knowd my background. Yet, when he hear'd about me becomin' a Christian, he de-cided ta take a chance on me. He knowd Christians is honest folks. He bel'eved in me. He bel'eved I'd be honest."

"Sounds like life is really turning around for you, buddy," Jake laughed. He glanced over at Eli standing at the front of the shop, watching them, armed folded across his chest. "Listen, Pudge, I've got to make this quick, on account of your boss. I'm trying to get some info about a Christian that disappeared about three days ago."

"Ya mean Alexander, the fella who had bacom' James' right-hand man?"

"That's him. That's who I've got to find."

Pudge quickly glanced up at Jake. "Dat deal is too hot.," he stated and then looked back at his work. "Ya don't wanna touch it. Nasty buz'ness." Pudge slowly wagged his head side to side. "Stay outa it."

"Why, Pudge?"

"Yar too young ta die."

"Listen, I've got a client. Pastor James is my client. I can't go back on my word to him!" Jake's face set hard and his eyes flashed a tinge of anger.

"Listen, buddy. I don't want ya gittin' kilt." Pudge said sharply to Jake. Then the potter looked over at Eli, still impatiently waiting for this conversation to wrap up. "Can't talk now. Meet me outside at lunchtime."

Jake didn't want to waste half a morning but so much of detective work in simply waiting and waiting. Waiting on stakeouts. Waiting for a message. Waiting and missing lunch. Waiting, losing an evening with Hannah. But Pudge had laid bare an ugly scenario that sounded deadly. It would be worth the wait of a few hours to hear all the toxic details from Pudge.

About a block down the street from the shop, across from the Royal Palace, Jake waited on the sidewalk at an elegant restaurant simply named Isaac's. The five-star restaurant needed no other designation. Isaac's was famous for its fine dining and its strategic proximity to the Royal Palace. It was a mecca for those of the higher echelon of society who visited the Royal Citadel.

As Jake waited for Pudge, the head waiter noticed the detective hanging out by Isaac's front doorway. The head waiter stepped out onto the sidewalk.

"May I help you, sir?" he asked Jake in an uppity tone.

Jake looked at the waiter. "No," he stated. "Can I help you?"

"Well, sir, I don't know if you realize it or not but you are blocking our front entrance," the head waiter smugly remarked. "I'm going to need to ask you to move along."

The detective dropped his head down slightly and gazed at the waiter through the top of his eyes. "You need me to do what?" he said with a laugh. "This is a public sidewalk and besides, I'm twenty feet away from the door."

"Don't make me call a policeman," the waiter retorted. "Our exclusive guests who come across the street from the Royal Palace don't need to have to deal with riffraff like you cluttering up our fine establishment."

Jake turned full face toward the head waiter and advanced a step closer to the man. He reached into his leather bag hanging from his belt.

The waiter stepped backward, hands up in front of him for protection. "Now, don't … get … violent," his shaky voice quivered.

"I'm not getting violent," Jake said with a smile. He pulled one of his business cards from his leather bag. "You look like a man who is in need of a lot of help. So, if I can help you in the future, here's my card. Name is Jake Jezreel, private detective. Just contact me at that address."

The head waiter's trembling hand took the card. He stared at Jake for a second, and then dashed back into the safety of Isaac's.

The detective smiled and then turned back toward the street waiting for Pudge.

In about five minutes, Pudge the potter sauntered down the street toward Jake. He eyeballed the restaurant where Jake was standing and as he approached he laughed. "Isaac's? You kiddin' me? Do ya think they'd let us in dis joint?"

"No, I know for a fact they would not let us into this joint!" Jake smiled. "We're too good for them. Where do you normally eat lunch?"

"Norm'lly out of my own burlap sack," Pudge said. "I'm a workin' man. I can't affo'd eatin' out."

"Well, today I'm treating you to lunch. How about Josiah's Deli, just a few blocks from here?"

"Sho', fine wit me."

As the pair sat in the warm sunshine at a small table outside Josiah's Deli, Jake once again began the questioning.

"Pudge, tell me all you know about Alexander's disappearance."

"Alexander ain't his name on da street," Pudge stated matter-of-factly. "His nickname on da street a'fore he surrendered to Christ was 'the Horse'. He was really good wit horses and he had even wormed his way into the royal stables. He worked for a gang. He was deep into the gang. He used his position at da royal stables to hep his gang members git the lowdown about the lives and riches of influent'al people 'round the city. As he learned about the riches of these impo'tant people, he'd pass that info over ta his gang members."

"Sounds like a perfect setup," Jake stated thoughtfully. "Nobody would even suspect the connection between 'the Horse' and the robberies."

"Dat's exac'ly right," Pudge said. "Den come da fly in da ointment. The Horse found Jesus Christ and totally found forgiveness fo' his sins! The Horse becomed a bran' new man! Saved by Jesus!"

"So, the Horse left the gang."

"Yeah, left 'em flat and it weren't easy," Pudge said, squirming in his chair. "He tried ta drop outa sight. But in dis town, evabody knows evabody. The Horse took his real name, Alexander, ta try ta throw da gang off his trail. He took up a new identity, workin' wit Pastor James, as James' assistant. An' he got real good at it. He was safe in da safety of da Christian comm'uity. But you knowd the gang. How day works …"

"They found Alexander, didn't they." Jake stated.

"Y-e-a-h …" Pudge's word stretched out in sadness. He sighed a dismal sigh. "You know. A guy can't never quit on da gang."

"Yeah, the gang won't let you quit on them," Jake said looking down at his uneaten food on his plate. "You're too much of a liability to them. You know too much about their operation. They can never let you go. You can never live a normal life again. Not if they have any say in it."

"Dat's why I tol' ya ta stay outa this deal," Pudge said looking Jake straight in the eye. "You mess wit' dis gang and you ain't gonna come out alive. Doze jokers means buz'ness. Day play fur keeps. And de'll always protec' dere in'trests. One way or tuther."

Jake stared squarely at Pudge. "But I have to find Alexander, Pudge" Jake stated frankly. "I have a client. You know I can't back out, now. I must honor that promise. I'm committed to see this through. But I really appreciate this inside information. It helps me an awful lot in getting the total picture of what I'm up against. Can you tell me who the leader of the gang is?"

Pudge scowled at the detective. "Now, I knowd you must be gittin' delirious," Pudge stated bluntly. "You knowd I can't do that. I ain't no stoolpigeon. Dez guys is dirty rats and day don't mess 'round when it comes ta squealers."

"Yeah, I guess I was a little delirious for askin' a dumb question like that," the detective smiled. "I know how a bunch like that works. They deal with their problems by letting their blades do the talking."

"Thank ya for seein' it my way," Pudge grinned.

"Well, if you hear of any more news about Alexander through any of your 'associates' please let me know."

"You got it."

4

TO CATCH A GANG

Five days of pounding the pavement turned out to be five blind alleys in Jake's investigation. He scoured the neighborhood around James' residence. He questioning every living soul within the immediate vicinity concerning Alexander's disappearance. No dice. If anybody did know anything, they weren't talking for fear of the gang's retaliation. Even when a resident reluctantly came across with some dope, that clue turned out to be a dry well. Nothing concrete turned up. In fact, Jake realized some of his leads were purposeful lies, sending him off in wrong directions.

As Hannah sat at her desk one day, she was startled by the office door abruptly sliding open from the hallway. A little, pudgy face peeped in the crack in the opening of the door. Then in one quick movement, the chubby man darted into the office and then rapidly slammed the door behind him. It was Pudge.

"Hello, Ms. Jezreel," Pudge stated quietly. "Is Jake in?"

"Yes, he is," she said putting down the file folder she had just pulled from the files. "Do you need to see him?"

"Yes. Immediately, I kin only stay a minute," Pudge whispered nervously.

"Come with me. I'll take you right in to see him."

Hannah hurried Pudge across her office and knocked on Jake's office door. "Jake, a man to see you," she announced as she opened the door and quickly ushered the round man right on into the detective's office. "Pudge said he needs to talk to you right now."

Hannah escorted the chubby man through the doorway and then melted back into her office, closing the door behind her.

Jake smiled as Pudge walked in. Jake figured his friend might have some news about Alexander.

"Have a seat," Jake said, pointing toward the armchair.

"Can't," Pudge stated breathlessly. "Can't stay. I come up da backway. If da gang knowd I wez here, I'd be in real trouble. But here's da lowdown. Da gang has sold Alexander into slavery. Dats how day got deir veng'ance on him fo' quittin' da gang."

"Sold Alexander into slavery!" Jake exclaimed, jumping up as if in protest. "Who was he sold to?"

"Don't know. I didn't git dat info," Pudge said holding up his hands, at a loss for an explanation. "I got dis info from some of my ol' buddies in crime. Day wouldn't talk no more 'bout it."

Jake heaved a heavy sigh, putting his hand up to his forehead in frustration,. Then he dropped his hand and stared blankly at Pudge. "There is no way of knowing who has Alexander? No way of knowing where he is?"

"No. I were lucky jus' ta git dat much skinny out of 'em," Pudge grimly said.

Pudge stood there suspended in motion like a short little round statue. His staring eyes gazed at Jake in sympathy. "I show wishd I coulda giv' ya more details den dat. I'm sorry."

Jake smiled at Pudge. "No, it's great that you could provide this much evidence for me to follow up on," the detective said. "And I know you took a big chance in coming to see me. Thank you for taking that risk. And thank you for giving me this piece of evidence to work on."

With a pleading expression, Pudge said, "I wishd I could do mor'. I gotta go."

Then without another word, Pudge spun around and hurried out of the office. Like a chubby flash, he was gone.

Hannah stepped into Jake's office. "That little man is in a big hurry," she said. "I don't think I've ever seen him move that fast before."

"A person can move pretty fast when the wolves are snapping at your heels," Jake stated. "Pudge brought me some information at the risk of his life, knowing a gang of degenerates might find out that he had helped law enforcement."

"What news is so vital that he would have to risk his life to tell you?" Hannah asked.

"He just told me that Alexander was sold into slavery," he said pointblank.

Hannah flashed a horrified expression. "What! Who could do such a thing?" she exclaimed.

"A gang of thugs that he had worked for in the past. They were getting even with him for crossing them."

"Alexander. Slavery," Hannah repeated in disbelief.

"In this Roman society that we live in, these things are very possible," Jake said shaking his head. "Just find the right buyer and you can sell anybody into slavery."

"That doesn't seem possible," she said matter-of-factly. "It's just not right."

"You are right, sweetheart. But it happens all the time in the underworld of this society. The slave trade is big business. You might be surprised how many people you pass on the street every day that are slaves. Some are slaves because they owe a debt. But some slavery is out-and-out buying and selling of people. Just prove to someone that a person owes you money, whether rightly or wrongly, and that person can be claimed as property and sold into slavery."

Hannah twisted her head to the side, as if trying to let this warped concept sink in to her brain. She stared back at Jake. "Are you telling me that some cruel people have sold Alexander and that he is now lost as a slave in the depths of the underworld? Can he never be free again?"

"It means I now have the monumental task of finding Alexander and dredging him up out of that underworld of slavery he's been plunged into," Jake stated. "I said earlier that this one smells like trouble. Well, now this case stinks to high heaven. And I've got to nose dive into the stench to free Alexander."

Hannah sat down in the armchair next to Jake's desk. She looked up at her husband. "Will you have to deal with the gang?" A tinge of fear edged her voice.

Jake hesitated. "I might," he said cautiously as he sat down on the corner of his desk next to her. "Somehow I've got to find out who Alexander has been sold to. That's going to be the rough part. I don't even know who the gang is that sold him. And even if I did know who they are, I don't know of a way to get that info out of the gang. They are certainly not going to say, 'Oh, hello, would you like to know where Alexander is?' No, I think I've got to do some deeper digging around in other places before I can solve this case. And it won't be with the gang!"

"Well, I'll do anything to help you, honey," Hannah said as she stood up and took her husband by the hand. "I'm a pretty good investigator myself, you know. Maybe I could snoop around and turn up something."

"Nothing doing, my dear," Jake stated. "We're dealing with cold-blooded criminals here. You need to stay clear of these degenerates. They are mean and vicious. They wouldn't care if you are a woman. If they thought you'd crossed them … well, it would be just too bad."

"You know you've got to tell Pastor James about Alexander being sold into slavery," she said sadly. "I'll pray for you when you go to talk to him and I'll pray for James that Jesus will give him strength."

Several days past. Jake had delivered the bad news to James and the whole church cascaded into prayer for Alexander. "We are all praying for you, Mister Jezreel, that the Lord will give you divine wisdom in finding Alexander," James told the detective.

Jake was encouraged. He knew that he would need every ounce of divine wisdom God could give him in solving this case.

Shortly after the Passover and the church's remembrance of the day the Lord Jesus rose from the dead, Jake got a break in the case.

One morning, Hannah knocked on Jake's door and stepped into his office. "Pastor James is waiting in my office to see you. He's got a very puzzling note he received from the gang that sold Alexander."

"The gang!" the detective exclaimed, jumping up. "Shoo him in, angel! Let's see what this is all about."

Hannah quickly escorted Pastor James into the detective's office and was about to leave when Jake told her to stay to hear this conversation.

"Mister Jezreel," James stated excitedly as he sat down in the armchair. "You asked me earlier if I had received a ransom note. I told you at that time that I had not. Well ... now I have!"

"What!" Jake exclaimed in surprise.

"How can that be possible?" Hannah asked.

"I don't know how it's possible, but here it is," James said, holding out the note. "I've received this ransom note demanding five hundred denarii for the release of Alexander." James flipped the parchment note onto Jake's desk. "Here, read it for yourself. I'm a little confused.'

Jake slid the parchment over to himself so he could get a clearer gaze at it. His eyes scanned the note and then he looked up at James and burst out laughing.

A strange expression swept over James' face. "Your response ... now I'm more confused."

"It is obvious that we are not dealing with the brightest rays of sunshine here," Jake smiled. "This gang thinks they can play both ends against the middle and win."

"I still don't understand," stated a very puzzled James.

"The gang must think that you don't know that Alexander has been sold into slavery," Jake explained, leaning over his desk toward the church leader. "They must think that you think they still have Alexander. They believe you think he is tied up somewhere and that you'll pay this king's ransom to guarantee his release. You see? They're trying to get double money. They've already gotten paid for selling Alexander into slavery. Now, they think they can squeeze more money from their kidnapping, because they believe you are unaware of the slave sale. They want you to believe that paying the ransom will guarantee his safe release."

A smile slowly crossed James' face. "I see. And by the look on your face, Mister Jezreel, I think you already have a plan in mind."

"Yes, sir, I sure do."

"Well, tell us!" Hannah exclaimed.

"We have been wanting to find out who the gang is who sold Alexander. This is our chance."

"You mean we're going to pay the ransom?" James questioned.

"That's right. That is the only way we can get a tail on the gang. Once we do that, we can hopefully catch this whole bunch of criminals. Maybe then we can wrangle the facts about Alexander's whereabouts out of them."

"This all sounds very dangerous," James stated skeptically.

"There will be no danger to you, sir," Jake soothed. "You would merely carry the money and drop it off. I would be waiting in the shadows and follow the pickup man back to the gang's hideout."

"Do you really think it will work?" James asked. "I've never done anything this outrageous in my life!"

"It is outrageous and risky but that's why it's going to work. I'm counting on this bunch of less-than-bright luminaries to not suspect a tail job. I should be able to shadow the pickup man with no problem. Do you think you can gather that much money together?"

"Yes, I think so. It is the Lord's money. So, I'm praying that He will bless this endeavor and your work. If you lack any wisdom, I always tell my church to ask God for His wisdom. So, brother Jezreel, ask God for His wisdom. He will give you wisdom overflowing!"

"I really will need the Lord's wisdom on this one," Jake remarked and then looking back at the parchment note he said, "The note says to 'bring the money in a burlap bag and leave the bag on the large stairway outside the Double Gate of the temple. The bag is to be placed on the third stair up against the ritual bath house wall.' The time of the drop is during the evening sacrifice in the temple. Humm. That is a very wide open area on the south end of the Temple. It's going to be difficult for me to hide in such a wide open space. There will probably be a lot of foot traffic coming in and out of the Double Gate and up and down that massive stairway leading to the Double Gate. Maybe that will help me stay hidden, if I just mill around in the crowd."

James and Hannah gazed quietly at Jake. They were still trying to process the detective's ad hoc plan.

"So, I will just leave the money on the stairs, up against the wall next to the stairs, and walk away," James stated, making sure he understood his part in the plan. "I just walk away. That's all I do."

"That's all you have to do."

James scrunched his face. "Don't you find it ironic that these men, this gang, wants to use the Lord's Temple to conduct their evil plans," James said, shaking his head in disbelief.

"Well, we will make them very sorry that they would ever do such an evil thing in the Lord's House," Jake smiled. "For that matter, we'll make them sorry that they ever got involved in the crime business."

"One thing puzzles me," James stated. "Once you follow this man who picks up the money and find out where the gang is located, what happens then? Won't you be in danger?"

"Yes," Hannah blurted out. "He will be in danger!"

"Take it easy," Jake tried to calm them both down. "The Lord has just given me an idea that will scoop up the whole bunch all at once. Now, just let me squeeze this idea through my brain to flesh out all the details."

The next day, Jake stood outside Governor Pilate's office door. He gathered his thoughts together to be sure his plan had been well formulated. He had already run the gauntlet of security guards but they were already familiar with Jake from his previous dealings with the governor. But Jake wasn't here to speak to Pilate. Jake had come to enlist the military assistance of Pilate's personal adjutant, Marcius. He pushed the door open into Marcius' office, just outside Pilate's inner sanctum.

Marcius immediately stood up when he saw Jake enter the room. Marcius was a well-built man. Muscular. Stood about five feet eleven, dark brown hair, clean shaven. His red Roman soldier uniform exuded an aura of power and respect. During the great persecution of the church, Marcius had helped Jake through that difficult time. During that same time of persecution, Jake had helped Marcius find Jesus as his savior. And now they had become fast friends.

Marcius strode over to the detective, extending his strong right hand to his friend and confidant. "Jake Jezreel, it is great to see you," Marcius said gladly.

"I'm very glad to see you, as well," Jake said and then he lowered his voice so the other office personnel could not hear their conversation. "What did you think of that sermon Peter preached this last Lord's day?" he whispered.

Marcius lowered his voice, as well. "It was absolutely great. I'm still growing in my faith since I surrendered to Christ. So, I'm just trying to soak in everything I can hear."

"The Christian life is so wonderful," Jake quietly encouraged. "The most important thing is for you to be serious in your spiritual life. Make your relationship with the Lord first and foremost in all you do. Make Him the sole reason for your living."

"I find it much easier to live for Christ when I have spent time with fellow Christians," Marcius said in a hush. "I am so encouraged in my spirit and I learn so much more from their study and experiences."

"You are so right," Jake said.

Marcius looked over toward his desk. "Come on and sit down at my desk and tell me the reason why you have come to my office."

Marcius sat down behind his oak desk, as Jake sat down in the wooden armchair across from him.

"I like the way you get right down to the point," Jake said, smiling.

"I'm a military man. It's the way I'm trained."

Jake laughed. "Well, I'm glad for that, because I've got a request that will require military precision to pull off."

"You intrigue me. Tell me more," the soldier remarked, leaning closer toward Jake.

Jake in turn leaned closer over the desk. "I think we have a golden opportunity, if we play our cards right, to capture a malicious gang that is operating within this city," he said in a low tone.

Marcius cocked his head slightly and narrowed his eyes, expressing his great interest. "I see. Tell me more."

"You do know of the disappearance of Pastor James' personal assistant, Alexander, right?"

"Yes, I do. Our entire church is praying for him."

"What if I told you that a nasty gang of degenerates kidnapped Alexander."

"I'd say that if we have the opportunity to capture and arrest them, we must do it."

"I like your attitude. And it's right to the point."

"From what you've told me so far, it sounds like you've already got a plan in mind."

"I do," Jake said confidently. "I believe this plan will work and with your help we'll drop the dragnet over them before they can blink."

"Okay. Let me take some notes. Go ahead ... shoot."

"Alright, now here's my plan ... ..."

5
STAKEOUT

The large, stone-paved plaza south of the Temple grounds bustled with humanity. People busying themselves with everyday concerns. Others making their way to worship during the evening sacrifice. Jake was there. He had stationed himself directly across the plaza from the portion of the Temple complex known as the Double Gate. The Double Gate provided an entrance through the thick Temple wall into the Temple precincts from the southern part of Jerusalem. This section of the wall was 912 feet long and at its southeastern corner, formed a drop of 140 feet to the pavement below. Across the top of this massive boundary wall, was a long portico known as The Royal Stoa, where the Sanhedrin, the supreme court of Israel, met in the central meeting hall of the portico.

Ascending up to the Double Gate from the south plaza, stretched an expansive, magnificent stone stairway. This stairway extended nearly 300 feet in length. On the east end of the wide stairway, a ritual bath house was situated for pilgrims to cleanse themselves before they entered the actual Temple precincts. On the third step of the stairway, next to the wall of the ritual bath house was the spot where Pastor James was to drop the ransom money.

From his vantage point across from the Double Gate, Jake had a clear field of view of the drop zone. The time of delivery stated in the ransom note clearly specified the money drop would be during the evening sacrifice, around three o'clock. Jake decided not to wear a disguise. His reasoning was that he should look like every other "man on the street". He figured he could draw in closer to the "pickup man" if he resembled a common Joe of the city.

Out of the corner of his eye, on his left, Jake caught sight of Pastor James striding across the plaza toward the Temple. In his right hand James carried a nondescript, bulging tan burlap sack. Judging by the stilted manner in which James carried the sack, it was obvious that the load of five hundred coins he carried was pretty hefty.

"Five hundred denarii ain't no pocket change," Jake muttered to himself. "James is getting his workout today carrying that load." Then he thought for a moment. "Maybe that hefty load will help slow down the pickup man and make it easy to tail him."

James hobbled his way over to the grand stairway leading up to the Double Gate. Jake stepped out of the shadow of the building he had been using as a blind and nonchalantly eased toward the drop area. People brushed past him in their busyness, going across his path, this way and that. He watched as James neared the stairway. The honored church leader stepped up one, then two, then three steps. Without glancing around, he drifted over to the bath house wall next to steps and gently deposited the bulging tan sack on the third step, nestling it against the wall. He looked down at the tan sack for only a moment and then turned and descended the steps. In a few seconds, James had disappeared into the bustling crowds in the plaza.

Jake stepped slightly closer to the drop off zone. He now was about halfway across the plaza, still trying to blend in with the flowing multitude. He could see the nondescript tan sack snuggled up against the bath house wall. Nobody seemed to be paying it any attention. A few worshippers heading into the Temple through the Double Gate glanced at the sack as they climbed the grand staircase. But they dismissed it and continued climbing the steps. Jake loitered in the area, floating around in the swirling humanity of the plaza.

Nothing was happening. The tan sack just sat there, staring back at Jake.

Several minutes dragged on. The crowds intermittently blocked Jake's line of sight. The throngs bumped and brushed Jake as he stopped to get a better view of the drop zone. Suddenly, Jake realized, as the crowd thinned out, that the sack was gone!

In controlled panic, the detective pushed his way toward the grand staircase. At the top of the stairway, Jake saw the back of a man, dressed in black ... hefting the tan sack! The man must have come from inside the Temple, through the Double Gate, and grabbed the sack in one swoop. Now, the pickup man was escaping back into the Temple area. Jake bolted through the swirl of humanity and tried to coolly follow the crook up the stairway. The man disappeared through the Double Gate and Jake trailed him as close as he dared. Inside the Double Gate ascended another set of numerous stairs that rose up and up into the main temple courtyards and into the expansive Court of the Gentiles.

During this time of day of the evening offering, the human activity in the Court of the Gentiles churned with a worshipful hubbub. As Jake climbed the final step in the stairway, he momentarily lost track of the crook with the sack.

"He's counting on the business of the crowd to hide his escape," Jake muttered to himself. "But not many man are wearing black clothing. I should be able to see ... Ah, there he is."

The man in black was cutting across the Court to the left toward another Temple gate simply known as the Upper Gate. Jake figured the Upper Gate would be the crook's escape route out of the Temple. The criminal now visibly seemed to be struggling with the heavy sack of coins, as he shuffled along in a halting fashion.

Suddenly, as the crook in black neared the Upper Gate and was about to exit the Temple grounds, another man, dressed in gray-tan clothing approached him. The pair exited the Temple precincts together. Jake momentarily lost sight of them, as the Upper Gate arched structure obscured them. He hurried to catch up and as he rounded the corner of the Upper Gate, Jake caught sight of the crook in black, but he no longer carried the money sack!

"They've switched off," Jake muttered. "Forget the crook in black. Now, where is the other guy?"

Jake scanned the crowds. Too many men in gray-tan clothing! They all blended together! He could not see the crook with the sack!

"The criminals are smarter than I thought," Jake said to himself. "They figured that someone might tail them and had a trick play up their sleeve. But I ain't done yet."

From the Upper Gate of the Temple a bridge-like archway descended down into the upper city. The structure of the archway narrowed the foot traffic into a tighter stream. Jake stopped for a moment to observe the walking manner of the people in the crowd. There were a lot of heads bobbing back and forth in the flow of humanity. But one head had that characteristic stilted movement of a man lugging a heavy sack. Jake focused in on the head that kept surging in its movement. He hurried in that direction.

The archway finally fanned out into the upper city. Jake easily picked up the trail, as he watched the crook with the money sack meander through the city streets. It soon became painfully obvious that the overloaded criminal now was struggling under the hefty load he was carrying. A few more twists and turns in various streets and alleys and the crook in the gray-tan clothing, now sweating profusely, set the money bag down to wipe his forehead. Jake realized quickly that the man's actions were a purposeful trick, meant to see if he was being followed. The crook glanced back in Jake's direction but the detective had already anticipated the ruse and had ducked behind a building corner. Jake waited a moment, giving the criminal time to feel safe and continue on his journey.

But Jake was surprised, when he peered around the corner, to see the criminal with the money sack, knock one time on a door halfway up the street. Quickly the door opened, the crook with the sack jumped inside, and the door slammed behind him.

Jake then slowly turned around and signaled behind him. Marcius drew up from out of the shadows, halfway down the street. Marcius was dressed in a gray regular working man's tunic.

"Your plan worked perfectly," Marcius whispered. "I saw the man with the money bag enter that doorway down the street. With me dressed as a common worker, I was able to follow you without detection.

My lieutenant is half a block further behind me. He's also dressed in a worker's gray tunic. And the rest of my soldiers are just behind him. I'll give the signal for all of my men to close in."

As quietly as Jake had ever seen a Roman military unit move, the ten red uniformed soldiers of the detachment fanned out down the street, starting near Jake and Marcius, past the thugs doorway, and then just beyond the door. They now had the door "surrounded." Jake, Marcius, and the lieutenant started to creep along the wall of the building until they were right outside the doorway. Marcius pulled out his dagger and then nodded his head at all his soldiers, indicating that they have their swords ready. Marcius glanced over at two of his biggest, beefiest soldiers directly across the alley. With a quick motion of his hand and a snap of his head, he signaled them to charge the door. The pair charged at full force and plowed into the wooden door, splintering it on its hinges and knocking it flat on the interior floor, dust flying. The pair immediately jumped up, as the rest of the soldiers poured into the room, swords drawn. Jake, Marcius, and the lieutenant followed quickly behind.

As Jake entered the murky room, the soldiers had already subdued the five members of the gang inside. The gang members all stood with the hands up and the soldiers' sword points nuzzled against their necks.

"Good work, men" Marcius stated to his soldiers. "Be sure they are all disarmed. And then have them sit on the floor. And keep them at sword point."

Turning to Jake, Marcius asked, "Do you see the money?"

Jake scanned around the tiny, dark grotto. In the middle of the dingy room, a small table lay on its side. Jake pulled the table aside and there lay the money sack on the floor.

"Here it is," the detective stated, as he picked up the bulging bag. "It must have been sitting on the table and got knocked over in the scuffle. This is Exhibit A in your arrest charges."

A sudden noise at the door snapped Jake's head around. Incredibly, the crook in black stood in the open doorway! He had arrived for his cut of the loot!

"Grab him!" Jake yelled and the soldier standing right by the doorway horse-collared the thug and slammed him to the floor.

"Just lay there r-e-a-l still," the soldier said calmly, as he slid the point of his sword up against the thug's jugular.

"Fine work," Jake said to the soldier. Then he glanced around the tiny room. "Now we've got them all. All tied up with a pretty ribbon."

Marcius stepped over toward the middle of the dimly-lit small chamber. He scanned all the crooks in the room. "Who's the boss?" he asked. "One of you has got to be the brains of this outfit. None of you look smart enough to run this gang on your own. But one of you must be the guy."

The thugs all looked around at each other, then at Marcius, scrunched their faces and shrugged their shoulders, as if to say, *I don't know who's the boss. Got no idea."*

"We *do* have ways of making you talk," Marcius said coolly, as he juggled his dagger in his hand. "We can do this the easy way or we can do this the hard way."

The thugs started looking at each other and then their eyes slowly glided over to one man, dressed in a beige, ratty-looking tunic.

Marcius's eyes locked on the man in the beige tunic. "Well? How 'bout it? Are you the ringleader?"

Defiantly the man gruffly growled, "If that's what these stool pigeons want you to think."

"Yeah, you'll do," Marcius smiled. "If you're not the real kingpin, we'll let you play the part today. Now, stand up and answer some questions." Then turning to Jake, Marcius said, "He's all yours."

Jake stepped up right beside Marcius and spoke to the shabby man. "You know your strategy on this deal was flawed from the beginning. You thought you could turn over a fast buck and double your money. You got greedy. That's how you set up your own trap."

"I ain't got no idea what you're talkin' about," the man in beige snarled, his stringy, greasy hair standing out like a porcupine. "You think you're some kinda genius? You go around being a mind reader?"

"No, I can put two and two together and realize that your greed did you in."

The ringleader stared at Jake. "You sound like you must be with the police. Ya don't sound like you're a Roman."

Marcius spoke up. "Have you ever heard of Jake Jezreel, the private detective?" he asked the gang boss. "Well, you're looking at him."

The gang ringleader's eyes grew wide in surprise. "Jake Jezreel. I've heard of you. You've got a real reputation all around this city. It's almost an honor to be taken down by you."

"Thank you for the compliment. And your name is what?" Jake asked.

"On the street I'm known as The Professor," the gang boss proudly stated.

"And I must admit that I've heard of you, too," Jake said almost respectfully. "You've got quite a reputation, too. They say you're one of the cagiest crooks in the city."

"Well, thank you. I do pride myself in being a highly educated crook. I've taken my education and applied it to perfecting the craft of being a criminal into an art form. I can come up with some pretty intricate plans for takin' other people's money. Ya don't have to work so hard for the money. Occasionally, some of my boys can get a little rough. Well, maybe even a little downright mean. And if somebody crosses us … well, that would be just too bad for them."

"Like, Alexander?" Jake abruptly asked.

The Professor shuttered and stiffened as he stood in front of the detective. "How did you know about Alexander?"

"I know a lot about Alexander and it is because of what I know about Alexander that helped me set this trap for you," Jake smiled.

The Professor lowered his head and wagged it side to side. Then he looked over at the detective with his head sideways. "My plan was perfect. Foolproof. Nobody could have figured it out."

"But I figured it out. There is one fact that you thought was hidden. And if that fact had remained hidden, this little scheme of yours today would have worked. But that one hidden fact is that I know that you first of all kidnapped Alexander and then, secondly, you sold him into slavery."

The Professor's face turned ashen, pasty white and his jaw dropped open. "You weren't supposed to know that. I had that high and mighty James thinking that we still had Alexander captive. That's why he paid the ransom today!"

"Sorry," Jake laughed. "You forget that I'm a detective. It's my job to dig around and dredge up muck from the gutters. It didn't take much to find out that the word on the street was that Alexander had been sold into slavery. Then when you demanded a ransom, I knew I had you cooked."

The Professor shook his head in disbelief. "I didn't count on James hiring you, the best private detective in this city, to investigate our snatching of Alexander. I thought I had all my angles covered."

"Yeah," growled one of the thugs in the background. "Mister smart guy. Smarty pants. Always braggin' how you got all the angles. How you could plan the perfect crime every time."

"Well, boys," Jake smiled, "that's where your greed sunk your perfect crime. You wanted more money from the ransom on top of your slavery sale."

Then Jake centered in on The Professor again. "The whole reason I was hired was to find Alexander. Since you've been caught and you *are* going to jail, you've got nothing to lose by telling me who you sold Alexander to."

The Professor stared at Jake, got a weird twist in his mouth, then rubbed the back of his neck, trying to think how to phrase his words.

"Come on, Professor," Jake prodded. "Maybe helping me may help you in court get a lighter sentence."

"It's not that so much, as it's gonna sound kinda funny."

"Go ahead. I can take it."

The Professor sheepishly heaved a heavy sigh and then said, "We sold Alexander to a racing team."

Jake shook his head to be sure he had heard the words correctly. "A racing team?"

"Yeah, a racing team. You know, a chariot racing team.'

"Why a chariot racing team?"

"Alexander was always good with horses. We always called him The Horse. He had a job at one time working in the royal stables. So, when we snatched him, we figured that we could get top money for him if we sold him to someone who needed a horse expert. The chariot racing world needs experienced and expert horse handlers. So, we sold him to a racing team and got big money for him, too."

"Man, I thought I could never be surprised again, but you guys just did it! You surprised me," Jake laughed out loud. "I've never heard such an outrageous story as that."

"Well, chalk one up for me, The Professor."

"There's just one more thing. Will you tell me which chariot racing team you sold Alexander to?" Jake probed.

"Sure. The chariot racing team we sold Alexander to is called The Black Diamond Racing Team. If ya ever been to any chariot races, their team racing colors are black silks."

Jake rubbed his forehead and then looked at The Professor. "Thank you for giving me that piece of vital information," he stated, smiling.

The Professor grinned. "Consider it – professional courtesy," he said with a salute. "One professional to another."

6

IN SEARCH OF THE BLACK DIAMOND

The dusty road from Jerusalem to the city of Samaria was about thirty-five miles. The windy road ran down the spine of the same mountain range which Jerusalem sat atop. Samaria nestled in this mountain range as one of the high points. The city of Samaria had once been the capital of Israel, back in bygone years. The metropolis stood on a hill 300 feet high. From its heights the terrain spilled out to the west into a wide basin valley which ran all the way from Shechem to the Mediterranean coast. Jake knew he would have to make this trip. This thirty-five mile journey was necessary. This dusty stretch of road led to Alexander.

Jake had done some nosing around in Jerusalem and discovered that The Black Diamond Chariot Racing Team was stabled on the outskirts of the city of Samaria. The team was well funded. The enterprise was owned by several influential businessmen from Samaria, who invested in the team with the expectations of making a lot of money in race winnings.

This meager amount of information turned out to be the only statistics Jake could squeeze out of his sources in Jerusalem. The rest of the story he would have to piece together on his own.

Jake had a plan for his trip northward and it included Hannah. "I'm thinking about bringing you along on this investigation," the detective told her. "Part of my cover would be that I am a married man who is looking for a job with the race team. With you being along with me as my wife, I'd be more convincing and maybe more likely to be hired. And then when I do get hired, you can help me in looking for clues."

"I'd be really happy to come with you, honey," Hannah said sweetly, "but who will look after the office while we're gone."

"Just close it up! Close it up! Put up a big sign that says 'GONE ON VACATION."

"You know somebody will ask us, 'Where ya going on vacation?'"

"We'll tell 'um, TSM!'"

"What is the world is TSM?"

"Top Secret Mission. Me and the wife are going off on vacation to recharge our marriage.'"

"It's gonna get recharged, alright," Hannah laughed. "Recharged with a swift kick in the pants if we ever get caught slinking around and pretending to be people we're not."

"Okay, so it's not the greatest vacation we've ever had but …"

"The vacation we've *never* had," she interrupted.

Jake smirked at her with his head turned sideways. "Okay, okay. We'll have that honeymoon vacation one day. And when we do, it will be a vacation you'll never forget!"

"And I know you, boss. That's your detective stall tactic hoping I *will forget* about it."

Jake threw out his hands to the sides in feigned exasperation. "Will you just draw up a sign and hang on the door in the corridor," he playfully commanded.

"I can do that. And it looks like I'm coming with you," she laughed. "But what is your plan. If I'm going to be part of this charade, I need to know what I'm supposed to be doing."

"My plan is very simple. I'm going to get hired by The Black Diamond Chariot Racing Team," Jake stated confidently.

Hannah half closed her eyes, faked a deadpan expression, and lowered her head slightly. "You're kidding me," she stated, barely opening her lips.

"No, I'm not," the detective said. "Now, hear me out. My plan is to take the leathercrafting skills your dad has taught me, you know, those same skills I learned when I've worked for him in the past. I'll offer my leathering skills to the race team. I have found out that chariot race teams require lots of leather. First of all, the chariots are very lightweight in construction. The chariot consists of a wood frame that is then covered with a thin skin of leather. That combination saves weight for maximum speed. There's not much to the construction but the leather stretched over the framework holds the chariot tightly together and allows for great flexibility of the chassis."

Hannah cocked her head and stared at Jake. She crossed her arms in front of her and asked, "Where did you learn all this stuff? What has happened to my husband who now thinks he's an engineer?" she laughed.

"You'd be very surprised what you can pick up off the street," he smiled.

"Yeah, and that's what I'm afraid of!" she smirked.

"Anyway, second of all, just think about all the leather on the horses, you know, the harness, all those straps, the bridle, the reins, and other leather stuff I don't even know about, yet. I'm counting on being able to get hired on the team roster and once I'm on the team, maybe I can figure out how to get Alexander free from his slavery."

"So, as a private eye, you're going to use the disguise of a leathercrafter," Hannah sat there smiling. "My dad will be so very pleased."

"Well, we can't tell him about what I'm doing until we get back from Samaria," Jake cautioned. "Otherwise, he might just blow our cover."

Hannah shook her head in disagreement. "We've got to tell him something," she countered. "After all, we're going to hang out a sign that says, GONE ON VACATION. You know he's going to be a little curious as to where our vacation spot is supposed to be."

"We'll just tell him the same as everyone else, 'We're going off to a secret hideaway for a vacation.'"

"O-k-a-y," Hannah sighed. "I sure hate to deceive my father. I'm a Christian. Deception goes against my grain."

"It's not deception," he refuted. "We're just not telling him all the details about our trip."

"Call it what you like."

"Would you rather have me get whacked when the team owners figure out why I'm really on their team?" Jake asked, trying to convince her. "Okay, listen, just to make sure you're not deceiving your dad, I promise to include a delightful vacation as a side venture before we come home."

"You mean I really will get my vacation?" she squealed.

"Yes, you'll get your dreamed-of vacation."

"Then the only thing left for me to do is make the GONE ON VACATION sign!"

And that didn't take her very long, at all.

The detective couple made the trip to Samaria in two days. They had to pass through the historic cities of Ramah and Bethel. The couple passed the ancient religious site of Shiloh and then Shechem, where Jacob's Well is located. At this point the road made a left turn and skirted the base of Mount Gerizim. After that, it was then only a few, short miles to the city of Samaria.

The entire countryside through which they traveled was lush with greenery. The pine and tamarisk and eucalyptus forests covered the lower sides to the ridge along the road in deep rich green foliage. The knurly calliprinos oaks, jutting out of the soil along the sides of the road, protruded up like giant tangled fans with their jade-colored limbs appearing to be knotted together. Everywhere the rockrose, honeysuckle, and thorny broom displayed vibrant pinks and whites and yellows. Woodlands spread out as far as the eye could see in all directions.

All this territory was new ground for both Jake and Hannah. They had never walked on this terrain before and for good reason. The province of Samaria, where the city of Samaria exists, had always been totally off limits to all Jewish people. Both Jake and Hannah had been raised under strict Jewish teaching. Jewish teaching stated that Jews were never to have contact or dealings with Samaritans. And Jewish people were forbidden to even travel through the province of Samaria.

Due to this upbringing, Jake and Hannah had never ventured into this area, the forbidden Samaria.

They had heard all the fascinating Bible stories of the life of the famous judge Deborah at Ramah and Jacob's dream of the ladder into heaven at Bethel. They remembered the stories of the original tabernacle being set up at Shiloh and then the story of Jacob buying land at Shechem and digging his famous well. As the couple followed the road between Mount Gerizim and Mount Ebal, they recalled the significance of these two tall mountains. Moses had commanded Israel when they first entered the land to use the valley between as a natural amphitheater for proclaiming the blessings of obedience to God and the curses for disobedience.

These places had always been wrapped in the mists of the ancient Bible world but Jake and Hannah had never physically seen them. Now, as they traveled these dusty miles, history came vibrantly alive and the trip took on a delightful and deep meaning.

"Jake, this is such beautiful country!" Hannah stated excitedly, as she swept her hand over the gorgeous countryside. "God has given Israel a spectacular land to live in! And we have been missing out on all this beauty all our lives."

"I am amazed at how magnificent the landscape is in this part of our country," Jake said. "And it's only because of our strict Jewish traditions that have forbidden us to venture into this lovely country. Now, as Christians, we aren't bound to those old, incorrect, man-made traditions that excluded the Samarian people from God's love. See what we've been missing? And the Samaritans have been missing out on learning about Christ and His salvation."

"For sure we're going to have to do some witnessing for the Lord Jesus while we're in this region," Hannah stated with a lilt in her voice.

Jake winked at her. "You must have been reading my heart," he smiled. "That's part of my plan. We'll have a prime opportunity to tell these Samaritans the good news about Jesus."

As the city of Samaria loomed up ahead, the duo stopped in the road. "We've got to pray that the Lord will lead us," Jake stated.

They bowed their heads right there in the middle of the road and prayed for God's guidance. As they opened their eyes, Jake just happened to look over toward the west. The view toward the west was magnificent, with mountains surrounding the city on three sides and a wide valley basin laying between them. Then Jake's eyes grew large at what he saw.

"Look, Hannah!" Jake shouted, pointing down into the wide valley. "Do you see what I see?"

"Jake, it looks like an oval race track!" she exclaimed.

"That's what it is! It's a practice track for chariot racing!" Jake pumped his fist in excitement. "Thank you, Lord! Thank you so much!"

"So, this is it!" Hannah laughed. "We've found The Black Diamond Racing Team!"

"Maybe. Let's hope so," he said cautiously. "That track may be used by several race teams. So, we'll need to scope out the situation before we begin talking to anybody."

The couple traveled a little further down the road toward the city of Samaria. As they approached the West Gate of the city, a road led out of the metropolis toward the west and down into the valley below.

"That road going off toward the west will probably lead us to the practice track in the valley," Jake said. "But I think we need to spend the night in town. We can take up our search in the morning."

"I'm with you on that, boss," she sighed happily. "My poor feet are killing me and I think maybe I could use a bath. And a good hot meal would do just right. I'm getting a little tired of these biscuit sandwiches you made before we left Jerusalem."

"I can tell you'd never last in the detective business," he teased. "When you're on a stakeout you have to be prepared to eat your lunch out of a burlap sack and like it. No frills."

"Well, I may be a woman but just you watch," she picked back at him, playfully narrowing her eyes. "I can take it just a good as you can. And I've proved it on this trip. I can eat out of a burlap sack with the best of them."

Jake laughed out loud. "I can't dispute that! Let's go see if we can find us a room for the night."

The couple entered the city of Samaria through the West Gate.

Inside the city they found a man selling vegetables in a small shop along the main street. The detective duo stepped into the shop hoping to get directions. They were greeted heartily by the owner.

"Welcome, friends," the shop owner stated magnanimously, as he approached them. "What can I do for you today? You two look like you are visitors to our fair city. You probably have been traveling all day. You are probably very tired. Can I interest you in some refreshing fruit that will revive you and invigorate your souls? Or maybe a ..."

Jake spoke up. "Yes, we would be very interested in trying some of your wonderful goods but first of all, we would like to find a room for the night. Could you direct us to an inn for the evening?"

The shop owner seemed a little disappointed for not making a sale. "I would be very happy to direct you. Go down this street toward the center of the city and you'll find an establishment called The Inn By The Ivory House. It is a classy inn, well-kept, and very reasonable."

"Thank you, friend," Jake said. "Once we get settled in the inn, we can think better about coming back and buying some of your produce for supper."

"That would be very nice," the shop keeper stated.

As Jake and Hannah turned to step outside, Jake turned back to the owner. "Oh, just one more thing. Why does the inn have the name The Inn By The Ivory House?"

The owner grew prune faced. "You two must be Jews," the man carped in a disdainful tone. "Only Jews would ask such a question."

"Well, sir, we're not really Jews," Jake said with a smile. "We are freed Jews."

"Freed Jews?" the man quizzed. "I've never heard of a freed Jew. What is that?"

"A freed Jew is a person who has been freed from all the religious trappings of the burdensome Jewish regulations," Jake said, still smiling. "Do you want to know how a person gets freed from all that heavy burden?"

The shop owner smugly gazed at Jake. "Okay, tell me."

"When a person, Jew or non-Jew, repents of their sins and surrenders his life to Jesus Christ as his Savior from sin, that person becomes a freed person, whether he is a Jew or not." Jake paused and looked hopefully at the shopkeeper, waiting for a response.

A long moment stretched out in silence.

"Okay," the owner finally grumbled and then quickly changing the subject, "To answer your question. The reason the inn is called The Inn By The Ivory House is because the ancient ruins of King Ahab's Ivory Palace are very close nearby. It's as simple as that. Now, I've explained it. Have a good day. Good bye."

"And you have a good day, also," Jake said cordially. "Please think about what I told you about becoming a freed person."

"I bid you a good day!" the shop owner snapped. "And I meant it!"

Jake and Hannah turned and stepped out of the shop, out onto the cobble stone street.

"Nice man," Jake stated, "but he really needs Jesus."

"Maybe we can visit him later and give him a more detailed look at Jesus' good news," Hannah winked. "He did seem like a nice man. He needs salvation from his sins."

The couple found The Inn By The Ivory House and checked in at the front desk.

"So pleasant to have you folks," the desk clerk's wafted. "Your room number is 14 on the second floor. It has a wonderful view of the ruins of King Ahab's spectacular Ivory Palace."

"See, honey," Jake said smiling. "You're really living now. You get to see the spectacular sites on our 'vacation'. I told you it would be a trip you'd never forget."

Hannah cocked her head in that 'Really?' look and just shook her head. "Spectacular," she mumbled.

After resting and cleaning up a little, the couple ventured back out into the street in front of the inn.

"How about a nice supper," Hannah said. "We passed a cute little café on our way to the inn. It's just a few doors down."

"Sounds great. We can check back with the fruit seller later."

But as they walked past a row of shops, Jake's interest spiked.

"Look, sweetheart, it's a leather goods shop," Jake exclaimed, stopping dead in his tracks.

Hannah got a wary look on her face, as she glanced over at the shop. "Are you thinking what I'm thinking?" she asked almost reading Jake's mind.

"We're tracking right together," he said, never looking away from the leather shop. "It's made to order. Just what we've been praying for. A contact in the leather goods market."

"I think supper will have to wait," Hannah eagerly said. "This is the Lord plopping His guidance right in our lap. We've come all this way to start our investigation right here!"

The couple drifted over to the little shop. The whole front of the shop opened to the street. Leather goods hung all over the front of the store, to attract customers to come inside. Jake started to admire some of the leather belts hanging outside the shop, speaking loudly enough to Hannah to arouse the attention of the store owner. The owner approached them.

"Good evening," the proprietor greeted them. "You look like you'd be interested in purchasing a belt. I've got a large selection in a variety of styles. Do you see anything that interests you?"

"I'm from out of town," Jake started. "I was noticing what fine workmanship has gone into designing and crafting these belts. The work is exquisite. I assume you are the craftsman."

"That would be correct," the owner stated proudly. "I do all my own work right here on the premises. You say you are from out of town. Will you be staying long in our fair city?"

"That depends," the detective played out his line, hoping to hook some prime information. "I'm actually looking for work. You see, I'm a fellow leather crafter myself."

"A leather crafter!" the proprietor exclaimed. "It's an honor to meet you. Where have you worked in the past?"

"Well, I apprenticed in Jerusalem under a master leather man. He taught me everything I know."

"Ahh, big city worker," the owner mused. "You can make a lot of money in Jerusalem. What happened? Why didn't you stay in the big city?"

"Chariot racing."

"Chariot racing?" the owner quizzed. "What do you mean?"

"I guess you could say that I've been bitten by the chariot racing bug," Jake laughed. "I've heard about the excitement and fame that championship chariot racing can bring a person. I just thought I'd try my hand at it and see what happens."

"Do you want to be a driver?" the proprietor asked.

"Oh, no," Jake said with a shrug. He then looked over at Hannah, who patiently watched this banter go back and forth. "No, me and the little lady, here, have an understanding," Jake said, patting his wife on the shoulder. "We agreed that I would not drive those dangerous rigs. We both agreed it would be too hazardous of a livelihood to risk life and limb every time I mounted up for a race."

"So, what's your point in trying to get into the chariot racing game?" asked the shop owner.

"Leather. I figured I could hire on to one of the teams using my leather skills," Jake said tilting his head as if fishing for more information.

"Oh, those race teams are always needing some of their leather equipment repaired or replaced," the shop owner said with a smile. "They are always coming to me asking me to fix a bridle or mend a strap. Chariot racing strains all that leather equipment to its limits and many times the leather pieces fail. So, they come to me for a quick fix. Or sometimes they have a new idea and want to try a new type of part. They come to me to manufacture the new piece, you know, make it stronger or beefier or thicker."

"So, you're in constant contact with all the local race teams, is that right?" Jake asked, still trolling.

"Oh yeah, personnel from the various local teams are in here several times a week."

"Do any of the teams hire leather workers to work for their teams?"

"The better financed teams can afford to hire extra people on their teams." The shop owner stopped and thought. "The Blue Team can afford it. So can the Green Team. And, of course, the Black Team can definitely afford to hire extra folks. That team is a big outfit."

"The Black Team?" Jake trolled even deeper.

"Yeah, they're actually known as The Black Diamond Race Team.

Their racing color is black, black silks, black chariot, and of course, black horses. Some of the prettiest black horses you've ever seen. They're a pretty famous race team. Maybe you've heard of them."

"Yes, I believe I have heard of them."

"If you're really looking for a job with a race team, you might try talking to The Black Team," the store owner offered. "Like I said, they've got the most money on the racing circuit, so they may be looking for a good leather man. There's a lot of leather used on a racing chariot and horses. But let me inform you. They've already got a full-time leather crafter on the team."

"Thank you very much for the tip," Jake said. "There might be a chance for a job opening. From what you've told me, that team may be the best place to start. Do any of The Black Team owners live in town?"

"Yeah, one of them lives over by the Forum on the east side of the city," the owner recalled. "His name is Diotrephes. I don't know exactly which house he lives in but you shouldn't have too much trouble locating him. He's rich and famous. Just ask around for him."

"Many thanks," Jake smiled. "I will look him up tomorrow. Me and the wife thank you very much."

"And when you speak to him, tell him I sent you," the shop owner stated. "He knows me. I do work for him all the time."

"Sir, you would do that for me?" Jake asked rather surprised. "You would recommend me. Sir, you don't even know me."

"I know, but you seem to me to be a good person, a genuine person. And besides, we leather men have to stick together."

"Who should I say has sent me?"

"Tell Diotrephes that his good friend Artemas sent you."

"Thank you, Artemas. You are too kind. And as I said, I will certainly look him up tomorrow."

"Oh, there is one more thing," Artemas stated as Jake turned to leave. "I realize you're looking to find a job that will pay you a lot of money. But if things don't pan out for you on The Black Team or another team, come on back and see me," Artemas said. "I'm always on the lookout for a skilled leatherworker. I can't pay you the big money like the well-funded teams can do, but you could make a good living for you and your pretty bride. Think about it."

"You are so very gracious, sir," Jake replied. "You have certainly helped a stranger in need. Thank you."

Hannah stepped closer to Artemas and with true sincerity in her voice she said, "We thank you, sir. You have helped us much, much more than you can ever know. We are *eternally* grateful."

And she truly meant it.

7

I'M LOOKING FOR A JOB

The bright yellow morning sunshine, found Jake and Hannah slightly disappointed. When they arrived at the home of Diotrephes, his servant informed the couple that the master of the house had already left for the race team stables. They had missed him by a quarter of an hour.

"We would like to meet with him this morning, if we could," Jake told the servant. "Can you direct us to the stables?"

"Certainly," the servant said happily. "Just follow this main street west and go out the West Gate of the city. There is a road that goes straight ahead from the gate and descends down into the valley. Just follow that road straight ahead and you will find the stables on your right about a half mile down in the valley."

"Thank you so much," Jake replied to the servant. And as he turned in the direction of the stables, the detective glanced over at Hannah and said, "And thank you, Lord for leading us on such a clear path."

Hannah just smiled and said quietly, "God is very good. I am amazed at how faithful He has been to help us find our way when we didn't know the way."

Jake's expression grew soft as he looked over at his attractive bride. "And I'm so very glad that we can experience His amazing leading together."

The couple exited the city through the West Gate and began the slight descent into the valley. Further down the road stood a red wooden barn like building and an unattached limestone office-looking room built off to the side. This was The Black Diamond Racing Team headquarters. Jake and Hannah approached slowly not knowing where to go, either into the office or the wide open barn door. Presently, a man dressed in a charcoal gray tunic walked out of the barn leading a beautiful, sleek black horse. The man did not see them.

"Excuse me," Jake spoke up. "Could you help me?"

The man turned to face the couple. "Sure, what can I do for you?"

"I was hoping to talk to one of the team owners, hopefully Diotrephes," Jake stated. "Are any of the owners here today?"

"Yeah, Diotrephes is here. He just arrived. You can find him in the team office over there."

"Thank you, friend," the detective smiled and he and his wife pivoted and headed for the office.

Everything about the race team grounds was spiffy and well-groomed. The immaculate red barn and clean, white office building projected money; it was all first-rate. Jake knocked on the office door and heard a voice from inside, "Push on it. It's not locked."

Jake pushed the door open and poked his head inside. "Are you Diotrephes?"

The man sitting behind his desk looked up and replied, "Yes, and to whom am I speaking?"

Jake quickly took in his surroundings. The office was large and roomy, clean and spotless. The desk across the room had a thick oak desktop, with beautiful oak paneled sides. There were plenty of parchment papers laying on the desk but they were all very neatly arranged in perfectly aligned stacks. The window directly behind the man at the desk had the curtains pulled wide open. The bright sunshine glare behind the man made him difficult to distinguish. The walls of the office had shelves with trophies and ribbons, indicating this team had a lot of race wins under their belt. Over to the left, two other men sat at a wooden table, looking at some papers.

Jake squinted his eyes, against the dazzling sunshine glare in the window directly behind Diotrephes. "Yes, sir, my name is Jacob Jezreel. I was told I could find you here. I'd like to talk to you."

"Please come in," Diotrephes stated, standing up. He moved around the side of his desk and Jake could now clearly see the man's features. Diotrephes exuded confidence, in his stance, in his voice, and in his attire. His voice carried a determined, commanding style. Yet, his speech projected a happy, pleasant tone. He stood about five feet nine. And though the man evidently was wealthy, his well-styled clothing was not showy or elaborate. His light brown tunic showed him to be a man who was part of the team, not someone lording over his employees. His closely cut black hair had threads of gray and silver. His carefully trimmed black beard was replete with more silver-gray than black.

"Did you say Jezreel?" Diotrephes asked. "Is your family from this area?"

Jake had to think fast. He quickly remembered his family's history, a chronicle he had used in the past in another investigation. "Yes, as a matter of fact, my family originally lived in Jezreel years ago, about twenty miles north of here. They actually lived more on the Plain of Esdraelon, which is in the proximity of Samaria."

"Well, that is quite interesting," stated Diotrephes, as he stood up to greet Jake. "So, you're a hometown boy?"

"Well, no, sir, my family moved to Jerusalem many years ago, before I was born."

"I see," the man said thoughtfully. And then he noticed Hannah standing behind Jake. "And who do we have here?"

Jake stepped aside to reveal his wife. "Sir, this is my wife, Hannah," he said gesturing toward her. "We have just arrived in Samaria yesterday and I brought her along with me today, since she knows no one in the city. Sir, I'm looking for a job. I was hoping to hire on with your race team."

"A job, huh. What type of work do you do?"

"I am a leathercrafter. I did my apprentice work in Jerusalem. And even though a lot of money can be made in the big city, I've become fascinated with chariot racing and thought maybe I could find work with the best chariot racing team in the business."

"Well, I wouldn't say we're the best in the business. We've raced at the hippodrome in Caesarea many times. Our wins have come there at that track. But our aspirations are to one day race against the very best teams in the Roman Empire at the Circus Maximus in Rome. Now, that would truly be the big time. Caesar attends those races at the Circus Maximus in Rome and gaining the emperor's favor would be the crowning glory for our team. On top of that, the famous Circus Maximus race track is where the big money can be made. It is every chariot race team's dream to race in front of Caesar and win the ton of money that can be won at that famous race track".

Diotrephes walked over to Jake and looked him up and down. "Leathercrafter. Are you good at your work?"

"I worked for one of the most skilled leather craftsman in Jerusalem, Hosea Haggai. We never lacked for work. He was that good. Our wares were coveted by every strata in the population, from the common worker all the way up to work orders for the Roman military and other government agencies. We always had plenty of work."

"I see," Diotrephes stated. "I really wish we had an opening but we've already got a superb leather man doing all our leather work. His name is Caleb. He's really good. We are quite pleased with all his work."

Jake nodded his head to indicate he understood that there was not more room on Diotrephes' team. "Well, I guess I can try the Green Team or maybe even the Blue team. I've got to find a job. You know, the little woman here … I've got to make some money so we can live."

"I'm sorry," Diotrephes sadly stated. "We just don't have any openings."

Jake threw out another line to see what he might hook. "You know, I wouldn't have come to you first, if it hadn't been for Artemas, the leatherworker in the city, encouraging me to speak to you. He even told me to tell you that I could use him as a reference for my job interview."

"Artemas sent you to us?"

"Yes, sir. Artemas said we leathercrafters needed to stick together. And he recommended that I talk to you first."

"Well, I don't know," stated Diotrephes.

Then one of the two men sitting at the table, listening to this whole discussion spoke up. "Ah, go ahead and give the man a try," the gentleman in a light brown cloak interjected. "We can always use another man as a 'gopher'. If he can help out with the leather work, then fine. And if he doesn't work out, well … we can just let him go."

Diotrephes looked over at the man. "Octavius, do you really want to spend the extra money on a new man?"

"It would only be on a trial basis," Octavius laughed. "Artemas does emergency work for us all the time. We know he's trustworthy. So, if Artemas recommends him, then maybe this man will be a safe bet. Invest a little money on an unknown and it may turn out to be a big benefit."

Diotrephes turned his attention back to Jake. "Okay, you're hired. And you can start right now. Let me introduce you to the other two owners of our race team."

Diotrephes escorted Jake and Hannah over to the table and the two men sitting there stood up.

"You've already heard from Octavius. He owns a quarter interest in the team. He knows the race game about as good as anybody." Octavius smiled and halfway bowed, extending his hands outward in a greeting gesture.

Diotrephes turned to the other man. "This gentleman is Linus. He owns a quarter stake in this team, as well. Linus is our money cruncher. He keeps the books, which sometimes can get pretty complicated."

"Very good to meet all you gentlemen," Jake said. "And thank you, Octavius, for taking a chance on me. I promise I won't disappoint you."

Then Diotrephes turned to Jake and Hannah. "I am the primary owner of the race team. I own fifty percent of this outfit. The three of us make all our decisions together but in all matters I have the final say so. That kinda puts me out on the point. It's gotten to where most everybody calls me 'The Captain.'"

"Well, sir, for right now, I think I'll call you Mister Diotrephes," Jake smiled.

Everybody had a good laugh.

"Well, let me take you out to meet the rest of the guys on the crew,"

Diotrephes said. "We have a good group of guys. A dedicated bunch. Totally dedicated to the team and to winning races."

They all stepped out of the office into the beautiful, bright sunny day and rambled over to the barn. "All the boys aren't here right now. Some of them are exercising the horses. But we will introduce you to those men who are here."

"About how many people work for you?" Jake asked as they walked.

"Right now, we have twenty employees," Diotrephes stated proudly. "We have one man who is our wheelwright. His name is Reuben. He builds our precision wheels. His wheels are strong and can take the brutal punishment of the race track. We also have one man who is our wainwright, who builds and repairs our chariots. His name is Ezra. He can build anything out of wood. His chariots are the best in the business. And then there is our leather craftsman, as I said, his name is Caleb. You'll be working with him and I'll introduce you to him later. We have our own blacksmith. He's a very big boy, like a muscle man. His name is Levi. He builds everything we need out of iron. Over along one wall of the barn we have our supply shelves and Sebastian oversees that inventory. Feed and other equipment purchasing is handled by Trophimus.

"We have one horse-master, whose name is Nathan. He is in total charge of all of our horses and their welfare. Some of our employees work with Nathan as horse trainers and exercisers. Their names are Eli, Jonathan, Leon, and Onesimus. Others groom and care for the horses. We've got twelve horses, at the present time, that way we can switch off for different events. Some of our people are responsible for the tack and other horse related equipment. Some keep the barn, stables and stalls clean. There's a lot to do in a big operation like this. It's important to be very organized. I like to run a tight operation."

As Diotrephes led the group into the barn, a couple of men were cleaning stalls. "This is Carpus and Zenas. They are hard workers and can do just about any job on the team." Turning to the two men, "This is Jake, a new man, who will be a 'floater' doing odd jobs for the moment. Then we'll work him in with Caleb."

Carpus and Zenas both greeted Jake and then resumed their work.

Over to the side, a handsome young man stepped out of the tack room and stood erect and smiling. Diotrephes pointed over at the young man and said, "Here is someone I really want you to meet. This is our team driver. He is rather new to the team but he is learning the skill of driving the chariot rather quickly. His name is Alexander."

8

CHARIOTEER

When Jake and Hannah got back to their room at the inn that evening, they couldn't contain their excitement.

"We've found Alexander!" Jake shouted. He hopped around the room as if he was skipping an invisible jump rope.

"Unbelievable!" Hannah squealed. "The Lord Jesus led us right straight to him." She held her hands upward, "Thank you, Jesus. You are so faithful!"

They embraced each other, spinning around in a happy dance. Then they looked at each other and caught their breath. As they gazed into each other's eyes, Jake said, "Now comes the really tough part. Getting Alexander out of here and back to Jerusalem."

Hannah stared at her husband. "With Alexander being a slave, he's considered property of Black Diamond Racing. I guess like any other property, he could be bought out of slavery. Then he'd be a free man again."

"That seems to be the only viable plan I can think of," Jake stated. "But let's play out this hand and see what happens. I've been hired on the team. Now I'm in. And what a brilliant stroke of God's intervention with you being hired on as the team cook!"

Hannah's face lit up. "Yeah, you just mentioned to Diotrephes that I was a great cook and the whole conversation spun off in that direction."

"I hadn't even planned to say anything about you," Jake laughed. "I just mentioned that in these first years of our marriage, you had really learned to be a wonderful cook and Diotrephes jumped right square into that conversation."

Hannah giggled. "I know. That's all it took," she laughed. "Diotrephes began thinking out loud. He started saying that they have been needing a team cook for a while. Then he mentioned that the team always loses a portion of their day when they leave work to eat lunch in the city. Then before I knew it, he had talked himself into it. He asked me to cook the team meals right at the racing facility. That way everybody could stay at work and not waste so much time breaking for lunch. I couldn't believe it!"

"I wonder Who put that thought into his head,"

"You know. Jesus, of course."

Jake stroked his chin thoughtfully. "With you hanging around the team office so much, I'm sure your little ears can pick up some really interesting facts and ideas from the team members"

"What do you mean 'little' ears," Hannah laughed. "When this girl gets into surveillance mode, I've got really 'big' ears."

Jake then took Hannah by both shoulders and turned her face squarely toward him. "For the moment, I don't think we should tell Alexander who we really are. I don't think it would be wise for us to reveal that we are here at the request of Pastor James. First of all, it would get his hopes up when those hopes might be dashed, if we can't wrangle a deal to free him from slavery. And second of all, Diotrephes might kick us out right away if he found out we were here to try to set Alexander free."

She nodded her head that she understood. "But I really would like to tell him. Maybe we at least could tell Alexander that we are Christians and we could develop a friendship with him along those lines."

Jake smiled. "I like your style, girl. That is a perfect idea. We can at least encourage him in his Christian life." He nodded his head at her and winked. "You're a really good partner, yes you are."

As the next few days past, Jake made a special effort to get to know Alexander more personally. The young man proved to be a very pleasant person to be around, always kindly and courteous. He was a handsome man. He stood about six feet two inches and quite muscular. A well-trimmed beard exhibited his square jaw and his thick, black eyebrows formed robust arches over his eyes. His eyes were black but exuded a wonderful kindheartedness. In his every action, Jake could sense the traces of Jesus Christ's life in Alexander.

Alexander also proved to be an excellent chariot driver. Jake already knew, from his conversation with Pudge, that Alexander loved to be around horses and it showed in his actions each day in the stables and on the practice track. Apparently, Diotrephes had decided to test Alexander's driving skills, even though the team already had a primary driver. Jake watched Alexander's precision driving each day in practice. He really was good!

The practice race track had been carved out right beside The Black Diamond Team's barn, stables, office and other facilities. It was a very simple track, scratched out of the dirt of the valley. It looked like two very long straightaways, each one about 1,000 feet in length, with a very tight hairpin turn at each end. These tight turns connected the two straights. A large stone pillar stood at the apex of each turn, for the chariot to practice racing around. Other local race teams could come and practice at The Black Diamond track – for a fee. But Alexander practiced nearly every day, driving the chariot and handling the horses. As Jake watched the young man putting the horses through their paces, the detective was greatly impressed at the exquisite driving skill Alexander had developed. The young man obviously loved his new job and he obviously loved the horses under his gentle care.

One day Jake greeted Alexander as he finished up his morning practice session. But he first waited for the charioteer to discuss his morning practice run with his racing crew.

"I'm going to need the two straps of the traces for the inside horse to be shortened up a little," Alexander said to his crew. "I'm not getting the control I need from the inside horse when we enter the turns. We seem to be losing the close unity of the team. I think that will help tighten the group of horses closer together. I think then the other horses can follow his lead better. The key is control of the inside horse."

"Okay, we can do that," Carpus affirmed. "I'll get Caleb on that leather project right away. Anything else?"

"No, everything else is okay. Oh, one more thing," Alexander said. "Let's try the larger wheels during the next practice. The dirt on the track is getting pretty well chewed up and the smaller wheels are digging in too much. When we travel to Caesarea to compete in the races at the hippodrome track, we don't know what the track surface is going to be like and we need to be ready for any possibility."

"Right," Carpus stated. "We'll install those larger wheels right away for your next practice."

"Thanks, I think that will greatly improve our lap times on this 'heavy' track."

Carpus pulled out a small papyrus notebook. "I'll make a note of these changes in my strategy book for future reference, when we travel to Caesarea to race there," he smiled. He and the other crewmembers got busy changing the chariot wheels.

Alexander stepped away from the chariot and began to wipe the sweat and dirt from his face with a cloth.

"Kinda hot and dusty out there," Jake stated trying to strike up a conversation.

"Whew! Yeah, hot and dusty is right!" Alexander said. "You've been on the team for several days. What do you think of our operation?"

"Very impressive," Jake stated. "The Black Diamond Team is impeccably organized. Diotrephes runs a well-oiled outfit, extremely well prepared in every aspect. Diotrephes demands precision of every facet. He seems to be a firm man but a fair man, also."

"Oh yeah, the boss is a good man," Alexander said with admiration. "He's treated me really good."

Jake wondered in his head about these adoring statements from a slave for his owner. He wasn't quite sure how to proceed in their conversation but he plowed ahead anyway.

"I understand you've been with the team only a short time," the detective continued. "Did you drive chariots for other teams?" Jake was fishing for information.

"No, I've never driven a chariot before in my life. But I've always loved horses. I grew up around horses and I guess you'd say I've got a sixth sense about them. I feel at ease around the big fellas and they seem to emotionally connect with me, too. When I came on the team, my relationship with the horses was almost immediate attraction. I love those big ol' guys!"

"That is very interesting. I've never experienced such an emotional bond with an animal," Jake said.

"Oh, yeah," Alexander shrugged. "I really can't explain it. But it's really a great feeling."

"You mentioned when you 'came' on the team, You used the word 'came'. What do you mean?" Jake still was angling, playing out his fishing line.

Alexander hesitated and looked down at the ground. He twisted his mouth in an uncomfortable display. Then he looked up at Jake. "Well, I wasn't exactly hired for this job." Again he hesitated awkwardly staring at the detective. "You see … I was … well …"

"That's okay," Jake said quietly. "Don't say any more. I catch your drift."

"You do?"

"Yeah, your situation is like that of about half the people in the Roman Empire. Nothin' to be concerned about."

"Then you know I'm a slave."

"Yeah, I kinda could figure it out."

"It may be hard to understand, but I'm happy here. I love my driving job. And I really believe I can become one of the best chariot drivers on the circuit."

"Well, from what I've seen, I believe you can do it! You can become the best driver on the racing circuit and maybe in the whole empire!"

"You are way too kind, Jacob. I've got a lot to learn about handling that lightweight chariot."

"But I think you'd be one of the very best because of your secret weapon."

"Secret weapon? What is that?"

"Your connection with the horses. Once those horses know and understand your affection for them, I bet they will do anything for you. I bet they will expend their last full measure to please you!"

"That is true," Alexander stated, gazing at his stallions with a smiling glow of admiration. "They will do anything for me! Anything! Those big boys are quite amazing. They are proud beasts and they like to showoff for me! They are concentrated power in horseflesh! And they love to compete … and beat any horse who challenges them. It's almost like a pride thing for them. They don't want any other horses to beat them in any race! And they can fly like the wind! It's incredible! When we are running together, we are like one tight, bonded unit! I love them!"

Jake had never experienced such a raw connection of a man and beast in such a fierce unity.

"Yeah, Alexander, you are going to be a winner!" Jake stated smiling. "You've already beat your competition before the officials even spring open that starting gate. You've beaten them physically and psychologically."

"Well, I love it!" Alexander laughed. "This is the most fun I've ever had in my life! And the boss treats me great, too. You'd never know that I'm a slave, as good as he treats me."

"I'm glad to hear it." Jake got a quizzical expression on his face. "You have such an unusual attitude in this whole situation. I would think you would be bitter, having been a free man and now having your freedom taken away."

Again, Alexander hesitated. "I guess the others haven't told you. But it's no secret. I've told everybody else on the team." The young man spread his hands out in an offering gesture. "I am a Christian. And my Lord Jesus is with me every step of the way. I could be bitter but I chose to rather rejoice in my new adventure that slavery and Jesus have brought me into. I am thankful to the Lord because I know He has my very best in store for me and that He is right here with me all the time."

Jake smiled. He couldn't be silent any longer. "Brother, you are not going to believe this. But I want you to know that I'm a Christian, too. And so is my wife," he stated quietly.

Alexander grinned big. "Wow, a fellow believer! I knew there was something very different about you from the first time I met you."

"The Holy Spirit who lives in you and me made that spiritual connection between us," Jake laughed. "Just like you and the horses have that unexplainable bond between you and them, so the Spirit draws His people together with an unseen affinity – an attraction of spirits."

"Oh, Jacob, those are such welcome and pleasant words to hear from you," the young man said with a pleasing sigh. "You just don't know how lonely it's been lately. Since I've been a slave, I've had no contact with any other Christians. And here in Samaria, these people are not Jewish, they're Samaritans, totally different. Oh, I thank the Lord for bringing you to me."

"And I'm very glad to have found you, too," the detective stated. "Me and the wife wanted to get into the racing game and we realized, to do that, we would have to leave all the comforts of Jerusalem and come to this area where they don't worship Jesus."

"Well, I've been trying to tell everyone I meet about Jesus," Alexander said scrunching up his face. "But these folks are not very receptive to the Good News of Christ's salvation."

"Don't be discouraged. That's pretty typical of people who are steeped in a false religion. They think they already know the 'truth'. They feel safe in their 'truth', as they see it. So, when someone, like you, comes along and tells them the actual Truth, they get offended and insulted and refuse to believe they might be wrong. They don't want to step beyond their 'safe' zone because in their mind, they already know the truth."

"Yeah, that must be what is happening," Alexander nodded in agreement.

"But don't give up, my friend," Jake encouraged. "Just keep telling the story of Jesus and His salvation."

"I will, but like I said, it's been so very lonely here," Alexander sighed. "But I've learned to rely upon the Lord each day, relying on His presence with me. I did learn some scripture before I was sold into slavery. Psalm 27 is a scripture that gives me great comfort. Verse 1 talks about God being my refuge and I shouldn't be afraid. A lot of the

Psalm explains how there may be enemies all around, but the Lord will defend me and hide me. I sing with the psalmist in verse 6, 'And now my head shall be lifted up!' But verse 8 is special to me. It says, 'When You said, Seek My face. My heart said to You, Your face, Lord, I will seek'. That teaching has been so very precious to me. I live to love the Lord and be in His presence!"

Jake smiled. "If that's what the Lord Jesus has taught you through this experience, I'd say it has been worth it."

Alexander just nodded and looked up to heaven. "Yes, it has been," he said with a glimmer in his eye. Then he looked back at Jake with a lighthearted look and said, "Would you like to meet the 'fellas'?"

"The 'fellas'?"

"My great friends, the horses!"

"Of course. Let's go!"

The two Christians moseyed over to the barn stalls, close to where they had been talking. Carpus and the rest of the crew had already cooled down and stabled the horses. As the two men stepped closer, all four jet black horses swung their heads in Alexander's direction and pricked their ears. One of them snorted. All of them had their heads hanging out over their individual stable gates, in a welcoming anticipation. Alexander eased up to the first horse in line and gently ran his hand over its nose.

"Hey there, big fellow," he spoke to the animal. Then without looking over at Jake he said, "This is Trooper. He is my inside horse, the horse closest to the inside of the turns on the track. He is the leader and commands the respect of the other horses. The other horses follow the lead of my inside horse. He's got a wonderful personality. A determined personality. Trooper is all black, no other markings." Again, without looking back at Jake, Alexander said to Trooper, "You're a good boy." And patted the stallion on the neck.

The two men moved down the line. "This is Rascal. He's harnessed next to Trooper. He tends to be very playful and energetic, don't you, big fella. We harness him in this alignment, so his boundless energy can be kept in check by the other horses. Rascal has three white stockings." Alexander ran his hand and arm under and around Rascal's neck. He patted Rascal's sleek black neck. "You really like to run, don't you, boy," he said affectionately to the horse.

Alexander moved down the row. "Next to Rascal we have Thunder. He's third in line and that is for a reason. Thunder is powerful, yet a very controlled animal. He knows how to race. His race instincts are excellent. And, most importantly, he listens to me quite well. They all listen well, but especially Thunder. As, you can see, Thunder has a thin, white streak down his nose. The white streak on his nose reminds us of lightning which generates thunder. Hence, his name is Thunder." The driver stepped back and looked Thunder straight in the eye. The horse pricked his ears again. "You and I understand each other, don't we boy," he said and the stallion whinnied.

"And finally, we have Swifty. He's my outside horse. Since Swifty is the outside steed, he has to travel the furthest. And because of that, Swifty has learned to stay synchronized perfectly with the other horses. He's a great follower, which makes him perfect for the outside. As you can see. Swifty has a tiny white star on his forehead. Swifty is so easy to work with. He's a joy to be around"

Alexander stepped back and adoringly spread out his arms over the four beautiful, sleek, black stallions. "There they are. My buddies. We run together. We win together."

Then the young man looked at Jake. "I really do love what I'm doing. I thank God for bringing me to this place. I'll just have to see where God takes me from here."

9
DIFFICULT REALIZATION

After a long day at the Black Diamond stable, Jake and Hannah trudged up the half mile road into the city of Samaria. They were both dog-tired. She had been cooking all morning, then serving lunch for the whole twenty man crew, then cleaning up the mess left behind, and then scrubbing all the pots and pans and dishes. Finally, her last daily duty was to straighten up the team kitchen and make it tidy for the next day.

"And what did you do today, my beloved one?" she asked, as they walked toward the city.

"Well, I've been working with our team leathercrafter, Caleb," Jake commented. "He's a really good guy. I like him. We reworked several of the bridles for the horses. The team is building another chariot, so, Caleb showed me how to stretch the thin leather covering over the chariot frame to form the dashboard. You stretch it tight and at the same time you tack it down to the wood frame. Pretty amazing stuff."

"I see. There were two of you." she said with a side tilt to her head.

"Of course."

"And you were in the cool shade, in the barn, with a nice breeze blowing through the barn."

"Right again."

She scowled playfully at Jake. "Why is it that I feel like I'm getting the short end of the stick, in this deal."

"Honey, what on earth could you mean?" he said sarcastically.

"I mean, I came along on this trip to help you do some investigating. Now, all I've investigated is the inside of a hot, steamy kitchen, slinging grease, cooking food, slopping food, serving hungry men, washing dishes, scrubbing pots and scouring pans. And now, will you look? Look at these formerly beautiful secretary hands. They're a mess! Red and irritated! Dishpan hands!" She feigned consternation. "Somehow, I don't think this is exactly the even trade I expected between your work and mine."

Then Hannah stopped walking along the road and folded her arms across her chest. She said with a prune face, "You told me this was also supposed to be our vacation. Vacation." She twisted her mouth to one side, which wrinkled her nose. "Doesn't look much like a vacation, does it."

"I know, honey, I promise you'll get your vacation. But what we are doing is the only way we can stay in touch with Alexander. And besides, we may not be staying around here that much longer."

"What?" she questioned. "What are you talking about? Not staying around here much longer?"

"Let's find a place to have supper and I'll tell you all about it."

The couple made their way through the city and landed at a small restaurant on the main boulevard called Hezekiah's Place. The café was a quaint little place with seven tables and a quiet atmosphere. Hezekiah owned the establishment and members of his family waited tables, cooked the food, and bussed the tables. Even the little six year old daughter was an integral part of the service, cleaning off tables and greeting folks. It was an old-fashioned family affair, which made the dining experience quite charming in this little evening retreat.

Jake and Hannah both ordered the Blue Plate Special and when the food arrived Jake began to unload his feelings.

"Hannah, I mentioned to you that we may not be staying around here that much longer."

"Yes, and your statement certainly shocked me. It raised some big questions in my mind."

"What I meant to say was that there may not be a need any longer for us to stay here in Samaria."

She cocked her head to one side and with a totally baffled look, exclaimed, "You're playing with words, now. And you're very confusing. What do you mean we 'may not need' to stay? What has happened?"

"Today I discovered that Alexander loves being here and is thankful to God for his new situation. He thoroughly loves working with the horses. He even calls them his 'buddies'. He seems content and happy in his new state of affairs. He's so happy, I don't think we could ever pry him out of here. And if we did, it would be against his will."

Hannah dropped her fork in shock. She shook her head to be sure she had heard Jake correctly. "You're telling me that we should just forget about taking Alexander home with us because he has become accustomed to his new lifestyle?"

"No, sweetheart, Alexander truly loves his new lifestyle. He has always loved horses. He grew up around the animals. Pudge even told me that Alexander had been working in the Royal Stables in Jerusalem. Then he was kidnapped by the gang. If he had been kidnapped and sold to anybody else, doing some menial task, he'd have been ready yesterday to get outa here. We probably could have negotiated a deal with his owners to buy him out of slavery and get him released. But he is truly happy here, working for Black Diamond Racing." Jake put one arm across his chest and brought his other arm thoughtfully up to cradle his chin. "I don't know what to say to Pastor James back in Jerusalem. I guess we'll tell him the truth about the situation and he will just have to accept it."

Hannah reached over and touched the detective's arm. "Slow down, honey. Let's hang around for a little while longer. We can at least give Alexander some Christian fellowship during the time we're here. Maybe we could even have some Bible studies with him and strengthen his new Christian life."

"Yeah, that is a good idea. We're not in any big hurry to get back to Jerusalem. We're both fully employed, making decent money. We can be his Christian buddies. We can play this situation out and see where it leads us."

They both went back to enjoying their supper. Hannah looked around at the other patrons who were also enjoying their supper.

"Seeing all this food reminds me of how much food I have to prepare each day for the team."

"And you are doing a very commendable job."

Then Hannah playfully looked up from her plate through the top of her eyes at Jake. "You know, folks around here in Samaria love pork. They like pork roast, pork chops, pork loin, pork ribs. I cook a lot of pork in the team kitchen. And you also know that I've never cooked pork before in my life. Growing up as Jews, I was never, never allowed to eat pork. I've never tasted it before, either. Well … you know what … add a little salt …"

"Hannah! You didn't!"

"Oh, yes, I did! You should try it."

10

SCORPIO

J ake began to notice that one of the team members seemed to be in a constant foul mood. Consistently erratic and confrontational. His name was Scorpio. He seemed to be brooding about something all the time. Nothing pleased him. Persistently discontented. He lived in a endless fuming anger. To the detective's mind, this man was a man to keep a close eye on. And Jake determined to figure out the cause of this man's problem.

Scorpio's discontentment showed in his appearance. He seemed to enjoy being filthy dirty. He flaunted the fact that he rarely took a bath. So as a result, a rank aroma followed him everywhere he went. "It keeps the other teams away from me," he would manically laugh. Of course, it kept everyone else away, too, isolating him. His wild, black hair blossomed out of his head in a long, stringy, greasy bush. His beard looked like a dirty black wad of brambles, knotted together by the wind. Scorpio always wore the same ugly charcoal gray tunic, which he never washed. And he always growled in a menacing, tough guy snarl. He projected the rough, course individual image – and he lived that way, as well.

Jake wondered to himself why Diotrephes continued to allow this antagonism to continue to infest the team. One day, as he and Caleb were working their leather goods, oiling down the horse bridles, Jake asked, "What ails Scorpio? He seems to be mad at the world, all the time."

"Oh, that sourpuss, he's angry with The Captain," Caleb stated matter-of-factly.

"What's he so angry about? Scorpio works for the best team in racing. He's got the best life in the chariot racing business."

"Well, he's always been an agitator. He has always thought that his ideas were better than the boss. And when he didn't get his way he'd stomp around and kick up a fuss. And then he'd take out his anger on the race track."

"Race track? What are you talking about?"

"Oh, I guess nobody has told you," Caleb stated.

"Told me what?"

"Scorpio used to be our chariot driver. When we got Alexander on the team, the boss demoted Scorpio as our driver."

"W-h-o-a," Jake slowly said. "Scorpio used to be your driver? That explains a lot."

"Yeah, Scorpio would take his anger and turn into a wild man on the race track. He raced with a wild, reckless vengeance in his driving, a seething rage. He took outrageous chances trying to prove to the world that he was the best driver alive. He'd dive his chariot in front of another competitor and if he crashed into the other guy and knocked him into the wall, that was the other guy's problem."

"And The Captain finally got fed up with his antics?" Jake asked.

"That's about the size of it. The boss had to fire Scorpio as our team driver. Scorpio generated too much animosity from the other race teams against our team. The Captain wants to maintain a good reputation. He is a good and honorable man. He likes to run a clean operation and he did not like the stain that Scorpio placed on our team. But then there also were the many crashes."

"Crashes?"

"Right. Too many by Scorpio. Look over in that corner of the barn. See those three crumpled and twisted hulks of chariots? Those are Scorpio's signatures. His dangerous driving would many times end up in wrecks and injured horses."

Jake shook his head, trying to process this new info. "Man, that is tough. How does Scorpio feel about being replaced by Alexander as driver for the team?"

"How would you feel?" Caleb stated, glancing at Jake in surprise. "Put yourself in his shoes. He's furious! He is a bitter, hateful man! And he lets it show at work every day, all day long. And his attitude toward Alexander? Well, Scorpio seems to take it personally, like Alexander is his personal mortal enemy. If Alexander comes near Scorpio, well, Scorpio's claws come out and you'd better hold him back."

"So, why does the boss let Scorpio still work for him?"

"The Captain is a gracious man. He will work with a guy and give him chance after chance, hoping the man's attitude will straighten out. As far as I'm concerned, Scorpio has used up all his chances. If I had to decide, Scorpio would have been booted long ago."

Several times a week Alexander practiced his driving skills on the race track. Jake could literally see degrees of improvement on each practice run. Alexander had developed a smoothness to his driving style. Every movement was fluid and effortless. He drove into the turns with powerful determination, combined with a calm confidence. As he stood in the chariot, reins in hand, behind his four faithful friends, Alexander displayed a quiet poise, even at full speed. He learned how to broad slide the chariot through the corners, kicking up two rooster tails of dirt. This technique helped the chariot slip around the corners quicker and exit the turn faster. He soon realized this driving style could also help him pass a competitor by broad sliding under an opponent's chariot on the inside. It became obvious that Alexander had quickly become a very savvy chariot driver.

But there was someone else watching, too. From the stables, while cleaning and mucking out the stalls, Scorpio watched and seethed. His brooding anger kept him hot. Diotrephes also was watching and walked up behind Scorpio one day, as the former driver worked and brooded and toiled and fumed.

The Captain said, "Scorpio, you are going to have to get hold of your temper."

Scorpio never turned around. "I got no respect for you … boss," he growled in a guttural low voice. "You shot me outa the saddle for no reason. I'm the best driver you ever had. And you know it. I mighta had a wreck or two but that ain't no reason to fire me from being your star driver."

"Scorpio, we have talked about this before," Diotrephes stated calmly. "You are a good driver but you cannot control you emotions. A great driver must learn to control his passions and not be reckless and wild. You have gotten a bad reputation on the racing circuit for winning at all cost, even if you have to run over people."

"Don't blame me for that guy on the Green Team who got his leg broke in that crash two months ago," Scorpio snarled, as he turned to face his boss. "He dove in on me and he just got in my way. It's just tough luck for him. I won the race, didn't I?"

"Scorpio, I'm letting you know that you are treading on thin ice. I've let you stay on the team in hopes that being demoted might humble you a little and maybe, just maybe, I'll give you another try at driving. But you've got to prove to me that this hotheadedness of yours is squelched and you can learn to control your feelings."

Scorpio jerked up straight in surprise. "Do you really mean that, boss? You'd let me drive again?" Scorpio asked in disbelief.

"I always say what I mean, you know that. I'm a man of my word."

"Boss, er Mister Diotrephes, I will prove to you I can be a good boy and not get mad."

"Okay, I'll be watching to be sure I see those improvements. And I want to see you treating Alexander much better than you have lately. He is your teammate. He is now part of our team."

"Oh, yes sir, Mister Diotrephes. I will show you I can be a team player. And I promise I'll treat Alexander really good. Like my kid brother."

"Good, glad to hear it. Now get back to work. We'll talk about this in a few days. I'll keep an eye on how you're doing in learning to control your temper."

During one of the days when Alexander was making some practice runs, Scorpio happened to be near the track, currying one of the other team horses named Champion. As Scorpio brushed the horse's mane, he couldn't take his eyes off of Alexander's practice laps on the track. Soon, the former driver stopped currying Champion and became transfixed with the activity on the practice track. Scorpio began to visibly become agitated. As Alexander rounded the turn, on one of his practice laps, Scorpio threw his hands up in exasperation and yelled at him, "Hey, you clown! You're doin' it all wrong! Drive those horses harder into the turn! What's wrong with you, you dumbbell!"

Alexander was so absorbed into his driving, plus the noise of the pounding hoofbeats and the rattling clatter of the chariot, he couldn't hear Scorpio. The next lap, Scorpio threw down his curry brush and dashed out onto the track as Alexander swooped by. With his arms flailing over his head, Scorpio darted out almost into the path of the charging horses and charioteer.

"Stop, wild man! You don't know what you're doing!" he shouted.

All Alexander could see was the blur of a man about to be run over by his horses. He reined the stallions hard to the left to avoid crashing into the man and stood the chariot up on one wheel, nearly flipping over. The skilled charioteer righted the tipping chariot and raced past the danger before he could get his team of horses slowed down and stopped.

Alexander jumped from his perch and ran back to see if he had inflicted any damage to the man he had tried hard not to kill. As he ran up to Scorpio, he stopped short.

"Scorpio! What were you trying to do!" a surprised Alexander shouted.

Scorpio screamed, "Why you! You tried to kill me," and he hurled himself into Alexander like he had been launched from a catapult. With a full body tackle, he leveled the young man to the dirt. Scorpio was shrieking, "You insane lunatic! You tried to kill me! You maniac!" He started to take a roundhouse swing at his prey on the ground, when some of the other team members grabbed him from behind and pulled him off Alexander. They wrestled Scorpio to the ground, pinning him down. Scorpio scuffled with them, too, violently kicking his legs and screaming, flinging dirt and dust everywhere.

"Settle down," Caleb shouted at Scorpio, as several other crewmen piled on to help hold the attacker down.

"Didn't you see it!" Scorpio screeched. "That assassin tried to kill me, so I couldn't replace him!"

Alexander stood up and looked down at the writhing man on the ground. "Scorpio, my intention was never to replace you. And I'm not afraid that you will replace me. We both could share the reins, if you'd let yourself ..."

Scorpio cut him off. "I'll get you for this!" he snorted while still being held down. "You tried to kill me! I'll never forget that! Murderer!"

Diotrephes heard the yelling and screaming out on the track and ran up to the scene.

"What goes on here?" he exclaimed. "And someone grab that team of horses and calm them down!" he ordered. "Let Scorpio up off the ground! Now, will someone explain to me what this ruckus is all about!"

The men released Scorpio and he sprung to his feet, dust and dirt flying. "That lame brain tried to kill me!" he yelled pointing his dirty, knurled finger at Alexander. "Murderer!"

"Wait just a second!" The Captain insisted. "I ask what is going on here. Someone tell me what started this whole uproar."

Caleb spoke up. "It's very simple. Scorpio ran out onto the track in front of the running horses and Alexander had to swerve the horses so he didn't hit Scorpio. Scorpio thought Alexander tried to kill him, when actually Alexander nearly killed himself in trying to avoid the crash. That's the short of it."

Diotrephes turned to Scorpio. "Is that the way it happened? Did you run out onto the track in the path of the horses?"

"Yeah, but I was tryin' to get that wild man you've got for a driver to listen to me!" Scorpio chided. "Then he tried to run over me."

"Why didn't you wait until his run was over and then give him your advice?"

"He needed to hear right then! He's a puny know-it-all! He just won't listen! And then he tried to kill me!"

Caleb spoke up. "Alexander did such a great job of avoiding Scorpio, that he near about flipped over but he kept his cool and kept control so no damage came to the chariot or to the horses."

Again Diotrephes turned to Scorpio. "It doesn't sound like Alexander tried to run you over. In fact, it sounds more like you were trying to cause more trouble for this team."

"But he tried to kill me to get me outa the way so I can't replace him!" Scorpio bellowed.

"No, my friend, you will never replace Alexander as our team driver," Diotrephes said firmly, "because I am firing you, as of right now. I've had it with you. You are no longer a member of this team. Come with me to the office and I'll give you your wages that are coming to you."

Scorpio stood his ground. He slowly wagged his head and gnawed at his bottom lip, as he looked around at all the team members surrounding him. "I see," he slowly growled through his teeth. "So, that's the way it's gonna be. Okay, you all will live to regret this, all of you. You haven't seen the last of Scorpio. You will all be very sorry you humiliated Scorpio." His eyes filled with rage and turned wild and fiery, as an evil sneer crept across his lips.

Then the crowd encircling him opened up and Scorpio started to inch away from the group.

"Follow me over to the office and I'll pay you your wages," Diotrephes called to him.

"Keep your lousy, stinkin' wages, Captain almight. I don't want your crummy dough. I'm gonna do just fine. Just you wait and see."

As Scorpio stormed angrily off the track, without looking back, he yelled one last parting shot, "You watch me! I'm gonna grind this lousy, second-rate team into the dust! I'll make all of you the laughing-stock of the racing circuit!"

11

DISASTROUS DISCOVERY

ll The Black Diamond Racing Team paused, speechless, quiet, as they watched Scorpio storm away.

Diotrephes sighed sadly. "Well, guys, that's that. It's been coming for a long time," he stated watching Scorpio stomp off the practice grounds, kicking dirt as he went. "But take note. We have seen the eyes of a vengeful man. He will be relentless in the future in getting his retribution. We can certainly count on payback of some sort."

"But how can Scorpio retaliate against us?" one of the crew asked. "He can't hurt us, can he?"

"The word I'm thinking of is *sabotage*," The Captain stated. "If Scorpio can sneak into our grounds or buildings, he could deliberately damage our equipment. He might even try to cut a leader or a harness or a rein so it will fail during a practice run or worse, in a race."

The race crew stood silent.

"What do we do, now?" one of them asked.

"From now on, we are going to have to protect against any attempted sabotage," Diotrephes said. "From now on, we will have to be on our guard. You all heard Scorpio's threats. And we all know how hotheaded he is. He definitely means business."

"But how do we do that?" Carpus questioned.

"Listen, Captain," Jake spoke up. "I have had some experience of doing surveillance work when I lived in Jerusalem. I picked up some skills at making myself invisible in the shadows so I could keep an eye on a certain area or people. I think I already know some perfect places to hide for keeping a lookout over the whole facility."

"Well, well. That is good news, Jacob," Diotrephes remarked with a smile. "If you think you can do it. We will need you to start tonight. Scorpio may strike tonight. He's mad enough to not waste any time in trying to damage our racing operation."

"Yes, sir," Jake said. "I've already got a plan in mind. If we can get all the horses into the barn during the night, it will be easier for me to keep an eagle-eye on them. We wouldn't want Scorpio sneaking around and nicking a horse's tendon with a knife. That would surely ruin a horse's career."

"Sounds like a good plan," Caleb stated. "I hadn't even thought that Scorpio might be such a low down dirty rat as to nick a tendon on one of the horses. But he's evil enough!"

"He'd better not try to hurt one of my stallions!" Nathan exclaimed. "I'll make him sorry he was ever born if he ever tried to do that! I'll nick him for good!"

"Simmer down, Nathan," said Caleb. "We'll make sure our horses are well protected."

"Okay, men, this plan that Jacob mentioned sounds like the best plan," Diotrephes stated. "By close of business tonight we will bring all twelve of our stallions into the barn. We know they will all fit in there. We have done it before when the weather is really fierce."

Nathan spoke up again. "The horses are my responsibility. Me and my trainers will get all our stallions safely in the barn and in their stalls for the night." Then Nathan clinched his teeth and growled, "Scorpio is not going to hurt one of *my* horses."

Turning to Jake, The Captain advised, "Jacob, you'd better go ahead right now and get some sleep, since you'll be up all night. You can go back to town and sleep in your room at the inn or you can sleep right here in my office area. But if you sleep in the city, be sure to be back here by nightfall."

Jake knew he could get better sleep back in his room in the city. He worked out a deal with Hannah for her to wake him up as she returned to the inn after ending her cooking shift at team headquarters.

Jake's first night on guard duty proved to be rather uneventful.

Jake's second night on guard duty proved to be even more uneventful.

Jake's third night on guard duty … well, this total uneventfulness went on for over a week.

Nothing suspicious happened.

On the twelfth morning of Jake's continuous stakeout, he returned to the office, as always, to report to Diotrephes the activities of the previous night.

He entered the office where the team owners, Diotrephes, Octavius, and Linus sat around the planning table in the headquarters.

"Ah, here he comes," Octavius proclaimed, looking over at Jake, extending his right arm in salute. "The midnight watchman extraordinaire."

"Yes, it's me," Jake said, blurry eyed. "I don't know about the extraordinaire part of it, but I sure can watch everything all through the night!"

Diotrephes smiled. "I take it you've got nothing new to report. No break ins. No overnight destruction."

"Not even a whimper from a mouse," Jake stated with a heavy sigh. "Nothing. Nighttime sure is beautiful but I'm seeing way to much of this silent night stuff and a whole lot of starry, starry night."

"Well, I'm not sure what to tell you," Diotrephes said. "We can't let our guard down. Maybe we could switch off with one of the other crew members and give you some relief from this night duty."

"That's sounds great," Jake said. "It may be kinda rough but maybe I can get my eyes accustomed to the light again," he laughed. "You know, sitting over there in that barn all night, your mind can start playing tricks on you. Like, I started to ask myself questions, just so I could hear myself respond and answer my own questions. It's kinda funny but this one question kept pinging around in my brain that I couldn't answer. It was the strangest thing."

"Well, what was this great mystery question that has proven to be such a mischief-maker?" asked Linus.

"The question rattled around in my brain all night. It is ... how did you ever come up with the name Black Diamond Racing for your team?"

"Well, that's pretty easy to answer," Diotrephes stated. "And it's no mystery. You see, last year we won the major competition race at the hippodrome race track at Caesarea by the coast. It's the biggest race of the year, a once a year extravaganza. One of the many prizes that were awarded to us for our victory was a magnificent Black Diamond Trophy provided by Caesar himself and presented by one of his illustrious emissaries. It was quite an honor to receive an award from Caesar, which came from his very own private collection."

"And the trophy itself is exquisite and very valuable," Octavius remarked. "The actual black diamond is extremely rare and it is mounted on a gold setting with a splendid pearl-white velvet backing. It is so valuable, we never leave it out, we always lock it up in a very safe place."

"Well, do you ever get it out just to admire it?" Jake, the ever inquisitive detective, asked.

"On occasion," Octavius teased, cocking his head while smirking at Jake.

"Well, do you kinda, sorta think that on this occasion you could look at it today?" Jake smiled sheepishly, raising his eyebrows hoping for an affirmative answer.

Diotrephes looked around at the other owners. "What do you think? Can we trust him?" he smiled as he gave a wink.

"I don't know. This guy may be a big security risk," Linus soberly stated, rubbing his chin.

"What kinda trophy is it, if you can't enjoy it and look at it once in a while," Jake appealed.

"Ah, let him see it," Octavius finally laughed. "Besides, I haven't looked at it in a good long while. Let's get it out and just drool over it."

"Alright," Diotrephes smiled. He reached into his desk drawer and pulled out a brass key. "The trophy is right over here in a safe place in the office. It's kept hidden away in a locked closet by this door over here that leads into the kitchen."

The four men stepped the short distance across the office and came to a standstill at a black curtain hanging over a recessed alcove along the far wall. Diotrephes brushed the drapery back. A thick oak door revealed itself behind the curtain. The Captain's key rattled in the lock on the door and the door yawned open. The light in the alcove was dim but to Jake it looked like there was nothing behind the door.

Suddenly Diotrephes yelled out, "The trophy is gone! The Black Diamond is gone!"

The other two owners jabbed their heads into the dimly lit closet and immediately cried out, "What! This cannot be! It's gone!" Unbelief swept over all of them.

Frantic questions spewed out. "How can this be? Who could have removed the trophy? Was it stolen? Who could have stolen the trophy? Who knew where the trophy was hidden?"

Jake exclaimed, "Maybe someone has moved it to a different place."

"No, no, no!" Diotrephes insisted vehemently. "We three owners are the only people who ever take the trophy out of the closet. We never let anyone else on the team handle the trophy. We have shown the trophy to the team occasionally but we always have maintained strict control of the security of the precious thing."

Jake grabbed a lamp and stuck his head into the closet. It proved to be a very small closet, specifically designed to house The Black Diamond Trophy. A nifty, petite display cabinet inside the closet had cradled the trophy. The display cabinet was lined with purple velvet, meant to set off the beauty of the trophy.

The other owners continued to frantically poke their heads into the closet in hopes that the trophy had fallen off the shelf of the cabinet and onto the floor of the closet.

"It's been stolen," Linus stated flatly. "There is no other explanation."

"Who could have stolen it?" Octavius questioned. "There has been no opportunity to steal the trophy."

"Listen, men," the detective commanded. "Don't touch anything. Let me look this crime scene over before anything is moved. I have had a little experience in investigative work."

The three owners backed up a little, still muttering among themselves in deep anguish over the loss of the valuable gift from Caesar.

In the yellow glow of the lamp light, Jake examined the entire interior of the trophy closet. Nothing seemed to have been disturbed. The display cabinet inside looked undisturbed, as well. He swung around and closely scrutinized the closet door and its lock. He ran his fingers over the lock to feel for any evidence of someone trying to jimmy the lock. He even felt along the edge of the wood of the door, looking for the tell-tale roughness of a pry bar being jammed into the crack between the door frame and the door. Nothing.

Jake straightened up. "Gentlemen, there is no evidence that this door has been tampered with or that the lock has been jimmied. That is very strange. Are you sure the trophy hasn't been moved for some reason?"

"Absolutely not," Linus said sternly. "We all guard the gift from Caesar with the utmost care."

"Well, with no evidence of tampering around the door or the lock, it looks like someone knew how to open the closet door. It's beginning to look like an inside job."

Diotrephes flared up. "What! Are you suggesting that one of our team members stole the trophy?" he asked indignantly.

Jake didn't answer his question. "Do you always keep that brass key for the closet door in your office desk drawer?" he asked.

"Yes, but then there is always someone in the office during the day. And then at night, we lock up the entire building," The Captain stated matter-of-factly.

"It's a real head-scratcher," Jake said. "It's possible that the person who lifted the diamond knew about the fact that you kept the key in your desk drawer. The robber must have waited until a moment when no one was in the office and swiped the key, grabbed the trophy and escaped, without a trace." Jake rubbed the back of his right thumb thoughtfully under his chin. "Yeah, that's the only way I can figure that the thief could have gotten away with it."

"Well, I cannot imagine when the office would *not* have had someone present during the day," The Captain stated with a puzzled look on his angry face. "Perhaps the thief was a burglar who broke in at night."

"Let me check around the office building to see if there are any signs of a break-in," Jake said.

Diotrephes stared at Jake. "How is it that you are so skilled in investigation? You talk and act like this is second nature to you" he asked.

"Back in Jerusalem, I did a lot of different jobs to make ends meet," the detective said, trying to be evasive. "Let me look around outside and see what I can turn up."

Jake was back in his element now – detective work.

He found no signs of a forced break-in from outside the office building. He found no signs of recent footprints outside the windows of the structure. All the exterior doors showed no evidence of tampering either of the doors themselves or the locks.

So, having hit a dead end, Jake asked permission from Diotrephes to expand his search out away from the Black Diamond facilities and into the adjacent area.

"You have my permission, Jacob," the boss said as he thoughtfully squinted at the detective. "I must say, the way you have approached this robbery reveals to me that you have been more than a casual observer of investigative work. I won't ask any more about your past. But I do believe you have the skills to find our trophy - our gift from Caesar. So, yes, please go and find out what you can."

"Thank you, Captain," Jake said but as he turned to leave, he pivoted back around. "Oh, just one more thing. Am I still on the payroll?" he smiled.

Diotrephes laughed out loud. "Yes, yes. You're still on the payroll. Now, will you get out of here?"

"There, I made you laugh," Jake grinned. "You needed to laugh. Glad to see it!"

Jake began his search by doing some nosing around in the city to hopefully get a lead on the Black Diamond Trophy and where it may have landed. It seemed very likely that whoever stole the trophy would want to unload it as soon as possible, since it was "hot". But then on the other hand, if the thief lifted the treasure simply because they loved the thought of it being a personal treasure from Caesar or he just loved gazing at the beauty of the black diamond, then the robber may never reveal that he had it. There are those evil types that steal simply because they like to collect beautiful things and gather those treasures around themselves.

But the more he thought about it, Jake's instincts began to drift more toward the idea that the burglar was a common laborer who needed money and was willing to sell the precious diamond trophy to the highest bidder. Still rattling around in his sleuth brain was the puzzle of how the intruder pulled off the theft, without a trace. He knew the robbery had to have been an inside job. But who could it be? Jake had his suspicions.

The best place to pick up clues would be in the markets and shops along the main drag in Samaria. Since he already had struck up a friendship with Artemas, the leathercrafter, the detective breezed into the leather shop for an "investigative" visit.

"Mornin', Artemas," Jake said as he walked into 'Leather Goods by Artemas'.

"Good morning, Jacob," Artemas smiled. "I haven't seen you for several weeks. The last time you came by you brought me that new design for a double ear bridle. How has that bridle worked out?"

"Perfect," Jake announced. "For our team, the double ear setup works better than a browband. You did a great job in the way you finished that new design. Caleb, our leathercrafter on the team said he can reproduce your finished design for the other horses on the team. He's going to call it the Artemas Bridle and promote it out on the circuit. His slogan will be 'Precision Performance by Artemas'. That will certainly throw some more business in your direction."

"Man, I like that! Sounds like a great plan," the leathercrafter smiled. "I might even add that catchy slogan to my own advertising. Now, what can I do for you today?"

"Well, sir, have you heard about the theft of the Black Diamond Trophy from my race team's headquarters."

"Oh, yeah, news like that travels like lightning in this town. I guess the loss was only discovered this morning but the news has already spread all over the city. How'd it happen?"

"Don't know," Jake said, shaking his head. "That's what we're trying to figure out. More importantly, where is the trophy?"

"It's such a tragedy," Artemas said, rapping his fingers thoughtfully on his front sales counter. "There was so much mystery surrounding that trophy. You know, it was a prized gift from Caesar himself. Everybody around here was able to see the trophy on display here in the city, after the Black Team won the prized award last year. It was displayed for several days. Ever after that, they changed the name of the team to The Black Diamond Racing Team. But after that one and only viewing of the trophy, no one in Samaria has ever seen it since. That alone added to the mystery cloaked around the royal prize. It's a wonder someone hasn't tried to steal it before now."

"People were that envious of the team having the trophy?" Jake asked.

"Oh, yeah," Artemas stated. "That expensive trophy caused The Black Diamond Racing team to become celebrities in the community. And it made a lot of people jealous. And envious. And even resentful."

Jake shook his head. "Wow, I didn't know all that. I just wondered if you had heard anything about what might have happened to the trophy. Any rumors?"

"No, just talk on the street about the robbery. Some people are sad about the theft. Others who are envious of other folks riches are visibly glad that Diotrephes and his company got their 'comeuppance.' That is sad to see. But to be perfectly honest with you, there are probably a lot of people in this city who gladly would have snatched the trophy, just out of envy or jealousy."

"A lot of people. That really narrows the field down substantially," Jake laughed sarcastically. "Okay, I'll work on that 'narrowed' field. But if you hear anything, please let me know."

"I'll do that. Good luck."

Two shops down the street, Jake turned off into the shop of the man he had first met in the city, the seller of fruits and vegetables.

"Hello, there, my friend," Jake greeted the man happily. "Remember me?"

"Oh, yes, I remember you," the seller of fruits and vegetables chided.

"You are one of those 'Freed Jews' who wants me to become a Christian. Well, I'm not buying. And I've got nothing more to say to you. I don't need your Jesus. I don't need your Christianity. It is a dead religion just like your dead leader, Jesus. Everyone knows He's dead. My religion suits me just fine. I'm good with it."

Jake smiled. "Actually Jesus is not dead. He is alive! I've seen him alive!" he proclaimed.

"Get out! Now, I know you're lost your mind!" the shop owner flared. "Seeing a living dead man! Get out! I told you once before in a very nice way to get out of my shop! Now, I'm telling you again to get out of my shop! If you don't leave right now, I'll call a policeman and have you arrested, Mister Freed Jew!"

Jake smiled again, pivoted and happily stepped outside the putridly toxic atmosphere. 'Huh, that really went very well,' he joked in his mind as he walked away. Next ...'

As the detective strolled down the street, he turned his ears wide open to listen to all the chatter in the crowds. He did hear some talk about The Black Diamond and knew the conversation had to be concerning the theft. But nothing substantial seemed to be discussed among the people.

Jake figured the clerk at the Inn By the Ivory House heard a lot of banter as clientele come in and go out. Besides, the Inn is a good place for people to congregate and talk over the news of the day. Jake sauntered into the Inn. The clerk was manning his post behind the front desk.

"Good morning, Mister Jezreel," the clerk greeted Jake. "Are you having a pleasant morning?"

"Not exactly," Jake said. "I guess you haven't heard about the theft of The Black Diamond."

"Oh yes, I have heard about it from one of our patrons. Theft of such a valuable item! That is terrible! Just terrible!"

"Have you heard anything else?"

"No, sir. Only the fact that the trophy has been stolen."

"Well, if you do hear any little bit of news about the theft that might be helpful in locating the whereabouts of the trophy, please let me know." Jake reached down and patted the small money bag hanging from his belt. "I'll make it worth your while," he said with a sly grin.

As the detective started to turn away, the clerk quickly said, "Ah, sir. I have an idea you may not have thought of. You might try checking with some of the jewelers in the city. Perhaps one of them may have had contact with a person trying to sell The Black Diamond. You never know. It's worth a try."

"Okay, thanks for the tip. If something pans out, I'll have a nice reward for you."

But as Jake walked away, the jeweler angle didn't make sense. Certainly a jewel trader would never admit to buying the stolen Black Diamond. He might buy it, but never tell. On the other hand, if someone tried to sell the diamond to a jeweler, Jake might be able to get a lead on a suspect.

After staying awake all the previous night on guard duty, Jake was practically asleep on his feet. He decided while he was here at the Inn, he'd get some shuteye. He cut "Zs" for most of the morning and afternoon. He woke up in time to greet Hannah when she came home from work.

"Hi, sweetheart," a blurry-eyed Jake yawned to Hannah. "I suppose you've heard the bad news from work."

"About the robbery? Yes. I've also heard you're on the case. I think Diotrephes believes you're some sort of detective."

"Yeah, he indicated that fact to me earlier today. I hope I haven't blown my cover. Several times I've gotten too eager about investigating stuff while I've been here. I just can't help myself."

"Well, just keep your head low," Hannah cautioned, "and don't talk so much like a detective."

"It's hard not to. The gumshoe in me just leaks out."

By the next morning, the city buzzed with the news of the theft. Jake didn't have to walk around questioning people. All he had to do was stand on the street corner and listen.

"I heard that The Black Diamond ended up over across town in a pawn shop."

"I heard that the governor stole it for his own personal collection."

"I heard that someone stole The Black Diamond and threw it into a 90 foot deep well, just to be mean."

"I heard that Neapolis Jewelers bought it for a thousand gold coins."

"I heard that The Black Diamond has already been spirited away to another country.

"I heard ..."

Jake realized all this yammering was ridiculous nonsense. None of this was true. It was only rumors, fantasized by wild imaginations, scattered by blabbering tongues, spreading like wildfire. None of this was productive. Only distractions.

With a fresh day ahead of him, Jake did decide to visit a number of the jewelry traders and gem shops in Samaria. If they hadn't been approached by someone to buy the stolen diamond, maybe they had heard if other jewelers in the trade had been contacted by the thief. Jake dropped by the city chamber of commerce and picked up a list of jewelers and gem dealers in Samaria. He worked the entire list, visiting every jeweler and gem dealer in the city. All day long the detective pounded the pavement. By six o'clock that evening, the end result was a big, fat zero. If one of the jewelers actually had been approached to buy the stolen diamond, everybody else in the gemology fraternity was covering for him.

Now that the day was pretty much spent, Jake could see the sun going down and decided to grab some supper. He had left a note in their room for Hannah to meet him at their favorite rendezvous, Hezekiah's Place. He waited for her, relaxing at one of the small tables, watching people pass by on the street. As he waited, the little six year old daughter of the proprietor skipped up to the detective and stopped in front of him.

"Hello, mister, ya gonna eat supper with us tonight?" she asked in a happy voice.

Jake sat up straight and looked her in the eye. "Yes, ma'am. You got anything good to eat tonight?"

"Yes, we do. But you'll have to ask daddy about what food you can have. Daddy told me to come out and light the lamp on your table. So, here I am."

The little girl carried a slender candle and lit the small lamp on Jake's table.

"Ooo, that glittering lamp looks just like a diamond," Jake commented.

"Are you talkin' about diamonds, too?" the six year old asked.

Jake looked surprised. "Why, have you heard other people talking about diamonds today?"

"Lots of people. But one man seemed to know something important about a black diamond. I never heard of a black diamond. Have you? But he sounded like he knew a bunch of stuff about it."

"Was he here at your restaurant?"

"Yes, sir. He was talking to another man at that table over there. They were whispering and I couldn't hear much. But they said something about horses and something about a team. I'm little. I don't understand much."

"Was the team they were talking about called The Black Team?"

"No, I didn't hear nothin' about a Black Team. But they sure did whisper a lot."

"Had you ever seen the two men before. Could you identify them?"

"Yes, sir, I've seen them before. But no, sir, I couldn't iden'afy them."

About that time Hannah arrived.

"Hi, honey," she said to Jake. And then kneeling down, Hannah smiled at the little girl, "And how are you doing this evening, Mary?"

"I'm doing just fine, ma'am. Me and your beau are having a good talk about pretty diamonds."

"Ohh. Well, don't let me interrupt. What else were you about to say?"

"That's all, Maybe daddy can tell you more. I'll get him."

In a flash the little six year old detective dragged her father, Hezekiah, out of the kitchen and over to the couple's table.

"Daddy, tell these nice people about the two whispering men who sat at that table over there."

"Hello, Mister Jacob. There is not a lot to tell. The two men sat in my café for over an hour. They didn't order anything but coffee the whole time they sat here. They just ordered more coffee. They kept scratching numbers on a papyrus sheet. Some of the numbers looked like large amounts of money. It was like they were working out a deal of some sort. But very hush hush."

"Your little girl mentioned that the men discussed something about horses and a black diamond and something about a team."

"I did hear something like that. Maybe they were horse trading. Maybe they were discussing the stolen Black Diamond, I don't know. Or maybe they were just negotiating about a valuable gem. But it all seemed to be very mysterious and secretive. Whenever I would bring them more coffee, they always tried to hide what they were doing. It made me suspicious but," Hezekiah shrugged, "what could I do about it?"

Jake leaned back in his chair and looked admiringly at the two café workers. "Thank you. Both of you. You both have given me a whole lot to think about. Much more than you'll ever know." Then he folded his hands in front of him on the table and said, "The wife and I would like to have some supper this evening. What's ya got that's on special for the night?"

12

THE JEZREEL DETECTIVES

All the way back to the Inn, Jake and Hannah spoke very little. The evidence they had discovered at Hezekiah's Place had opened up a whole new direction in the investigation. When the couple arrived back to their room in the Inn, Hannah seemed a little puzzled.

"While we were eating supper tonight, you said you didn't want to talk about Hezekiah's thoughts in public," she stated with an inquisitive glint in her eye. "Okay, we're not in public now. So what do you think it all means?"

Jake sat down on the edge of the bed and looked up at his wife. "Those two guys Hezekiah was talking about are mixed up in this business somehow," he said confidently. "The three things the little girl said she heard the men talking about were horses, a team, and most importantly, a Black Diamond. There is only one Black Diamond in existence in these parts. The stolen Black Diamond. Whoever those two men were, they quite possibly were plotting a deal about the Diamond. I wish Hezekiah could have put the finger on at least one of the men. But at least, this may be a good sign that after two days since the discovery of the theft, the trophy is still in the vicinity of the city of Samaria."

Then Hannah frowned, as a memory swept across her mind. "Jake, what day was Scorpio fired?"

"Day? Ohh, that was about two weeks ago. Why?"

"Uh-huh. I thought so. Something very odd happened the day Scorpio was fired. I didn't think much about it at the time. At that moment, I didn't even know Scorpio had been fired."

"What did you see?"

"I was working in the kitchen preparing lunch for the boys. You know there is a door connecting the owner's main office and the kitchen. While I was over in the corner of the kitchen pulling several loaves of bread out of the oven, Scorpio burst through the door from the office area in a big hurry. He had a burlap sack slung over his shoulder and the contents appeared to be bulky and heavy. He rushed on through the kitchen and out the back door. It seemed odd to me but as far as I knew he was just lugging something work related."

"Did he see you?"

"I don't think so. He was too busy getting out of the building in what seemed to be a big hurry. However, as he exited the back door to the kitchen he glanced back toward the office doorway. But I still don't think he saw me in the kitchen."

Jake brought his hand up and began to stroke his chin, as he thought about Hannah's experience. "This all happened on the day Scorpio got fired."

"Uh-huh. Of course, I never put two and two together at the time that Scorpio had done anything wrong. That was two weeks ago. No one discovered that the trophy had been stolen until just two days ago. I had nearly forgotten all about Scorpio's run through the kitchen, but now it all makes sense!"

"Man, this tells us a lot," Jake stated as he jumped up from the edge of the bed. "When the facts are fairly obvious, then you've got to reason that they are correct. Scorpio may have stolen The Black Diamond Trophy the day he got fired. Since he was part of the team, he probably knew where the trophy was stored. He also had probably been in the office enough to have seen the key in Diotrephes' desk drawer. And the day he stomped off the practice track, he was wild with anger and threatened all of us. He saw his opportunity to get his revenge when he entered the office and saw that no one was there. All the owners had left the office and had run to the practice track to find out what the fight was all about."

"And that's when Scorpio probably stole the trophy," Hannah said. "That's why he was in such a gigantic hurry to escape through the kitchen, lugging that heavy burlap sack."

"Bingo! You've said it in a nutshell."

"What are we going to do? We can't go accuse Scorpio of any crime," Hannah stated. "You've taught me that much about circumstantial evidence."

"And even if we tried to accuse him, we wouldn't be able to. Scorpio has disappeared. Nobody has seem him since the day he got fired. I wonder if one of those two men sitting in Hezekiah's restaurant was Scorpio? It really would make perfect sense if one of the men was him."

A puzzled gaze crossed Hannah's face and she began to move her eyes all over the room. Through her tightly pressed lips, she finally said, "Looks like we've got a bunch more digging to do."

Jake now knew his search had narrowed greatly. Scorpio would be the detective's main focus of investigation. Jake decided that his best lead would be to go back to Hezekiah. Following his hunch that one of the men in the restaurant the day of the secret meeting was probably Scorpio, the detective hoped he could jog the restaurant owner's memory with a few more questions. When Jake arrived at the café, Hezekiah was working in the kitchen, but the little six year old was wiping off tables in the front.

"Hello, there, Mary," Jake said as he knelt down to talk to the little girl.

"Hello, Mister Jacob. Are you back doing more perspecting?"

Jake laughed. "Yeah, missy, you've got me pegged. I just wanted to see if you could remember anything more about the men who sat at that table over there, you know, the ones who were talking very quietly."

"No, sir, I told you as much as I could remember the last time you were here. But let me get daddy. We were talking about it and he did remember some other things."

The little girl disappeared but quickly reappeared with Hezekiah in tow.

"Hello, Jacob," Hezekiah stated. "Mary told me you had come back, asking more questions about the two men."

"I just thought I'd ask you about one of the men's appearance," Jake said. "Did one of the men have long, stringy hair?"

"Well yes, it is rather odd but the main thing about one of the men that I can remember is that he had greasy, bushy long hair."

"And did he look and talk gruff and tough?"

"Yes, like a snarling beast."

"And did he smell? And was he kinda dirty?"

"Yes, smelly and dirty is the right description."

"Sort of looked like he just came from a pig pen?"

"Yeah, and that's how he smelled. He smelled like a pig pen!"

"Did he have on an old ratty, charcoal colored tunic?'

"Yes, as a matter of fact, his clothes were a dirty, charcoal color. Does that mean anything?"

"It indicates a lot. That greasy, bushy hair, the smelly odor, and charcoal clothing sounds a lot like our old racing team driver, Scorpio. He got fired …"

"Daddy! Daddy!" the little girl interrupted. "That's the man!" she yelled pointing outside. "There he is on the street!"

Jake jerked around in time to see Scorpio glace over in the direction of the yelling little girl. Scorpio saw Jake and immediately bolted into a frantic sprint.

Jake yelled, "Stop, Scorpio!" and hurled himself out of the restaurant, in full pursuit of the suspected thief. "Stop! I want to talk to you!"

Scorpio never turned around but ran in determined strides down the main street of Samaria. He dodged around unsuspecting shoppers, even knocking some of them down. Jake tried desperately to avoid the fallen people and yet keep up his chase. Scorpio ducked around a corner up ahead. Jake slowed up, realizing Scorpio could be waiting around that corner with a brickbat, ready to crown him. The detective made a wide turn around the corner, staying away from the side of the building. As he rounded the corner, he caught a glimpse of Scorpio far down the alleyway, making his escape. Jake knew he had lost too much time at the corner, but still tried to catch up to the fleeing suspect. Then Scorpio ducked around another corner a long distance away. At that point, Jake knew there was far too much daylight between him and Scorpio. He was hopelessly behind to ever catch up.

The detective made his way back to Hezekiah's restaurant. The little girl and her daddy still stood looking longingly down the street.

"That looked like a bunch of fun!" the little girl squealed in delight.

"Oh yeah, that was a real blast," Jake gasped, out of breath. "I didn't catch him, though. I don't know what I would have done even if I did catch him."

A bewildered gaze etched Hezekiah's face. "That was the man that you were looking for," he stated in a deadpan. "I'm positive that was the man who sat in my café."

"Yep, that was Scorpio, our ex-team driver. I just wanted to talk to him. But maybe I will at a later time. I want to thank you, both." Jake looked at the little girl and said, "And especially to you, missy, for putting the finger on the man I was looking for."

"Put the finger on the man? I must have a v-e-r-y long finger!" the little girl laughed.

Jake left the little café with a much clearer direction for his next move. He tried to put himself in the shoes of Scorpio. What would motivate this ego maniac? Racing and revenge! Nothing but racing and revenge for a hated racing "enemy"! Jake knew that Scorpio's flaming passion was chariot racing. Scorpio even promoted himself as "The Demon Driver", a self-inflicted moniker that was meant to scare the competition. He would be hard pressed to ever give up driving a chariot. If a chance to continue to race presented itself, Jake knew Scorpio would grab it quick. But in the tight knit racing business, tracking down Scorpio's whereabouts was not going to be so easy. Team secrets kept the other race teams guessing. If "The Demon Driver" had landed on another team, "team secrets" may keep this news under wraps for weeks before the news would leak out.

Jake also knew Scorpio's new flaming revenge was to grind Diotrephes and his Black Diamond Team into the dust on the race track. If Scorpio was now driving for a rival racing team, he would use racing as a means to get his revenge on Diotrephes and his team. That is what Scorpio meant when he said, "You all will live to regret this. You haven't seen the last of Scorpio." Scorpio fully intended all along to get his vengeance on Diotrephes. Stealing The Black Diamond Trophy was part of that revenge. The obvious fact was "The Demon Driver" would be out for blood. No greater satisfaction could inspire Scorpio than to obliterate his hated enemy, his old boss and his old team.

More snooping around. The racing rumor mill provided a great source of information about changes to personnel on some of the other teams in the vicinity. Several race teams were headquartered in and around the Samaria area. Other teams headquartered their outfits outside of Samaria, in other adjacent towns. But the major race teams working out of Samaria, other than The Black Diamond Team, were The Red Team, The Green Team, and The Blue Team. Jake figured, if the other man meeting with Scorpio in Hezekiah's restaurant was a member of one of those race teams, then more than likely Scorpio was cutting a deal with him. That hunch narrowed down the span of investigation even closer to right here in Samaria.

Playing his instincts, Jake dropped by the leather shop of Artemas. The detective knew that all the other race teams in the area came to the leathercrafter occasionally to have emergency repairs or other work done to their leather racing gear. It was worth a try to see if Artemas might have picked up any news as the team members past through his shop.

"Well, hello, Jacob," Artemas called to the detective as he walked in the shop. "How's tricks?"

"Everything is running smooth, like a well-greased chariot wheel."

"Man, that does sound smooth. Is your race team getting ready for the upcoming big, annual race at Caesarea in a few weeks? It's the annual event called The Grand Judean Chariot Races at Caesarea. All the teams have been starting to come by and have me make fresh leather pieces for their racing equipment."

"Yeah, we're gearing up pretty good. Caleb, our leather man on the team, said he's got a new design for a unique breast collar and forked neck strap for the horses. He will probably come by this week with his new design to see what you think of it. Did I hear you say that other race teams have been coming by? Did you pick up any rumors from the other teams?"

"Ahh, I see what you're doing," Artemas laughed, raising his eyebrows. "You're doing a little nosing around about the competition. That's normal. Anything to get an edge on your racing rivals. Right?"

"I guess you could say that. My approach wasn't too subtle, was it?"

"No, not too subtle. Well, let's see. The Red Team had to build a new chariot. Seems like their driver clipped a wall with their chariot in practice. Kinda made a mess out of the chariot. That team also got some new horses. They bought several 'barbs', the best horses money can buy. The Green Team had a team member fall and break his leg. And … Oh! I know you'll be interested in this! Scorpio, your former driver, well, the Blue Team has hired him as their new driver! I just heard that news this morning. Quite a news flash, huh."

"Yeah, quite a news flash," Jake muttered.

"I imagine Scorpio will definitely give your driver, Alexander, a run for his money! That should be some great racing! Worth the price of a ticket, I'd say!"

"Did you learn any of the details about how Scorpio worked a deal to drive for that team?"

"Only rumors from other teams. Somebody mentioned that Scorpio bought his ride."

"Bought his ride? You mean he paid the team to let him drive for them?"

"Yeah, I have heard of it being done. It's not a normal practice. However, if a team is strapped for operating cash and in need of money, I have heard of drivers bringing money with them to buy their way onto the team. It sounds like Scorpio did the same thing. The rumor is he brought money with him and bought his way onto the Blue Team as their driver."

"Fascinating," Jake stated, shaking his head. "I've never heard of that one before. Paying to be hired for a job. You learn something new every day. The question is, where did Scorpio get enough money to buy his way onto the team? He certainly doesn't have much money, at all. In fact, he's been living hand to mouth lately."

"Search me," Artemas said, shrugging his shoulders. "I only spread the rumors. I report, you decide."

"Thanks, Artemas, you've been a big help."

Now the real mystery began to grip Jake. If Scorpio had stolen the Black Diamond, did he sell it to get enough money to "buy his ride" with the Blue Team? If he sold the valuable trophy, who did he sell it to? And where was the trophy now? Who had possession of it? Time was of the essence. The valuable Black Diamond may be slipping away into another region. Another country. Lost into the fog of obscurity forever. This mystery suddenly had gotten very complicated.

Jake knew Scorpio was far ahead of him and the trail seemed to be getting cold. Two weeks had passed since Scorpio got fired. And interlocking Hannah's story of Scorpio's suspicious actions on that same day, Jake realized he had lost two weeks of valuable time and that he had fallen very far behind Scorpio. His investigation now was seriously handicapped. Two whole weeks had been wasted. The detective now had to dig through the wasted time and uncover the non-existent trail.

Jake again made a sweep of all the jewelry dealers and gem shops in the city of Samaria. He was willing to pay handsomely for any information about the precious gem, but none of the jewel traders had any inkling of what had happened to The Black Diamond.

One jeweler stated, "I'd never buy a stolen diamond like The Black Diamond. My reputation would be ruined if I traded in stolen goods. And even if I would buy it, I could never sell it because it is too well known and famous. A diamond that is that celebrated would have to be hidden away in a secret collection, solely for the private collector. My best guess would be that whoever has The Black Diamond has secretly coveted the precious stone for some time. They found an opportunity to acquire it, and may now have it concealed in a safe hiding place. Then this person can enjoy the prized gem at their leisure for their own pleasure."

Jake explained the situation to Hannah in their room that evening.

"What the jeweler described to me made sense," the detective told his pretty wife. "If The Black Diamond has not surfaced on the market by now, it may very well have gone underground in some private collection. The trail has to start somewhere."

"But where?" she asked. "Anybody with money could be a private collector. And they're not going to advertise it."

"Let's connect the dots. The first logical place to begin investigating would be the team where Scorpio landed, the Blue Team," Jake reasoned as he paced the floor. "Somehow, The Black Diamond is tied to Scorpio's new employment as the driver of the Blue Team. Who is the owner of the Blue Team? Is the team owner *the* private collector willing to conspire with Scorpio just for the pleasure of having The Black Diamond in his personal possession?" Jake shrugged. "Maybe that's true. But the next burning question is, how can I approach the Blue Team without rousing their suspicions?"

"Sounds like a rats' nest to me," Hannah stated with a scowl.

"Yeah. I never have liked rats."

"And rats can attack and bite in bunches."

"Do you have any suggestions as to the way I can wiggle into the Blue Team headquarters and not get a brickbat across the back of my head?"

"You've really drawn a short straw on this one, honey," Hannah said placing her index finger up to her mouth. "However, there is one aspect that you may have playing in your favor."

"What's that?"

"The men who work on the Blue Team probably don't know you. You've only been in this region for a short while, and during that time you have mainly been holed up over on the Black Diamond Team. You've had no interaction with any of the other teams in the area. So, you would be an unknown person to the guys on the Blue Team."

"And what are you suggesting?"

"Maybe you could find some excuse to go nosing around the Blue Team headquarters"

Jake looked at Hannah as if she was loony. "Come on, honey. That's a joke, huh. Not very funny," he said with a deadpan expression. "Those guys on the Blue Team may not know me but Scorpio sure does. He works there. All it would take would be for him to recognize me and that would be curtains! He'd squeal on me in a flash. And then my goose would be cooked. No telling what might happen."

"You could always run real fast," she laughed.

"Yeah, I'd have to flee using the old adage, 'It's a sorry pair of legs that let's a body get hurt!'"

"Well, I just come up with the ideas," she said with a smirk. "I don't guarantee that they will work."

Hannah sat down on the edge of the bed and clarified her thought. "Actually what I really meant was that you could find some legitimate excuse to be there. Some ploy where you would be at the Blue Team's facility only once in a while. You know, like being a delivery man. You could deliver stuff to the team and snoop around while you're there in the team headquarters."

Jake ran that idea through his head. A little flash of light flared in his brain. "You know, you've got something there, sweetheart. I like the delivery man scheme. Now, I've just got to figure what I can deliver and then make my delivery when Scorpio isn't around."

13

THE JEZREEL DETECTIVES
IN ACTION

very morning, Artemas opened his leather goods shop bright and early. Jake remembered that Artemas had told him that all the teams had been starting to come by and have him make fresh leather pieces for their racing equipment in preparation for the upcoming Grand Judean Chariot Races at Caesarea. That event was the grandest chariot race of the entire local racing season. Huge amounts of prize money and other awards enticed every competitor in the region. All the local teams stood to win more prize money at that one event than they could win in an entire year of racing.

In addition, Caesar had contributed another spectacular trophy for this year's race from his private collection. It was called The Golden Cup of Caesar. This gleaming, gorgeous, gold cup stood two and a half feet tall. The gold cup was shaped into a tapered vase-like design with its top circumference measuring eighteen inches across. There were two soaring gold wing-like handles on either side and the base was made from a sparkling square, gold ingot. The trophy was estimated to be worth over 2,000 denarii. A handsome fortune by any of the racing participants standards. This stunning golden cup had every race team salivating to win that magnificent prize donated by Caesar!

With so much customer traffic from the race teams coming through

Artemas' leather shop, Jake figured he could maybe work out a deal with the leather merchant. Jake hoped he could talk Artemas into letting him deliver any order he might have from the Blue Team.

"Well, what do you think, Artemas, could I do a delivery for you? It's a new idea, I know. But I'd do it for free."

"You can't fool me," Artemas laughed. "I know what you're up to. Always trying to get a leg up on your competition, huh. I must admit it's a novel way to spy on your competition. And which team did you want to spy … er … I mean, deliver my orders to?"

"I've really got a hankering to make a delivery to the Blue Team. You know, just a little friendly free delivery service. No charge to them. And especially no charge to you. What do you say."

"I say, what can it hurt?" Artemas shrugged. "I win all the way around. And it just so happens that I've got several brand new leather bridles ready for delivery to the Blue Team. Their man was going to pick them up this afternoon. I guess you can go ahead and deliver the new parts to the Blue Team this morning. I'll wrap them up and you can go ahead with the delivery."

The Blue Team's headquarters lay directly north of Samaria on the main road, a quarter mile outside the city limits. As Jake approached the team facilities, he noticed their buildings were much more austere than those of the Black Diamond Team. There was a sturdy, gray-weathered wooden barn and a large, limestone office building but everything on the property emitted an atmosphere of disorganization. The exterior of all the structures on the property was weather-beaten and dirty. Equipment lay scattered around in the long, tall uncut grass surrounding the buildings. Leaves and trash littered the grounds. There seemed to be no effort to clean up the facility. A few team personnel were exercising four bluish-gray horses around a makeshift dirt race track beside the barn but other than them, Jake saw no one else.

Then came the risky part. Jake wanted to see inside the main office building. As he neared the office structure, he had no idea who may be waiting inside. If Scorpio was there, his plan was to quickly dump the package of leather parts on the doorstep and run like the wind.

"Not much of a plan," he muttered to himself. "But here goes."

Jake walked through the main office door into a semi-darkened room. One window streamed yellowish morning sunshine into the chamber. Making a quick scan of the room, Jake didn't see Scorpio. But a thin, wiry gent sat at a desk across from the doorway in the shadows. The man looked up.

"May I help you?" a squeaky voice emitted from the darkened figure in the shadows.

"Yes, I'm here to deliver some new bridles that you had ordered from Artemas," Jake said, his eyes glancing around the room. "Artemas told me you wanted him to make four new sets of bridles, with all the associated straps. So, here they are."

The wiry man stood up and emerged from the shadows around his desk. "Is this some sort of new service Artemas has started? Is he now delivering orders to his customers?"

The thin man stepped more into the light. "My name is Dominic. I am the owner of the Blue Racing Team," his high-pitched words squeaked.

Jake was astonished by the strange little man standing before him. The tiny man's eyes bugged out of his thin, narrow face. His bugged-out eyes reminded Jake of a hoot owl. His skinny, oblong head perched on top of a slender little stem of a neck. His ears stuck straight out. He had a high forehead with a pronounced receding hairline. His nose poked out of his face in a sharp point and his mouth resembled a thin slit. When he talked, he barely opened his mouth but his shrill voice sent chills up Jake's spine. As he spoke, Dominic perpetually leaned forward in a threatening manner. And his voice had a sinister, aggressive edge to it.

"Good to meet you, Mister Dominic," Jake said, his eyes shifting around so he didn't have to look at this strange creature standing there. "Yes, Artemas said that all the race teams were in a time crunch during these days just before the big race at Caesarea in a few weeks. So, I offered to deliver these parts to your team. To save time, you know."

"Yes, very interesting," Dominic squeaked. He aggressively stepped to within a foot of Jake and leaned forward, his bug-eyes expanding wider into protruding orbs. "Seems like I have never seen you before."

"No, I'm really new to this region. I'm just trying to find work. Pick up a job here and there."

"Do you work for Artemas?"

"No, I don't work for him. I just pick up a little work now and then and I was talking to Artemas and he told me about teams needing their leather parts in a hurry. So, I offered to deliver these parts to your team."

"I see. Okay, well, thank you." The strange little man backed away. "Tell Artemas that I appreciate this new service of his. Do I owe you anything?"

"No, you've already paid for the bridles up front. Ahh, there is one more thing, though. Could I trouble you for some water. That walk out from the city was hot and dry."

"Yes, I can get you some water."

As Dominic turned around to retrieve a cup to pour water into, Jake took the opportunity to shoot little darting glances all over the office. Over to the left of the chamber sat a table and a chair. To the right of the room were some cabinets along that wall and a cozy, confined corner with oak panels. A small window let in dim light in the confined corner. There was no other furniture in the office.

Dominic returned with the water. "There. Drink your water and be on your way. I'm a busy man," the shrill, piercing voice grated.

"Right. Thanks," Jake said as he gulped the water. "Have a great day."

The detective hurriedly turned and exited the building. It was a relief to get out of the presence of that bizarre, little man. Jake quickly scanned over the property outside, hoping Scorpio was no where around. Thankfully the former Black Diamond driver didn't appear to be anywhere in sight.

All the way back to the city, Jake ran the evidence he had just discovered through his mind.

In their room at The Inn By The Ivory House, the detective shared his evidence he had uncovered with his wife.

"Hannah, it's been a rather strange day," Jake said, as he began to talk and pace around their room at the Inn. "First of all, I met this weird little man who is the owner of the Blue Team. His name is Dominic. It's hard to describe him. By all appearances, he seemed to be very erratic and rather sharp-edged. He's the type of person who is always 'in your face', leaning into you nose-to-nose, even in a regular discussion. But while I was there I was able to check out the office. His office has very stark and lifeless. Very little furniture. If The Black Diamond Trophy is on the premises, I think I may have seen a possible place it could be hidden. I can't be sure but if the Trophy is there, the only logical place it could be hidden is somewhere on the right side of the office. That is the area that caught my attention the most. It's the only storage area in the office. That area is a cozy little alcove where some cabinets are pressed up against the wall. The rest of the alcove is decorated with ornamental oak paneling. There is a small window in that part of the building, over on the right side, close to the cabinets."

"Okay, but what can you do with that information?"

"Well, I've got a plan to find out if the Trophy actually is in that building. And I really think it will work. Are you up for it?"

A startled Hannah stared at Jake for a moment. "You want *me* to be part of your plan?"

"That's right. I'm going to need you to help me pull this one off."

"Okay. I'm all in," she said warily. "But we don't really know if the Trophy is in the Blue Team building. How can we find out for sure?"

"Dominic is going to show us where the Trophy is hidden."

"What? Dominic will show us? Why would he do that?" she asked, cocking her head.

"He will not be able to resist showing us. I know this plan will work. Do you want to hear it?"

"Absolutely," Hannah said with a wry smile.

"Okay. This is my plan …"

At dusk the next day, a gaggle of men approached the Blue Team's property on the main road. Jake and Hannah closely trailed the group of five men which Jake had hired for his scheme. In the evening twilight, the cluster of people, with torches in hand, drew near to the main office.

"When we get close to the building," Jake told Hannah, "hide down in the tall grass beside the building, until we all get into position. Do you have the bundle of flax?"

"Sure do. And I know what to do with it."

"Good. May God go with you."

Close to the office structure, Hannah ducked down into the thick, waist high grass that hadn't been cut in months. The rest of the men, including Jake continued on, wading through the uncut grass, toward the building. They had to hold their torches high so they wouldn't catch the tall, dry grass on fire. All of the men were talking very loudly, arguing among themselves as they reached the front door of the structure.

Dominic had not left work yet and still was in the building. He bounced out of the front door. "Hey, what is all this commotion about!" he shrieked. "It's late! I'm getting ready to go home! Get out of here!"

"Dominic, we've got a bet goin'!" the paid rowdies yelled. "Some of us say that you're gonna win at the big race at Caesarea! And some of us say you ain't gonna win! You ain't got a chance! What's it gonna be?"

"Are you trouble makers drunk? You know I believe we can win. But I have no way of knowing what will be the final outcome! Now, get out of here! You're disturbing me!"

"Are you a welsher? Are you scared to give us the odds on you winnin'?"

Pandemonium broke out. Yelling and arguing intensified. That was Jake's que to drop his torch into the tall, dry grass next to the stone building. Smoke began to rise. Suddenly, the grass burst into flames!

"Fire! Fire! The grass is on fire!' the rowdy bunch all yelled, jumping around.

"Put out that blaze!" Dominic screamed in panic.

"We'll stomp it out!" yelled the band of paid rowdies.

Around the side of the stone structure, Hannah crept up to the window on that end of the office. She was able to look inside the building and watch the smoke from the fire outside, billowing through the front door into the office. That was her signal to light the bundle of flax she carried and toss it in the window. The smoldering, smoking flax landed on the floor and quickly filled the room with thick, white smoke. She could hear Dominic yelling and clawing his way through the dense fog of smoke toward her end of the building. Coughing and choking, Dominic fumbled his way over to the secluded alcove and quickly opened a sliding oak panel. Through the thick smoke, Hannah could see inside the panel. There stood The Black Diamond Trophy nestled inside! Dominic started to rescue the Trophy from destruction in the flames. As he grabbed the Trophy, Dominic suddenly spun around and realized that there was no fire inside the room, only smoking flax. He hurriedly shoved the trophy back in place and grabbed the unlit end of the bundle of flax and carried it out of the building.

"You rowdies! Who tossed this burning bundle inside?" he screeched. "Put out those flames in the grass!"

The rowdy bunch finally stomped out the small flames in the grass. "We got it up out, Dominic," they chuckled through the lingering smoke. "Nothin' to worry about. Just a little, tiny grass fire."

"Get out of here you ruffians!" Dominic screamed. "You've caused enough trouble! Get out! Get out! Don't ever come back!"

The gang started to meander away. They hurled some parting shots back at the team owner. "You sure do get mad easy," they mocked. "Just a little grass fire. No big deal!"

Jake and Hannah already had fled the scene. They met on the main road and began to run back toward Samaria.

As they ran, Jake asked, "Did you get to see where Dominic had The Black Diamond Trophy hidden?"

"Of course."

"Well, where is it hidden?"

"You were right," Hannah stated. "In that secluded corner of the office, just like you suspected. One of the oak panels slides to the side. The panel has a hideaway handle. It has to be pushed in to unlatch the panel."

"Well, we will now have to figure out a way to go back …" Then, in the darkness, Jake noticed that Hannah had something black in her hand. "What is that?"

"The Trophy."

"What! The Trophy?" Jake exclaimed, screeching to a halt. "How did you get that?"

"Well, it was easy," Hannah remarked with a confident smile. "In the smoke I saw where Dominic had hidden the Trophy behind that panel. He carelessly left the panel half open when he ran back out to the front. He was distracted just long enough for me to crawl in the window and grab the Trophy. He conveniently had this black bag inside the panel. The bag made it much easier to carry the Trophy away."

"Girl! You've got some real nerve! You're the best!"

"We're just returning the Black Diamond to it's rightful owner," she stated matter-of-factly.

"That's exactly true. Here, let me carry that heavy load! And let's g-e-t o-u-t-a here!"

Jake kept looking over his shoulder, as they ran. "Nobody is following us. I guess the smoke still has them all distracted."

"And thank God for the moonless darkness to help hide our getaway," Hannah gasped. "I haven't run this much in years."

"Running is good for you," Jake puffed and laughed at the same time. "And right now, running is the best medicine for saving our lives."

As the couple dived into the safety of their room, Jake laughed out loud. "That was thrilling! And girl, you surprise me every day. I knew you were spunky but this proves that to me. You've got real courage. You're quite a woman! Great job!"

"It was all for a good cause. We were just righting a wrong. I don't feel bad about putting the wrong back right."

She glanced at Jake with a gleam in her eye. "Would you like to take a peek at The Black Diamond Trophy?"

Jake's eyes lit up. "You bet I would! I do believe I'd like that," he said, his words salivating his desire.

The detective reached into the black burlap sack and gently lifted the precious Trophy out into the open. Hannah clasped her hands together in awe as her eyes fell upon the gorgeous, valuable award. Her mouth formed an 'o' but no sound came out from her lips. Jake sat the treasure on the small table in their room and stepped back to take in the magnificence of the Trophy in all its glory. He, too, could not find words to express his amazement engulfed in the beauty sitting there before them.

Hannah got down on her knees to be on the same level as the stunning gem display. Finally she found words. "It is soooo beautiful," she gushed. "Just look at it. It sparkles even in this dim light. It draws your eye straight to it. And the diamond is so clear you can see right through it, even though it is an enchanting black color. I just am blown away! It is so absolutely stunning!"

As Jake stood back and admired the treasure, he commented, "Look at how the gold setting mounts the black diamond perfectly on its gold pedestal and gold base. Look at how that foot high gold pedestal lifts the black diamond up to show it off against the pearl-white velvet backing. And look at how the velvet backing halfway surrounds the diamond and its setting, pulling your eyes right to the gem in the middle. I don't use this word much, but I'd say this treasure is 'exquisite'! What an absolutely rare beauty."

Hannah reached out and tenderly rotated the Trophy on the small table. "It is so beautiful," she said softly. "And to think I grabbed it so roughly when I was escaping from Dominic's hiding place. I'm glad I didn't hurt it." She turned the trophy around a little farther. "It is sooo gorgeous," she said, her voice trailing off.

That night the couple radiated such excitement, they could hardly sleep. They knew they had to guard their treasure during the long, dark hours. They tried napping in shifts, taking turns. First Jake stayed awake while Hannah dozed. Then they traded off. But neither Jezreel detective got much sleep. They begged for the morning to come. They had one more part of their rescue plan to fulfill.

14

BACK HOME AGAIN

I t was a day, like most days, at The Black Diamond Racing office when Jake and Hannah walked in the next morning.

"Well, if it isn't the two missing persons," Octavius joked. "We sent out an All-Points Bulletin on you guys just this morning. We've been missing you two."

"We've been missing all of you, too," Jake said looking coy. Hannah stood next to her husband with a very silly smile on her face, her eyes open real wide.

Diotrephes, Octavius, Linus, and several other members of the crew all stopped what they were doing. There seemed to be something very strange about the way the couple stood quietly in the office doorway.

Diotrephes squinted at them, realizing they were up to something. Then he looked down at the black burlap bag dangling in Jake's hand at his side. "What is that?" he asked pointing with his eyes at the bag.

"It's the Trophy," Jake stated almost casually.

The entire room gasped in unsuspected shock. A long stunned silence suspended time for a moment.

"What did you say?" Diotrephes yelped. "The Trophy! Jacob, how in the world did you ever get the Trophy back?" he exclaimed.

"Boss, you really, really don't want to know how we got it. We just got it!

"I can't believe it!" The Captain yelled. "I just knew it was gone forever!"

Jubilation exploded in the room! Every man in the team office began shouting in exaggerated celebration! Exhilaration! What was lost was found! The Black Diamond finally was back home!

"Open the sack, Jacob!" Diotrephes exclaimed, his voice now quivering slightly.

Jake dug down deep into the black bag and carefully lifted the beautiful Black Diamond Trophy up and into the open. He lifted it even higher, over his head so everyone in the office could gaze and be transfixed by the magnificent Trophy. Hoots and hollers erupted again as every man in the room celebrated the return of their treasure.

One of the horse trainers, who was jumping around in the office, bellowed, "I've got to tell all the other guys!" and dashed out the office door, headed for the barn.

"This is incredible!" shouted The Captain. "I don't know how you did it, but now I know you must be a genius, Mister Jacob Jezreel!"

"I couldn't have done it alone. My pretty wife had a very big hand in it!" Jake laughed. "She's actually the one who snatched it. She's pretty smart!"

"She must be very smart!" exclaimed Octavius.

"Men," Diotrephes announced to one and all, "the Jezreel detectives in action! I salute them both. And a special salute to the little lady, Ms. Hannah, for her bravery!"

Jake paused for a moment. "I know I told all of you that we couldn't tell you how we got the Trophy back," he stated. "But I can tell you this much. All the evidence led us to believe Scorpio stole the Trophy. So, we played a hunch as to where the Trophy ended up. Dominic and the Blue Team had it."

"I am not surprised," The Captain said matter-of-factly. "The rumor is that Scorpio has been hired by the Blue Team, so it makes perfect sense that our Trophy ended up there."

"But the important thing is — we've got the Trophy now!" Jake exclaimed.

"Yes! Yes! Let us all celebrate!" The Captain shouted, dancing a little jig.

For a full half hour the celebration continued. All of the helpers from the barn and all the horse trainers crowded into the team office and rejoiced together in the victory.

"This is like winning The Black Diamond Trophy all over again!" shouted Octavius.

Shouts of joy rang out across the lower valley outside the City of Samaria for a very long time. The loud party probably could be heard all the way across the rolling countryside at the Blue Team's headquarters!

As the celebration began to wind down, Diotrephes made a proclamation. "Men, we are no longer going to hide this magnificent Trophy away in some dark closet. It is far to beautiful to keep under wraps. I want all of you to be able to gaze at this beauty any day, anytime. After all, you all helped win this beautiful treasure. It belongs to all of us. I'm going to figure out a way to display it here in the office, so you can enjoy the fruits of your hard work whenever you want to."

"How 'bout an iron bar trophy cage-like box?" suggested Octavius.

"I can build that!" burly Levi the blacksmith chimed in. "That's my department. If it's made outa iron, I can design and build the most beautiful metal display case you've ever seen!"

"There you go! That project is taken care of!" team owner Linus stated, brushing his hands together as if he was dusting them off. "Levi, you're the best iron man in the whole region. You'll do better work than anybody in the whole province of Samaria!"

"Perfect!" Diotrephes exclaimed to all the team in the office. "This way we can display this beauty and still secure it's safety from sticky fingers."

As the crowd dispersed back to their work duties, Diotrephes took Jake by the arm and said, "Please come over here with me. I'd like to talk with you both for a moment." He led the couple over to his desk. In a halting voice he said, "Please, sit down for a moment." He pointed to two chairs next to his desk. He hesitated for a moment. He cleared his throat. Then in great humiliation he started.

"There is no way I can thank both of you enough for rescuing this team treasure, this Trophy. It means so very much to all of us. But it's more than that. It's an award from Caesar; a personal gift from the Emperor. It holds great significance, as well as being an item beyond value. I am personally very grateful to you both. And I am profoundly impressed by your loyalty to me and to the team. I am indebted to you for what you have done. I know it must not have been easy to retrieve what was stolen from us. I fear that you may even have risked your lives to rescue our property from the hands of evil men. I am truly indebted to you. I cannot thank you enough."

Jake smiled. "Sir, I speak for my wife, when I say it was our pleasure to be of service to you."

"I want to echo my husband's sentiments," Hannah said. "You are a friend. We did it because you are a friend and we wanted to serve you. We are Christians and our Lord Jesus taught us to be loyal, not just to Him but to each other. And we will gladly continue to be loyal to you."

"Besides, what are friends for," Jake added.

Diotrephes gazed at the pair with a pleased expression on his face. "I knew there was something different about you two," he said. "I have heard about Christians, how they love. I've seen that quality in you two. What you did for me in rescuing our Trophy shows me that you two really do have love in your hearts."

"And you have shown love for us, as well," Jake said, "when you took a chance and hired two strangers to work for you. And we appreciate you doing that for us."

It was then that Diotrephes paused and his facial expression dimmed from the smile he had been wearing. He stood up and began to slowly pace back and forth behind his desk. With great effort he turned toward Jake and Hannah, cleared his throat, and spoke.

"It's because of what you have done for our team and of my great indebtedness to you that I find it hard to even say these next words to you." He paused with a look of dread on his face. He sat down for a moment but then got back up and started pacing again. "You know earlier when I announced, 'The Jezreel Detectives in action'. That wasn't a slip of the tongue. It was something that was on my mind."

Diotrephes paused again and faced the couple. "You see ... I know who you are. You are Jacob Jezreel, the famous private detective from Jerusalem." Diotrephes sat down at his desk and breathed a heavy sigh. He looked grave and ashen, disturbed by what he was saying.

"You see ... I began to get suspicious when you so willingly wanted to track down our stolen Trophy. You even made some comment that you had done some detective type work in the big city, specifically in Jerusalem. I wondered why a detective would leave the big city and come here to take a job that paid only minimum wage."

Diotrephes paused once again and looked down at his desktop. He would not look up, as he continued. "You see ... I did some checking up on my own. I sent one of my men on horseback up to Jerusalem to ask around if there was a detective in the city who went by the name Jacob Jezreel. My man didn't have to poke around very long before he got the information he needed. And he also probed around enough to find out why you are here in Samaria. You have come for Alexander."

Jake didn't say a word. He just placed his right arm across his chest and rested his left arm on his right, stroking his chin with his left hand. He heaved a sigh. "You've got us pegged," he finally said. "But your final conclusion about Alexander is not quite right."

"What do you mean?" the Captain asked. "I know you are here in Samaria to attempt to purchase Alexander and take him back with you to that Christian leader, that Pastor James fellow."

"Sir, your man did an admirable job of detective work," Jake smiled. "But he missed one clue that was here, right under his nose. Alexander loves his job here on your team. He loves his horses. He has told me that much. And his horses love him, too. When a man is so well satisfied with his job, it would be wrong to take away the profession that makes him happy. And he is happy. You have given Alexander new meaning in this life. You have given him the profession he loves and that he excels at."

"I don't understand," Diotrephes said, very puzzled. "What are you saying, then?"

"What we're saying," Hannah stated, "there is no way we would attempt to buy Alexander away from you or this team. You've been very kind to him and he has responded to you by becoming an excellent charioteer."

"He is too valuable of an asset to you for him to be taken away," Jake interjected. "This team has worked hard. They have built the team around Alexander. They deserve to win that championship race at Caesarea in a few weeks. You deserve to win that race. And I know that Alexander is fired up. And he's got the moxie to do it!"

Diotrephes stared at the Jezreel detectives for a long moment, processing what they had just said. Then a large grin flashed across his face. "Oh, my," he said putting his right hand up to his forehead. "What wonderful news! I was so scared we would have a major confrontation! I surly didn't want to fight with you. But I didn't expect this!"

"And we certainly didn't want to have a fight with you," Jake laughed. "We've come to greatly admire you. You're such a good man, a fair man. And you have become our friend, as well as our employer."

"Well, I dreaded this conversation even more after you had rescued The Black Diamond Trophy," The Captain stated. "I am truly relieved that we are all still on the same side."

"And we always will be on the same side, boss," Jake said. "That is if you'll still let us work for you. After all, you've discovered the real reason why we've come here in the first place. You know our first motivation and our history."

"We've all got our past histories. We've got to move past it. The main thing is we keep moving ahead and keep working together."

"We are on board with that," Jake said.

As the three sat reveling in the happiness of the moment, Diotrephes had a new revelation.

"You know, Jacob and Hannah," The Captain stated leaning over his desk toward them, "sooner or later, Scorpio and Dominic are going to find out that The Black Diamond Trophy is missing and no longer in their possession. It won't take long for the racing rumor mill to spread the news like lightning that we now have the Trophy. And the Blue Team is going to hear about it. They are going to be fighting mad!"

"Don't you just love it!" Jake laughed. "Those guys are crooks They are thieves. It will give us great satisfaction to see them all get angry. They deserve to have the tables turned on them."

"That is all true," Diotrephes mused. "But the one fact that we do know for sure is that we now have a determined, aggressive enemy, who in the future will want revenge. They will be out for blood. Scorpio, Dominic, the whole Blue Team are going to be boiling mad when they find out we now have The Black Diamond. You can count on the fact that they will try every dirty trick in the book to get revenge on us. We already know that Scorpio is a wild man on the race track. This might tip him over the edge into a raving lunatic! I'm sure he will have team orders from Dominic to drive dirty in the big race at Caesarea. Consequently, we've got to be ready for it. We must plan on Scorpio driving like a wild maniac with revenge in his eyes."

As Jake and Hannah walked back toward the city, Jake had an idea. "Angel, I'm not going to wait for this news about The Black Diamond to trickle over to the Blue Team through the rumor mill. I'm going to spread the word. Let everybody know the Black Diamond Team has Caesar's Trophy back safe and sound."

"But that's just going to stir up the Blue Team and make them super angry," Hannah said with a puzzled expression.

"That's good. Let them get mad. When a man gets angry, he's driven by emotion. Emotion causes him to not think straight. He *can't* think straight. And when a man doesn't think straight, he makes all kinds of foolish decisions. I like it that way. That will give us an advantage."

"Okay, honey, but I still like the silent approach. Less things get broken that way. Like your head!"

As the couple hit the city limits, Jake started announcing to every merchant along Main Street that the Black Diamond Team now had recovered their famous trophy that had been stolen. He stopped by the leather shop of Artemas.

"Great news, Artemas!" Jake proclaimed. "We've got our stolen Black Diamond Trophy back! Great news!"

"Fantastic news, Jacob! How did you find it? Where was it?"

"That answer, my friend, will linger in the annals of time as an unsolved mystery forever!" Jake floated his answer, as he waved his hand toward the sky and eternity.

"Too bad! That really would have made a great headline for the Samaria Evening Gazette, 'FAMOUS STOLEN TROPHY FOUND'. But I guess we'll have to let that news flash slide on past."

"Yeah, it looks like that story won't even make the back newsroom waste basket."

"That's really too bad. That would have been a sensational, splashy news story!"

"Well, why don't you sound the alarm, Artemas. You spread the word! You announce the splashy news story. You told me once that you just spread the rumors. Well, spread this one! You let people decide for themselves."

"I sure will! Man, people love gossip. It draws people into my shop, too! It helps my trade! Folks might even buy a belt or a perfect pair of sandals while they're here!"

Jake and Hannah rambled on down the street spreading the news about the stolen Trophy that had been found. Jake took one side of the main boulevard and Hannah took the other. Within a half hour of scattering gossip like fertile seeds throughout the metropolis, the entire city of Samaria buzzed with the news of The Black Diamond Trophy recovery.

As the couple settled in for a cozy supper at Hezekiah's café, they could hear the swelling murmur rustling through the crowds outside on the street.

"Well, I think we have done our job," Jake commented. "By tonight the infuriating news about the trophy should be filtering into the Blue Team's headquarters. I'd like to be a fly on the wall to watch Dominic's angry expression when the news hits his protruding little ears that we've got the trophy back, safe and sound. He will run to his little cabinet and find out the trophy is really gone. And then he will probably blow a gasket!"

"Don't forget Scorpio," Hannah smiled. "He of all people will be the most angry. He intended his stealing The Black Diamond Trophy to be the ultimate revenge when Diotrephes fired him. Now, his revenge has failed. He ends up with a hand full of air. What does Scorpio do now, when his revenge suddenly doesn't work out and boomerangs right back at him? He and Dominic are left with nothing."

The couple sat at their table and smiled at each other in great satisfaction.

"We do good work together," Jake beamed with a pleased expression.

"Very good work," she said.

"Now that we've spread the word, we don't have to wonder when Dominic will try to get back at us." Jake stated. "He can't catch us unaware. We'll be ready for him."

"What do you think he will do?" she asked.

"Cause trouble, for sure. No telling what kind, though. He might try some sort of sabotage."

"You mean he might try sabotage, right away?"

"There's a good possibility."

Jake looked at his bride and wrinkled his nose in a smirk. "Kinda does your heart good to see justice done. We really do work pretty good together, sweetheart. We did it. We were the agents of justice in setting things right."

15

TIMES, THEY ARE A-CHANGIN'

The first strike! The very next day!

Everyone was on high alert, expecting reprisal and ready for it. All the members of the Black Diamond Race Team reported for work early. Each man started his work but kept a keen eye out for any kind of looming trouble. Dominic and his bunch surely had heard by now of their loss of The Black Diamond Trophy. And more importantly, who now had the treasure. Carpus and Zenas had stayed the night locked inside the team's main office, where the trophy was sealed away safely in its special cabinet. Meanwhile, Nathan and two of his horse handlers stayed the night in the barn with all twelve stallions safely protected inside.

The work at the facility started up at this very early hour. Several men in the barn had already begun their normal duties. Jake and Caleb had started fabricating a new leather chest band to replace one that had gotten old and needed replacing. Everyone busied themselves but, slung in their belts, each man carried a tool of their trade to use as a defensive weapon. Brawny Levi, the blacksmith, had a dagger of his own personal design and craftsmanship strapped to his side.

Jake looked around at all the members of the crew, working hard but keeping a sharp eye out for trouble, with one hand ready to draw his tool as a side arm.

Jake remembered a Bible story he had heard many years before as a kid. "Caleb, look at all our guys," he said to his partner as they worked. "They are all working but spoiling for a fight if Dominic tries to stir up a fracas. This is like that story in the Bible about the people of Judah under Nehemiah's leadership when they were working to rebuild the wall around Jerusalem."

"Seems like I remember hearing some legend about Nehemiah and the Israelites rebuilding the wall around Jerusalem in the record time of fifty-two days," Caleb mused.

"Well, it's not a legend. It's a historical fact," Jake stated confidently. "And, as the story goes, all the men working on the wall carried a sword ready to drop their tools and fight the enemy who surrounded them."

Caleb glanced around him at his fellow team members. He smiled big. "Yeah, our guys do look just like that old story from long ago. Ready for a fight."

Without warning, Jonathan, one of the horse trainers, dashed through the open barn door and shouted, "Get ready, boys! Dominic and his gang are coming!"

Within seconds, an angry tornado of ten roughnecks from the Blue Team stormed through the open barn door, looking for trouble. Dominic and Scorpio led the group. All the men flashed fire in their eyes. They all shouted loud obscenities, spoiling for a fight.

"Where is your worthless leader, Diotrephes?" Dominic snidely spouted to the men in the barn.

"What do you want with him?" Jake called from across the barn.

"I want to have a word with that worm!" Dominic screeched. "Is he in here, in this barn!"

Jake advanced on the group. He still carried his curved leathercraft knife in his hand. "I don't think Diotrephes wants to talk to you," he stated with a sneer on his lip, holding his knife out at a menacing angle.

"You tell that four-flusher we're coming to get him," Dominic seethed in his screechy voice. His oblong head teetered on his thin pedestal neck as he ranted. His eyes bulged out even further in a red-faced rage. "He stole our Black Diamond Trophy from our racing office. That trophy belongs to us and he stole it!"

"The trophy was not stolen from you," broad-shouldered Levi stated, still clutching his blacksmith tongs in his massive hand. "That trophy was restored to its rightful owners. So, scram, get outa here, you bunch of weasels!"

"I'm warning you! I will get my revenge!" Dominic yelped. "I will get Diotrephes. Maybe not today. Maybe not tomorrow. We'll get him when you least expect it. You have declared war on our team. If you want war, you will get it!"

The entire Black Diamond team advanced toward Dominic's seething horde. Big Levi flexed his burly muscles and growled to the team, "Come on, boys! We can take 'em! Right now!"

"Wait a minute, guys!" Jake shouted to his team. "Seems like Dominic has a real sensitivity problem. Before we pummel these degenerates, maybe Dominic can explain to us what his big beef is with our boss."

Dominic puffed up like a blowfish! "Everybody knows that the Black Team stole that big race at Caesarea from our team last year!" Dominic shrieked, his high-pitched screeching piercing the air. "You all know it. Your team unfairly grabbed the lead from our team on the last lap by throwing a 'slider' right in front of our horses, spooking our horses causing them to pullup. That momentary loss of speed caused our Blue Team chariot to lose the big race and forfeit The Black Diamond Trophy. That Trophy belongs to me!"

"That racing move last year was perfectly legal," Caleb stated, as he advanced on the Blue Team roughnecks with his hammer poised in his hand. The other Black Diamond Team members began to form a line of defense facing off against the Blue Team men. Caleb kept talking, "Besides, Scorpio was our driver last year, driving and winning against you. You seem to have forgotten that fact. You should file a complaint against him. Oh yeah, he's your driver now."

"Scorpio believes that Trophy belongs to him!" Dominic shrilled. "He is the man who won it! It belongs to him!"

"It *is* mine!" Scorpio shouted, his black, stringy hair flying around as he yelled. "It's mine! It's mine! It's mine!" He began stomping his feet like a two year old throwing a temper tantrum. "It's mine! I won it!"

Caleb advanced yet another step closer. "Scorpio, you know our whole team won that Trophy. It was a team effort. You drove the race but we all supplied the best equipment and finest horseflesh so you had something to win with!"

"Yeah, we gave you everything you needed to win!" Carpus snarled. "You should be grateful!"

"You lowlifes are a bunch of thieves and cheaters!" Dominic squeaked, his bug eyes bulging out further. He looked ready to pop a cork. "We will never forgive you for last year's trickery and robbery of our rightful Black Diamond Trophy. This year's race … we will mop the track with you clowns this year. We will grind you into the dust of the race track until you're like powder. Everybody will ask, 'Where is the Black Team? I thought they were here. But they just disappeared into the dust.'"

Alexander stepped through the line of Black Diamond men and faced Dominic and Scorpio. "You boast of grinding me into the dust," he said smoothly. "I don't even know you Mister Dominic. This is the first time I have met you. Do you hate me? Why would you hate me? I've done no wrong to you."

"We're going to crush you because you're associated with these vermin," Dominic seethed. "Anyone and anything that is part of the Black Team must be smashed! And we have many ways we can smash all of you." An ugly snarl contorted the slit of his vile mouth. "You'll never know when or where we will strike. But I guarantee that the Black Team will not win the Caesarea race this year or Caesar's gold cup. Mark my words. You'll never know what hit you!"

"I think it's time for you to go," Caleb stated matter-of-factly, stepping even closer. He raised his hammer, cocking his arm back. "You've left your message. Now, go."

The other Black Diamond Team members all began to close in on Dominic and his bunch to within ten feet. They all still carried the tools they had been working with.

Dominic started to back away. "Let's go men," he said as he retreated backwards. "I don't want to spend another minute around this stinking bunch."

In a quick moment, Dominic and The Blue Team turned tail and left the barn. The men of the Black Diamond Team followed them out into the open air, outside the barn and watched them until they were out of sight down the road.

"Somebody needs to go tell The Captain about this confrontation by Dominic," Jake said. "What he said was more than a wild threat. It was a horrible promise of sabotage. We can absolutely count on it."

"I'll tell the Captain and the other owners," Caleb said and started for the office building.

"I'll go with you," Jake stated, as he tagged along.

When Diotrephes and the other team owners were told of the Blue Team threats, they immediately called the whole team together for a meeting in the team office.

"Men, we will soon be under attack from the Blue Team," Diotrephes started. He stood behind his desk. All the rest of the team stood or sat around the perimeter of the room. Hannah was there, as well. She was a team member, too, and needed to know what the plan was going to be.

"It appears that Dominic and his gang are a bunch of vicious sore losers and cannot accept the fact that they lost the championship race at Caesarea last year," The Captain continued. "And apparently they have been angry about losing for this whole past year! That could be the very reason why Dominic so gladly received our Black Diamond Trophy that Scorpio stole from us.

"Now, that he's lost the trophy and we have the trophy back in our possession, Dominic is flaming mad. We have beaten him, again, at his own game. But he won't let it go. He will get his revenge. He has told us that, loud and clear.

"Thanks to our good friends, Jacob and Hannah, they spread the word that we had the trophy back. That way we didn't have to wait for the news to drift over to The Blue Team. We could be pretty sure about the precise time Dominic would receive word that we had the trophy. Now, we don't have to wait around wondering if and when the Blue Team got the news. Or when they might retaliate. As we saw this morning, we didn't have to wait very long at all. They played right into our hands. They showed their evil intensions right away – today!"

"So, here's the plan," Octavius stated, standing up next to The Captain. "We are going back on guard duty every night. We can expect an attack against our facilities and it will probably be sometime during the night. You know how evil loves darkness to do their evil deeds. We'll have to rotate you guys. Most of you will be working the day shift but several of you will be working the night shift as a security team. We've got to protect our facilities and our horses from sabotage by the Blue Team."

Linus stood up next to the other team owners. "I've worked out a rotating shift schedule, so none of you will have to work more than three nights in a row. To be truthful, we can't spare you for very long at your normal assigned jobs. So, we'll rotate you guys back to days as much as we can, so we don't lose the efficiency of our operation."

"Any questions?" Diotrephes asked of the group.

Silence in the room.

"Okay, if Dominic wants a war, we will give it to him!" The Captain stated firmly. "We have two and a half weeks until the championship race at Caesarea. These two and a half weeks will be the critical time that members of the Blue Team might strike. We've got to be on our guard. We cannot let down our vigilance."

Jake volunteered to take the first night shift. He had already pulled that shift earlier when Scorpio got fired. Jake figured he could slide right back into that nighttime routine. Three other crewmen pulled the night shift with Jake. They made sure all twelve horses were stabled inside the safety of the barn. They lit lamps all around the interior of the barn to help themselves keep a watchful eye on the most precious asset on the race team – their magnificent black stallions. Two of the night shift guys stayed inside the barn. One man stationed himself in the office building, guarding the headquarters and also the precious Black Diamond Trophy.

But Jake chose to roam outside in the darkness around the entire perimeter of the race team property. He pretended this was a giant stakeout, where he kept his eye sharp for any movement in the dark and his ear tuned to any sound in the night. He wandered the team grounds, regularly circling the barn, the office, and the equipment sheds. Occasionally, he checked in with the guards in each building.

At about two AM, he knocked on the locked door of the office building. "Hey, Joe. It's me, Jacob," he called through the door. "Just checking in to see how things are going."

Joe, one of the stable men opened the door. "Hi, Jacob. Everything is as quiet as a graveyard. And that's pretty quiet."

"Sounds great for the first night on security duty," Jake smiled. "Keep up the good work."

"Hey, I think you got the good duty," Joe said. "At least you can walk around to stay awake. Me – I've got to stay awake by singing to myself. And I can't sing!"

"Why don't you try walking around, like me?"

"Have you ever tried to walk around in a little, tiny space? In one hour I'd make a million laps around this office."

"Tough duty, man," Jake laughed. "Well, good luck. If you need some toothpicks to keep your eyes open, I've got some. See ya."

The whole night dragged on in the same fashion. Jake drifted over to the barn and exchanged pleasantries with the guys there later that night. This first night slid quietly on with no excitement or incident to report.

The first rays of gorgeous, yellow daylight peeked over the horizon, finding Jake propped up against one of the equipment sheds. As the warm sunshine began to blanket him, he straightened up and shrugged his shoulders to work out the kinks. He had been snuggled up under the eve of the equipment shed roof to stay dry from the falling dew. Now as the detective stepped out into the short grass, he noticed his feet getting wet from the dewy blades.

But the night had not been a total waste of time. Jake's active brain had been calculating.

He met The Captain at the office door when the boss arrived at work that morning.

"How'd it go last night?" Diotrephes asked. "Any activity to report?"

"Nope, you'll have to check with the other guys, but I circulated around all night and nobody reported any problems."

"Well, that is good news."

"Boss, have you noticed the heavy dew on the grass this morning? In this territory, what does that indicate?"

"It's a good indicator of potential rain coming. The heavy moisture in the air usually can be a forerunner of some rain showers blowing in from the coast. Why?"

"I was just thinking that rain might hinder Dominic from pulling any pranks on us. For sure the rain would stop him from lighting any fires around our buildings."

"But think about this. The rain would stop us from getting the valuable practice Alexander is going to need for the upcoming championship race at Caesarea. He is a rookie, with not much experience. The rain would be like a double-edged sword."

"Okay, well that was only one of the things I've been thinking about all night in the dark, black of nighttime. I've got some really revolutionary ideas that could make our chariot run faster."

"Run faster? Sounds great. Let's go inside and you can explain it all to me."

The two men stepped inside the office building, greeting Joe as they entered. Diotrephes sat down behind his desk and pulled out a large, clean sheet of papyrus, laying it down on the desk top.

"Alright, don't just tell me your idea. Draw it out on this sheet."

"Well, boss, this is gonna be radical. So, here goes. Right now, we run our horses exactly like everybody else, four abreast. Like this." Jake scratched out a top view of four crudely drawn horses. He drew a roughed out sketch of a chariot behind the horses, connecting the horses and chariot with a T-shaped drawn line. "This line resembles the tongue fixture attached to the front of the chariot.

"Okay, now here's my radical idea. What if we modified the tongue fixture, making it longer, actually twice as long, made in two parts, with a hinge connecting the two parts. And then ..." Jake paused as he redrew the idea beside the first drawing. "What if we ran the horses in two pairs, one pair ahead of the other pair, like this." Jake drew the four horses in two pairs, a lead pair and a trailing pair with the chariot following right behind the new arrangement.

"With this arrangement of the horses, they all would be pulling the chariot more evenly, from a central point. The four horse power would be centralized and concentrated around the center tongue fixture. There would be no wasted power."

Diotrephes stared at the crude drawing in amazement. With his head down studying the sketch, he brought his left hand up and began stroking his short beard. "Remarkable," he finally said in a measured tone. "It does make sense. It makes good sense. It is incredible that no one else has thought of this concept. Maybe it took someone who is from outside the racing status quo to envision something this new and fresh."

Joe had been looking on from the side. He spoke up. "That arrangement would make our chariot team more narrow. Make it easier to slip in between the other teams."

"Great observation, Joe," Jake stated. "I hadn't even thought about that aspect."

"We would have to design a new harness arrangement for the horses," Joe continued, "but we could do that easy. The horses may think it's a little strange at first but those guys are pretty adaptable. They're smart. They'll figure it out."

Diotrephes held up the sketching and admired it for a moment. "I like it!" he exclaimed. "You've got a great idea, Jacob. I think we'll try it!"

Then turning to Joe The Captain said, "I know you've been up all night on guard duty. But will you do one more thing before you go home and get some sleep. Take this drawing over to the barn and show it to all the guys and get their opinion about it. And also check with Caleb to see what he thinks about him designing a brand new setup for the harnesses and reins. And tell the guys to keep this idea under wraps. If this new concept works, it may give us an extra advantage over our competition."

Diotrephes' weather predictions came true by that same afternoon. The rains came – in buckets. For the next three days, thundershowers surged in waves across the Samarian valley gusting in from the sea coast. All training sessions came to a standstill. All the outside facilities were flooded. So, The Captain and his team decided to take full advantage of the rainy down time. The whole team went straight to work on designing and manufacturing Jake's experimental proposal. Caleb did some of his own additional sketching to Jake's drawing, inventing new leather harnesses for the unique arrangement of the horses. Ezra, the wainwright, designed a new, hinged chariot tongue that would flex in the middle to allow the chariot to negotiate the tight turns on the race track. Levi, the big blacksmith, forged new experimental hardware to bolt the whole rig together.

One hope among the Black Diamond Team was that the rains also would dampen any probabilities of sabotage by the Blue Team. The guard duty shift work still continued but the team hoped the messy weather outside would "bog down" sabotage attempts by the Blue Team.

During one of the rainy afternoons, Jake had another brainstorm. He dodged the raindrops to get to the main office building. "Boss, I've got another idea that might give us even more of an advantage over our competition," he announced to Diotrephes.

"Jacob, you're just full of ideas, aren't you."

"Well, my detective brain won't quit working on the pieces of a puzzle. And to me, chariot racing is like many pieces of a puzzle."

"Alright, what piece of the puzzle are you focused on with your new idea?"

"The wheels."

"Wheels? We already have great wheels. Reuben, our wheelwright, builds precision wheels, the best in the business. His wheels can take the brutal punishment of the race track. Do we need better wheels?"

"No, sir. We need two different sizes of wheels."

"Reuben already builds two sizes of wheels. A smaller size for a fast, hard-surfaced track and a larger size for a heavy, softer-surfaced track. So, what is your idea?"

"Make two pairs of wheels, a small pair and a large pair, but each pair would be slightly different in diameters. For each pair, the inside wheel, the left wheel, would be slightly smaller in diameter than the outer wheel. This arrangement would help the chariot to corner more efficiently. The inner wheel always travels less distance in the turns than the outer wheel. This pairing would help distribute the weight of the chariot and driver more to the left in the left turns and," Jake held out his hands in a proof positive gesture, "Alexander will be able to fly through the turns with greater speed and less effort." He paused for a moment. "Well, what do you think?"

Diotrephes sat at his desk and just shook his head with a dazed expression. "You've got to run all that info by me one more time. I've never heard anything so far from normal thinking. Nobody thinks like that!'

"I'll be glad to explain it again," Jake said. "No, wait, I'll show you."

Jake found a clay drinking cup on the meeting table over along the side of the office. He brought it to The Captain's desk and laid the cup on its side.

"Now, notice, this cup is slightly larger in circumference at the top than at the bottom. In fact, the top of the cup has a slight flare to it. Now, watch when I roll the cup across your desk top."

Jake gave the cup a gentle shove and it rolled across the top of the desk, but … it rolled automatically in a circle, not in a straight line.

"See, as the cup rolls, the larger top has to travel further than the smaller bottom of the cup. The cup turns on its own. The action is automatic. There is no extra effort expended to make it happen. The same action will apply out on the race track with wheels that are slightly different in circumference. The smaller wheel on the inside of the track. Larger on the outside. The chariot will negotiate the turns, basically on its own, with less effort and greater speed."

Diotrephes squinted his eyes at Jake, still with a dazed expression. Then he gazed back down at the sideways clay cup laying on his desk.

"It is just not done this way," he said slightly shaking his head. "This is too mind-boggling. Too far out of the mainstream of conventional thinking. But then again, it looks like it would work. Man, I don't know. It seems too radical, but then, is it really? I don't think there is a rule against it, either."

"We've got to stay one step ahead of the competition, especially the Blue Team," Jake said. "As long as we stay within the rules, we're good to go! Couple this idea with our new harnessing for our horses, this new wheel concept should put us miles ahead of the other teams."

"Well, like I said earlier," The Captain remarked. "Maybe it takes someone who comes from outside the racing world to see these new ideas. Let's head over to the barn and talk to Rueben about your idea for building these staggered wheels. See if you can convince him that you know what you're talking about. And let's take that cup along with us."

16

SABOTAGE

Jake laid down his leather working tools and he and Caleb drifted over to the big, open barn door. They had heard Alexander running some practice laps outside in the team's newly modified chariot. The rains had finally stopped and the dirt practice track outside had dried out rather quickly. The two men reached the door and admired the skill of their young charioteer. They also admired their handy work in the newly designed "four up" harnesses.

"I must admit," Caleb mused, "I've never seen horses running in pairs like that, one pair behind the other. It looks strange not to see the horses lined up four across."

"It just seemed to make sense to apply all that horsepower down the center line of the chariot," Jake stated. "I guess these test runs will give us a good indicator as to whether this idea will work or not."

"Well, one thing is for sure," Caleb laughed. "I designed a really great set of harnesses that will make your idea work. Now, these practice runs will show us if our hours of labor spent on that lovely leatherwork was wasted or not."

The two leather men stepped further out into the glorious morning sunshine. Alexander zipped around the track effortlessly. The new, revolutionary wheels had also been installed and from where Jake stood, Alexander glided through the sharp hairpin turns at either end of the track with ease. Occasionally, Alexander would rein in his mighty steeds for a quick conversation with Diotrephes, who stood by the edge of the track. Reuben, the builder of the new "staggered" wheels, also waited at trackside. During one of these confabs, Jake heard The Captain say, "Drive it into the barn."

Diotrephes hopped on the chariot with Alexander and rode it into the barn.

"We've got to make a change," The Captain stated to Ezra, as he hopped off. "Alexander suggests that we remove the extra length of chariot tongue between the lead horses."

"I can do that," Ezra said. "I'll get with Caleb and figure out a new configuration of leather straps and wood pieces."

"Yeah, I don't think we need that extra tongue," Alexander explained. "Based on the temperaments of my horses, I've got Trooper and Rascal paired together, as my lead pair. I noticed my lead horses seemed to be bothered by that new tongue dangling between them, whenever we cut around those sharp turns. What kind of new arrangement could we come up with if we removed the tongue extension?"

Caleb knelt down to inspect the area of the chariot in question. "I think Ezra and I can design a ring connector so we can attach a second double tree hitch to the front of the original chariot tongue. That will eliminate the tongue extension. We can hook up the two lead horses to that new double tree hitch. Jacob and I will get to work on the new leather pieces of the apparatus right away."

Jake had to ask his burning question. "How did the new asymmetric wheels work for you?"

Alexander's eyes grew happy. "Smooth, really smooth," he said with a big grin. "The chariot wants to make the turns on its own. I believe I can make even sharper turns now than I could before." He gave Jake a thumbs up, "Really great idea," he laughed with a twinkle in his eye.

Reuben arrived in the barn from trackside. Alexander saw him walking up and said, "Rueben, you are the best! You built some superb wheels. With these new 'staggered' wheels, I'm driving now with more confidence than I ever have before."

Reuben crossed his arms proudly and smirked. "Only the best for you! You dream 'em up and I'll build 'em!"

Progress on the new double tree connector moved quickly, but couldn't be finished by close of business for the day. By nightfall, everybody began to put away their tools and get cleaned up for the evening. A new swing shift crew now took up the evening security duties. Jake was so involved with his work on the new experimental second hitch connector that he decided to curl up in a corner of the barn and sleep there for the night. "Tell Hannah, I'm sleeping in the barn, tonight," Jake told Diotrephes. All twelve of the team's stallions had been safely stabled in the barn, so Jake found an empty stall in the corner and lay down on the soft hay.

Suddenly around one o'clock in the morning, Jake heard yelling in the midst of his sleep. *'What a weird dream,'* he thought to himself. Then the pungent scent of hot smoke smacked his nostrils. Jake woke up with a start.

Bleary eyed and half asleep, the detective jumped up. Across on the other side of the barn, the corner of the building was ablaze! Smoke billowed, filling the barn. The horses franticly pranced and shrieked in terrified whinnies in their stalls. In fear, they began rearing up, panic-stricken, trying to escape. The two crewmen on guard duty were yelling instructions to each other, grabbing water buckets and dousing the flames with what little water was in the barn.

Jake yelled to the men through the smoke, "I'll get the horses. I'll turn 'em loose outside!" He threw the barn doors wide open and began releasing the stallions from their stalls, letting them run freely out the door into the night.

Carpus, the third man on duty, came running in from outside. "I saw men outside, but I was too late to stop them!" he screamed in disgust. "They looked like some of Dominic's men

"Well, we'll deal with that later!" Jake yelled to him. "Go help battle the blaze. I'll get the rest of these horses outa here!"

Fortunately, there was a corral-like enclosure outside the barn, some distance away. Jake was able to whistle to the horses and call them into that enclosure, without too much difficulty. "Thank you, Lord, for giving me herding skills I've never had before," Jake thought out loud.

The bright blaze lit up the night sky and many of the town's people responded and rushed to the blaze in an effort to save the barn. The Black Diamond crew arrived on the scene from the city, also, and began a bucket brigade carrying water from a nearby well on the Black Diamond property. The rains had brought the water levels in the well up significantly. So, swilling water from the well was much easier.

"Get more buckets out of the maintenance shed!" yelled The Captain as he rushed in from the city, into the smoke-filled chaos. "Some of you get around the outside corner of the barn and throw water on the fire from out there!

Nathan dashed into the barn. "Where are my horses?" he shrieked.

"They're all outside in the corral!" The Captain hollered to Nathan. "Go take charge of your horses! And you two men, go with him and protect those horses! Get them calmed down! Lead them further away from the fire to quiet them if you have to!"

Diotrephes stood in the middle of the chaos barking orders and slinging his arms, pointing in all directions, as he took command of the turbulent situation.

"More water over here!" he screamed, as he ran into the barn, glowing embers falling all around him. "Stomp out those burning sparks!"

Jake dashed in behind Diotrephes and yelled to him midst the roar of the blaze, "Boss, get back outside! We need you to call the shots from out there! We don't need you getting hurt!"

Diotrephes made a grimace, staring wild-eyed at Jake. "Okay, okay! But put more water over there in that corner! That's where the fire is the hottest!"

The bucket brigade had formed a flimsy line from the well to the flames in the barn corner. Already the blaze was licking at the loft and toward the roof.

Caleb rushed into the barn from the city. Jake saw him run in and yelled to him, "We've got to get up to the loft!"

Both men scrambled up the ladder into the hay loft. They threw a rope down to the firefighters below so they could attach buckets of water to it. One by one Jake and Caleb hauled bucket after bucket of water up to the loft, dousing the hay and the raging blaze. Little by little they started to knock back the flames. More towns folk climbed up into the teeth of the smoke and flames in the loft to help. Muscleman Levi ran back and forth to the well lugging two oversized tubs of water at a time, so the firefighters could dip into the tubs. Finally, slowly, the blaze began to subside. They kept pouring gallons of water on the whimpering flames, knocking them down gradually. Through the heavy, choking smoke, someone yelled, "I think the fire is out!"

Jake shouted, "Halleluiah! Praise God!"

From high up in the fog of smoke, Jake caught sight of Hannah, as she ran into the barn from the city. He could barely see her through the smokey haze but he yelled down to her, "Hannah! I'm up here, in the loft! God has helped us!"

"Jake, are you okay?" she asked in a frenzy.

"Yep! Safe and sound! And I think everybody else is safe, too!"

Jake, the firefighter, slid down the ladder from the loft and ran to Hannah. As he reached her, they hugged each other tightly. "I'm so glad God protected you and helped all of you to put out the fire," Hannah said, gazing into Jake's black smudged face.

"Everybody was quick to respond, even the folks from the city!" he said. "We couldn't have put it out without their help."

At least fifty people, some crew members, some town folks, continued to swarm over the smoking, smoldering embers. They poured so much water on the blaze, in the loft and in the corner stables that streams of water ran in wide rivulets out the barn door.

Jake turned to all the many town's people heroes who showed up to fight the blaze. "Thank you, everybody!" he yelled to all the group. "Our team wants to sincerely thank you all from the bottom of our hearts for coming to our rescue! This barn would be nothing but a smoldering cinder right now if it wasn't for you! We owe this community a very big debt of thanks and gratitude. And I thank God for Him sending you to us and for making sure none of us got hurt!"

Diotrephes chimed in. "I personally am very grateful to all of you, people from the city and people from our team. We did this together.

And all you people from the city made an investment in this race team tonight. You invested your lives into this team. You risked your safety to help us. That is a very big investment, much more valuable to me than gold or silver. Tomorrow, I am going to go to the city mayor and his city council and commend all of you for your bravery and heroism. And when we race in the championship race in Caesarea in a week and a half, our team will dedicate our race to you, the people of the City of Samaria!"

A wild cheer erupted from the crowd assembled inside and outside the barn. In the midst of their celebration, the fire brigade continued to douse water on the fading, dying coals until the entire burned out area was drenched.

Hannah contemplated Jake's sooty face and clothes. "Wow, honey, you look a mess. What do you suppose started the fire in the first place?" she asked.

"I have my clues to work on. I'll investigate this case just like I would any other. But I've got good info to go on."

"Well, come on home and get cleaned up and get a good night's sleep," Hannah said in a comforting tone. "You need to relax and unwind. I can't even imagine how terrifying it was for you, waking up and having to immediately fight that fire."

Jake breathed a relaxed sigh. "It was scary. But when I was in there, fighting the fire, it was like I knew I had a job to do and I just did it. It's only now that I'm getting a little shaky."

"Well, you come on," his wife said calmly. "You deserve a break. There's still plenty of night for you to relax and sleep. You can start your investigation bright and early in the morning."

The dazzling light of day revealed the seriousness of the damage to the barn. Jake and The Captain walked the grounds, surveying the destruction. Now in full-on detective mode, Jake was extremely careful not to disturb the scene of the investigation. As the two men stood outside the barn, they studied the fire-swept, blackened corner of the structure. The entire burned corner was gutted with a gaping hole big enough to see through into the interior of the barn. The charred remains could be shored up temporarily. Thankfully the roof seemed to have escaped any damage.

"Boss, I think we dodged the big one," Jake stated. "It could have been much worse."

"Wet wood," The Captain mused, gazing at the blackened corner of the barn.

"Wet wood?" Jake asked.

"I think one saving grace about this incident is the fact that the structure of the barn was still very saturated with water from three days of rain," The Captain stated. "Wet wood – I am very thankful for it. If the wood of the barn had been dry, it might have burst into flames like a tinderbox. And all of our valuable and beloved horses would have been destroyed in one fell swoop. We were very fortunate."

"Great point, boss. That proved to be very fortunate."

"Everybody's help is also what saved the barn from total destruction."

"Don't forget the Lord God's help," the detective remarked.

"Yes, the Lord God," Diotrephes said, as he looked away and glanced heavenward.

The two men began to search the ground for clues to the cause of the blaze. "Boss, just to let you know, Carpus told me that he saw men sneaking around outside the barn. And he also told me that they looked like some of Dominic's men. That fact would be hard to prove, since it was a totally dark night, with no moon. But we'll still look around and see what we can find."

The fact-finding pair skirted the perimeter of the site of the investigation and walked a little further away from the area. "Look here," Jake observed, "the ground is still soft from the rain. It's even muddy in spots and see these footprints in the mud. There are several sets of footprints, going toward the barn and then the prints trail away from the barn. It appears that one of the men slipped and fell. See here, the skid marks of sandals sliding in the soft ground and here are knee prints and a hand print where the man fell to the ground."

The pair walked a few steps further. "And what is this?" Jake stated in a voice of discovery. The detective knelt down and fished around under a brambly bush. He dragged out a broken clay jar.

"Hmmm, this looks very interesting," he said, holding up the largest fractured portion of the jar.

"What is that jar doing way out here under that bush?" Diotrephes asked.

"I think we may have the found the answer to the mystery of the fire," Jake mused. "Look inside the jar. The inside is covered with soot, as if there was a fire inside the jar. Now, let me think ..."

Jake stood quietly for a moment paging through his brain for historical facts. Slowly an ancient story from the scriptures came to light in his thoughts.

"There is an old story from the ancient history of Israel about a Judge in the land named Gideon. Gideon was engaged in a battle with an enemy army of hundreds of thousands against his tiny army of three hundred. As the story goes, Gideon had his tiny army creep up on the enemy at night, with blazing torches hidden inside clay jars. Just at the right moment, all the men of his army smashed the clay jars and held up the torches, screaming loudly, 'The sword of the Lord and of Gideon!' The enemy army, seeing bright lights all around them in the middle of the night, panicked in the darkness of their camp and started killing each other. The key to Gideon's victory was how his army hid their torches inside the clay jars."

Diotrephes' eyes opened wide as he realized Jake's point. "So, you're thinking that someone set the fire in the barn. And they did it Gideon-style!

"That is the way it appears," the detective stated, "Whoever did this, must have snuck up to the barn in the darkness using a clay jar to camouflage the lit torch they were carrying. The clay jar hid the torch's glow. Once they got up close to the barn, they threw the lit torch through a barn window! The firebugs made their hurried escape into the night, but the guy carrying the jar must have slipped in the mud, smashing the jar. In the hurried confusion, he must have just flipped the broken jar up under this bush, hoping to hide it."

"Who could have done such a terrible thing?"

"We only have Carpus' word that the men outside the barn looked like Dominic's men," Jake said. "That assumption would be hard to prove, since it was a moonless night. Carpus assumed the men looked like some of Dominic's team members. Carpus, being one of the horse trainers, surely is mostly upset about the fact that he almost lost all of his precious horses in the fire. To Nathan and him, they are their precious babies."

"We all would have been extremely upset if we had lost our horses!" The Captain exclaimed. "They **are** the treasure of our racing team. We have nothing without them."

Then a grimace rushed across Jake's face in a horrified expression. "Do you suppose that was the *real* objective of someone setting the fire? To destroy all of our horses. They must have known that we had stabled all of our horses in the barn for their safety. Why didn't they try to burn down the office building? Why choose the barn to burn down?"

A burst of rage flashed across Diotrephes' face. He grit his teeth together and said through angry lips, "How horrifying! How evil! Whoever would do that is lower than a snake! They can come after me, if you must get revenge! But don't try to destroy my stallions!"

The two men stood there in the mud, shocked and dazed at the possibility of such an inhumane, vicious act.

"We've got to be calm about this, boss. We can't prove Dominic did this, although all the evidence points straight back to his doorstep."

"Yes, I know. But we do know Dominic does mean to inflict harm to us and our team. So does Scorpio. They are the only ones who would want to engineer such a vengeful act."

"Once again, I think we should thank God for helping us to spoil the evil plans brought against us," Jake stated. "God helped us to outsmart our enemy. Our enemy may have burned a corner of the barn but God helped us safe the horses from destruction. God has blessed us! Blessed us, absolutely!"

The Captain nodded his head. "Yes, I believe you, Jacob. Our enemy intended destruction for our team and God shielded us from the worst possible catastrophe. A burned out corner of a barn is a small tradeoff for the safety of our horses."

Jake looked down at the shattered piece of pottery dangling from his hand. "I think I'm going to hang on to this little souvenir. I think I can use it in the future to our advantage."

17

DECISION TIME

With just a week and a half until the championship race at Caesarea, the Black Diamond Racing Team shifted into high gear. There was no time to repair the charred and burned out corner of the barn. Time was too precious. Just let the wind blow through. Besides, the cavernous hole in the corner gave the barn better ventilation and kept the barn cooler.

Nathan lightly exercised the horses every day, to keep them loose and in shape. Every other day Alexander practiced with the new "four up" configuration. The new setup seemed to be working extremely well.

"When we get to Caesarea," Nathan stated with a glint in his eye, "we're going to surprise all of our competition with this radical new hitch!"

"I like it!" Alexander exclaimed. "I really do like it. My lead horses, Trooper and Rascal, are w-a-y out there in front of me and I think they like the extra freedom of running in a simple pair. My wheel horses, Thunder and Swifty, seem to enjoy playing follow-the-leader, too. We're all having fun. I can tell the horses love to give me everything they've got. They love to compete. They are r-e-a-l aggressive competitors. And it's almost like they keep asking me, 'When are we gonna race for real?'"

"We'll be racing for all the marbles very soon," Nathan said. "We will be leaving for the coast in four days."

Everybody made their last minute checks of their equipment and replacement parts. As they made their final preparations, they began loading all the gear into the transport wagons. Diotrephes kept a checklist on all the essentials. But with only a few days before departure, The Captain arrived at work in a depressed mood. Jake stepped into the office to give the boss the latest progress report. As he crossed the threshold, he immediately realized the boss was dejected about something.

"Boss, you look a little down today. Is there anything I can do to cheer you up."

"No, just a little problem at home. It'll pass."

"Do you want to talk about it? You seem awful sad. Sometimes just talking about a problem can provide a solution."

"Oh, it's the age old problem between a man and a woman. A woman marries a man hoping to change him, but he doesn't. The man marries the woman, hoping she *never* changes, but she *does*. It's a constant battle. He wants her to stay just exactly like she was when they first met, but she changes into something different. She marries the man trying to mold him into the kind of man she ideally wants him to be, but he doesn't change." The Captain sighed. "Everything is wonderful in the beginning. But romance has nothing to do with real life. One day you realize that marriage is nothing more than a struggle for control. Just vying for power. And if anything goes wrong, it's always my fault. I wonder sometimes if she's ever had respect for me. It's frustration all the way around."

Jake just sat in his chair, looking at the floor, contemplating. Listening.

"I've always heard that the longer a married couple lives together, the more they become like each other," Diotrephes sadly stated, hanging his head. "It is not true. I'm here to tell you, it is not true. Maybe if there was respect for each other in the marriage that would be true. But with no respect ... all you do is fight and grow further apart. And when your wife shuts off her heart, there's nothing you can do about it"

Jake sat quietly, listening.

The Captain raised his eyes and stared thoughtfully at the ceiling.

"You know, sometimes I wonder if an indebted kind of love is better than a romantic love. Romance fades. Dwindles away into everyday complacency. But when a person is indebted to someone else, it is the foundation of a relationship of gratitude and respect. Every man wants respect. Romance seems like it's all about fuzzy feelings and delirious emotions. Who can make a wise decision when your mind is so messed up? So clouded and overpowered by euphoria?" Diotrephes stopped and heaved a long sigh of sadness. He looked over at Jake. "No, it is better to build a relationship on an indebtedness, where the man does something to help the woman out of a tight spot. He helps her by saving her from her perplexing problem. Then in gratitude she wants to devote her whole life to the man who helped her, respecting him for saving her from her dire straits – her helpless situation – she was in. That will bring about a lasting devotion. It cannot be shaken. That bond will last. Neither person is trying to outdo the other and change them. There is a thankfulness in the relationship. A true devotion. A bond of thankfulness, gratitude, and respect binds the two together."

"Sort of like the story in the Bible of Ruth's devotion to her husband Boaz," Jake commented.

"There is such a story in the Bible?"

"Oh yeah. It's a really great story of devotion because a man helps a woman out of a terrible situation of personal ruin."

"See, that's what I'm talking about," Diotrephes stated. "That kind of relationship is not formulated out of romantic, feel-good euphoria. That kind of relationship is founded on a basis of mutual gratitude and respect. Romance can come and will come after the relationship of thankfulness and respect have been established. Devotion bonds the two lives together. Romance will come later as the spawn of that devotion."

Jake gazed at The Captain and asked, "So, what is the problem?"

"Here lately my wife seems to want to turn everything that happens into a conflict," Diotrephes continued. "Everything is a struggle. She's irritated about my racing. My wife has been nagging me to get out of the racing business." Diotrephes lowered his head and rubbed his hand across his brow. "She's tired of racing. She says we've made our pile of money and that I should get out of racing all together. She wants me to sell the team and just walk away. She was a sweet thing when I married her. Very reasonable. Very accommodating. But now she has become plenty unreasonable. She doesn't understand. Racing is what I do. It's all I've known. My life *is* racing. Racing is what makes me happy. Gives me meaning. Something to live for. She wants to change me. Make me into a merchant or something. I could not do that."

Jake continued to sit quietly, listening, staring at the floor.

"You know, with you and Hannah it's different," the boss continued. "I don't notice conflict with you and Hannah. You two seem to be in harmony. What makes you two different?"

"Love is a choice," Jake said quietly. "We have learned to not compete against each other. We choose not to. Since we work together so much, we have learned to use the old adage, 'Complete one another, don't compete.' So, we try to complete each other and not compete against each other. We try to complete each other by trying to work as a team. We try not to be competitors, like two people grappling to prove one of us is better than the other. Just like this race team. Everybody on the team has their assigned duties, but we all work together for the same goal. We team members complete each other, we don't compete against each other. Nobody is trying to prove we are better than anybody else on the team."

Diotrephes sat behind his desk, head bowed, thinking about Jake's comments.

"Very interesting," The Captain said, looking up. "So, how did you two get to this point in your marriage?"

"Jesus Christ," Jake simply stated with a pleasant smile on his face.

"Jesus Christ? How does He play into all this? I thought He was dead."

"Have you not heard that Jesus Christ is alive?"

"Only rumors about some myth that He is alive. Here in Samaria, we don't get a lot of news from Jerusalem or Jews for that matter. The Jews despise us Samaritans so much, they never travel through our country. In fact, you're the first Jew I've known in years."

146

"I was a Jew. Now, I'm a completely free Jew. I now believe in the risen Christ. In fact, I have seen Jesus alive and I have spoken to Him."

Diotrephes stared at Jake, with a stunned expression. "You have actually seen this Jesus of Nazareth living, in the flesh?"

"Yes, I have. Jesus is God. He is powerful and controls life and death. He has divine authority, so He conquered death by His mighty authority. And now, He is alive and invites people to surrender their lives to Him, so He may empower them to live a new life of freedom. And not just in this life. Jesus promises eternal life in Heaven with Him! In this life, Jesus gives freedom for a life of peace. Freedom to have His divine blessings. Freedom from the power of sin. Freedom to love each other, even your wife."

Diotrephes dropped his head and gazed at the top of the desk. "Can all that really be possible?"

"Do you see living proof of Christ's reality in Hannah's and my relationship? Do you see Christ in her life, in my life, in our lives together?"

"I do. Very much so."

Diotrephes stood up slowly and began to thoughtfully pace back and forth behind his desk. He stroked his short chin beard, contemplating Jake's remarks. He stopped and looked over at the detective.

"I have been observing you while you have worked for me. You are a loyal man. You always do what you say. You work solely for the team and the good of the team. Look at the new innovations you have introduced to assist the performance of our race team. And, incredibly, you proved that you truly care about our team when you and Hannah rescued The Black Diamond Trophy from Dominic at great danger to your own lives. I learned then that I could truly trust you. That powerful experience branded in my brain that you are a loyal, trustworthy man. I can trust you."

The Captain sat down in his chair behind his desk and breathed a thoughtful sigh. "All of those factors about you help me want to believe you about Jesus Christ. Can you tell me more?"

Jake's smile turned into a glorious grin. "Absolutely. Jesus Christ's mission as God was to come to earth for the express purpose of being the sacrifice for our sins. We all, Jews and Gentiles, were all alienated from God because of our sins. There was nothing we could do to pacify the anger of God over our sins. So, Jesus, as God, came to be the sacrifice Himself for our sins to satisfy the rage of the Almighty against our sins. When He did die on the cross, God Almighty saw His Son's perfect, selfless sacrifice and turned away His vengeance and wrath against sin. Jesus' sacrifice satisfied God's wrath against our sin.

"Now, because of Jesus' sacrifice, God Almighty only looks at a person's relationship to Jesus. Has that person accepted Christ's sacrificial, finished work on the cross? Or does that person still stand stubbornly against the gracious act Jesus did for them? In God's eyes there are only two kinds of people. Those who have repented of their sins and surrendered their lives to Jesus Christ as their Lord and Savior. And those who stubbornly refuse to accept Jesus Christ as their personal Lord and Savior. It's a simple plan. It's really Good News. It's really not hard for anyone to understand."

"It's only hard because it requires a person to surrender their whole life to a Man they don't know," The Captain said quietly.

"But this Man sacrificed His life to save your life."

"True," Diotrephes stated. He thought for a moment. "In some ways, I can see a parallel by the way you and Hannah risked your lives to rescue The Black Diamond Trophy. You did that for me and our team. You didn't have to do that. I told you at the time that I am deeply indebted to you for your act of loyalty. I guess, as I realize the sacrifice and loyalty Jesus showed to me by dying for me, I am equally indebted to Him for His absolute display of devotion to me." He paused and sat quietly at his desk.

Diotrephes looked straight at Jake. "I have not been satisfied with my religion for a long time. I've tried to be a good man. But as the years have gone by, I cannot say I am happy in my religion. There is this gnawing feeling inside that I am not in good favor with the Lord God. I have felt that I need someone or something to help me get to God, like a savior. This moment you have told me who the Savior is. And at last, at last, I know His Name! His name is Jesus!" Diotrephes breathed the name Jesus with a sigh of total recognition.

Diotrephes stretched out his hands toward Jake in a pleading fashion. "Jacob, what must I do, now?"

"Pray."

"Pray? That's all?'

"It's what you pray that counts. Right here, at your desk, you can pray to the Lord Jesus and tell Him you are coming to Him in repentance of your past sins. Tell Him you want to surrender your whole life to Him, to make Him your Lord and your Savior. Ask Him to show you how to live. And guess what? He will do all that, right here in your office. He hears you right now. Do you want to pray to Him, now?

"I do."

Diotrephes lowered his head and prayed a very simple prayer to Christ. His prayer flowed out in a heartfelt stream of deep confession of his sins and an earnest surrender of his life to the Lordship of Christ. As his prayer ended, he looked up at Jake with an expression of amazement on his face.

"Jacob, I just spoke to Jesus! And I know He heard me! It was like He was with me right here in this room!"

"That's because His really is!" Jake exclaimed. "You are His now. And at the moment you prayed, you stepped across the line into eternal life! And at that moment, Jesus placed inside you His Holy Spirit. He promised He would give you His Holy Spirit to empower you with His divine authority to live this new Christian life that you now have!"

Diotrephes placed his hands on his cheeks and closed his eyes. "I do know this, I felt a warmth in my heart like I have never before experienced when I prayed."

"That was Jesus, confirming His presence in you. And remember this, Jesus has given you eternal life when you surrendered to Him. The Holy Spirit inside you guarantees Christ's eternal life exists in your soul! Your eternal life began the moment you prayed!"

The Captain lowered his head and raised his hand up to his forehead. He began to cry. "This is all too wonderful to take in," he said through his joyful tears. "I am overwhelmed."

The two men sat quietly together. The experience truly was too wonderful to explain.

Diotrephes looked up at Jake, wiping away his tears. "I'm going home and explain to my wife what just happened to me. I'm a Christian, now! I'm going to make an effort to rectify any hurtful differences I have caused her and try to get our marriage back on track. Maybe we can work out our differences with Jesus' help. And maybe with Jesus' help, she will become a Christian, too!"

"All that is wonderful news, Captain. I certainly will be praying for you that God would give you His wisdom as you speak to her."

In a sudden moment of euphoria, Diotrephes jumped up. He looked at Jake and exclaimed, "I want to call a team meeting, later on! I want you to explain this same Good News about Jesus to all the members of this race team! They all need to hear this wonderful message about Jesus Christ! Imagine if Jesus ran our racing team! What a fabulous experience we all could have together!"

18

OFF TO THE RACES

The twenty-three mile ride to Caesarea by the Mediterranean coast took about a day to complete. The team had packed all the necessary equine equipment, chariot spare parts, and other racing essentials in two wagons. Fifteen members of the Black Diamond Race Team made the trip to the race track. Nathan and his horse trainers carefully led the valuable stallions along the road. The team brought six horses, four designated as the starting team, and two in reserve. The rest of the horses were left behind at the Black Diamond stables with five of the team members. On a separate wagon rode two magnificent chariots, the personal handiwork of Ezra, the constructor, and Caleb, the leathercrafter. One was the primary chariot and the other was the backup chariot, in case it would be needed. One of the team members, Lucas, had painted a special name on the right side of each chariot's leather dashboard, "City of Samaria", in honor of all the courageous folks back in Samaria.

"I told the people back in the city," Diotrephes said, "that I would dedicate this race to all those wonderful folks who risked their lives to save our racing team from destruction. And I meant what I said. We'll carry their name with us in the race."

Alexander rode in the wagon with the chariots. "We've got to take care of our driver and let him take it easy for now," The Captain was heard to say.

The team wanted to arrive at the race track three days before the actual championship race. The official title of the annual event was, *The Grand Judean Chariot Races at Caesarea*. When the team got to the stadium track, rumors were flying around that Tiberius Caesar himself may attend the event this year. The rumor was that Caesar would present the grand prize, The Golden Cup of Caesar. A spectacular rumor, if it was true.

When the Black Diamond Team began to unload their equipment in their assigned stable, Jake noticed Dominic and his Blue Team pulling in, as well. The Blue Team began to unload their equipment several stables away. The Captain watched with interest as Dominic supervised his team's setup.

Diotrephes turned to Jake, with a smile on his face and said, "Watch this. My Lord Jesus has given me a warm forgiveness in my heart. I'm going to go over and wish Dominic the best of luck in the big race."

"Boss, that's risky," Jake stated. "Do you want me to go with you?"

"No, I think Jesus and I can manage this," he grinned.

Diotrephes pivoted and began to stride over toward the entire Blue Team, arrayed in front of him. They all noticed The Captain approaching and called to their boss. All of them gathered in a defensive posture. Scorpio shrunk back behind them. Dominic stepped forward ahead of the line of his men, his tiny, oblong bubble of a head bobbling on his spindly neck. Diotrephes continued to advance, never slowing down. At a distance of about six feet, The Captain stopped.

"Good morning, Dominic," Diotrephes grinned. "Fine weather to contest our racing program. Your team looks very well prepared. I want to wish you and all of your team the absolute best of luck in the upcoming contest. And Scorpio, I wish you the very best, too." He continued to stand straight and confident, still grinning. He then swept his hand out over all the line of men on the Blue Team and stated, "May the Lord God bless and reward all of you in your upcoming competition."

A moment longer and then The Captain swung around and headed back to his team members. As he approached Jake, Diotrephes gave a large, visible expression of relief, thankful that he had met the enemy and survived. Without looking back, he asked Jake, "Are they still looking this way?"

Jake threw a glance back toward the Blue Team. "Yeah, they are still standing there, looking at you, I guess they're in shock. What did you say to them?"

"I told them that I wanted God to bless and reward them in the approaching race," he smiled, still looking away from Dominic and his men. "I don't think I could have done that a week ago before I met Christ. I think they must have thought I wanted to pick a fight. Now they must think I'm just loony! But I have a wonderful new Lord and a wonderful new eternal life that Jesus has given me. I've got a new life! I don't need to fight!"

"What you just did is something Jesus taught about," Jake smiled. "When I followed Jesus in Galilee, I often heard Him teach us to love our enemies. That's exactly what you just did." The detective glanced past The Captain again and continued, "They all look bewildered, not knowing how to respond to your kindness."

"Well, I'm so glad Jesus gave me the grace to forgive Dominic," The Captain stated. "What a wonderful, freeing feeling it is to forgive someone. I feel like shouting, I'm so happy!"

Jake grinned and just shook his head in joyful understanding. "We'd better get our equipment unloaded," he said, "before all this happiness subsides."

The Black Diamond Team began to unpack their equipment and set it up in Stable Number 51. The stable was incorporated into a long line of stables in the paddock area, a stone's throw from the track. The stable area bustled noisily with an overflow of racing personnel, horses, and assorted wagons and paraphernalia. Electric tension sparked in the air.

Caleb watched Jake as the detective surveyed all this hurried activity. "Like a beehive, ain't it," Caleb stated.

"Wow, I've never seen anything like this!" Jake exclaimed "The excitement! The noise! The crush of people running everywhere! It's unreal!"

"There are race teams here from all over Judea," Caleb observed. "Crowds of racing personnel busying themselves, preparing, all intent on winning ... and winning big! Prize money. Contingency awards. Fortunes to be won. This business is big business. Money flows around here like floods of ocean waves.

"And then there are the crowds of chariot racing fans from all over the place. They have come to throw around their money and wager their hard-earned cash on the races. During this two day race meet, there will be twelve races on the racing card each day. That's a bunch of races and that's a bunch of chances for the fans to bet their money. A few will win. Most will lose."

Jake just shook his head. "I don't know what to think! If you love noisy crowds and excitement, this is the place to be!"

"Let's get the chariots unloaded," stated The Captain to team members. "Back 'em in to our stable, Stable Number 51."

Jake turned to Caleb and asked, "Is there something extra special about Stable Number 51? The boss seemed to take pride in that number."

Oh, yeah," Caleb laughed. "That is our stable number from last year when we won the championship race and when we won The Black Diamond Trophy. The boss specially requested that we get Stable Number 51 this year. You know. Racing people have their little quirks."

In about an hour, the team had completely unloaded all their equipment and chariots. Nathan took care of the horses, getting them settled into their new stalls, their new home away from home. Trooper, Thunder, and Swifty all seemed to settle in without any problems. But Rascal started being a rascal almost immediately. It was his first time away from the safety of his familiar surroundings. The loud racket, the unsettling turmoil, and the commotion of the frantic activity around the stable area, caused him to grow increasingly fretful. He could not be quiet. He pranced in his stall. The incessant clamor around him, unnerved the beautiful animal. Nathan tried to calm the high-spirited steed but Rascal wanted nothing to do with being tranquil. So, Nathan decided to take Rascal out for a run, to blow off steam. Nathan, a skilled horseman, slid onto Rascal's bare back and took off at a slow trot.

"I'll see you guys in a little bit," Nathan stated as he rode off, riding bareback. "We might even take a lap or two around the race track."

"Maybe that run will help Rascal get acclimated to his new

environment," Caleb stated hopefully. "Running off some nervous energy will be the best medicine for Rascal and probably for Nathan, too!"

"Wow, I've never seen anyone riding bareback before," Jake said. "I always thought you had to have a saddle to stay on a horse."

"Not for Nathan," Caleb laughed. "I think he was born on a horse. He is a great horseman. And Alexander can ride bareback, too. But I don't think the boss wants Alexander goofing around, riding bareback right now, just before our big race!"

Caleb smiled as he saw Jake watching Nathan ride off out of sight. "Would you like to go take a look at the race track? We could watch Nathan and Rascal take a few laps."

"You bet I would!" Jake yelped. "I've been ready for this moment for quite some time!"

The pair of leathercrafters exited the paddock with its long row of stables and trekked about a hundred yards south to the race track grounds. As they approached, the vast expanses of the Caesarea Hippodrome spread out before them.

"Man!" Jake stated in an awe-inspired declaration. "This place is utterly breathtaking."

"Yeah, it's quite a place," Caleb observed. "It stretches out before you and it is spectacular. We're standing on the north end of the track and it is from this part of the track that they start the races. In fact, these are the iron starting gates here behind us. Now, look south. The track stretches out 950 feet long in front of you and is 165 feet wide. As you can see, right down the middle of the facility is a divider, known as the spina. This divider separates the race track into two long straightaways that are each 80 feet wide. The charioteers race around that long divider. As you can see, at each end of the spina divider, there are tall, stone column turning points, called metas. It's at these turning points where the crashes often occur."

The two men walked out onto the track. "Look at all those seats along the front stretch," Jake said in astonishment. "I count twelve rows of seats. And the seating extends way down to the other end and curves around in sort of a U shape. How many people will this place seat?"

"I'm told this stadium will seat about 5,000 people," Caleb stated, "and that's not counting the standing room crowd. Notice, for the safety of the spectators, there is a five and a half foot tall stone retaining wall, separating the crowd from the racing charioteers."

"It must get pretty intense out here during the races," Jake stated thoughtfully.

"Yep, the drivers can sometimes become overly aggressive and that's when violent wrecks will happen. Like I said earlier, there is a lot of money riding on these races. A lot of personal pride and prestige pushes some drivers to take big chances. Bad things can happen. This is a dangerous sport."

At that moment, Nathan and Rascal galloped by, making the tight turn in front of them around the spina. Rascal really turned on the jets as he accelerated down the long, 950 foot straightaway, kicking dirt clods soaring airborne from his flying hooves.

"That long straight is known as the West Straightaway and, as you can see, it is bordered by the Mediterranean Sea to the West," Caleb explained. "The horses seem to run more freely on this side of the track because it is so much more open, with no grandstands down the sea side. Of course, as you can feel right now, there is a constant breeze coming in from the ocean. Sometimes that breeze can cause problems during a race. Most of the drivers rely on the streamers and pennants that are flown on various poles on the spina and the metas to tell them how stiff the breeze is when they approach the hairpin turns around the spina."

"But there still is a five foot high wall all the way down the length of this oceanside straightaway," Jake observed.

"That retaining wall is there to keep the drivers and horses from drifting out too far and plunging into the ocean," Caleb stated. "The drivers have to be careful not to swing out too wide or they will crash into that unforgiving wall!"

Nathan and Rascal galloped by again and this time the rider waved nonchalantly. Jake and Caleb returned the salute.

Both men turned to exit the facility, but in turning, they now faced the row of twelve iron starting gates constructed on the north end of the track. Behind each gate, lay a small compartment in which the chariots backed into, to line up for the start. Jake's detective mind couldn't help but ask a question.

"How do these gates work? Do all the chariots start at the same time?"

"Yeah, these iron starting gates are called carceres. The Romans have come up with a nifty system of insuring a fair, even start. The starting gates are spring-loaded and operate on the same principle as a catapult. When all the horses and chariots are loaded behind their starting gate, the sponsor of the race event drops a cloth, and the starting gate operator hits the lever and all the gates fly open at once. That way it is a clean, fair start every time. Pretty neat, huh."

Wonder etched Jake's expression. "This is a brand new world to me," he said, with his mouth gaping open. "I'm going to have to be a fast learner if I'm going to be any good to you guys and this team."

"I think you'll do alright," Caleb laughed. "Everything we have thrown at you since you've been on our team has been brand new to you. And I think you're a good, quick study in every situation we've dumped on you."

"I try," Jake said. "I just try to bob and weave and roll with the punches!"

As evening approached, Octavius and Linus arrived in Caesarea from Samaria. They had left team headquarters later in the day to bring a wagon loaded with the personal gear of all the team members. They brought along the team cook, Hannah.

As the wagon from Samaria pulled up in front of Stable Number 51, Hannah dismounted and ran to her husband.

"Kind of a dusty trip," Hannah said, as she brushed the grit from her beige tunic, "and I never thought we'd get here. But, we made it!"

"And I'm glad you made it! I haven't been to our hotel room, yet. But Diotrephes has booked enough rooms for all of us on the team in a hotel in downtown Caesarea. The Captain really does know how to treat his team members just right."

"Well, I can't stop right now. It's almost supper time and I've brought supper for all the gang. I still have got to set the food out for the guys. I've got their supper over in the wagon. Cold cuts and bread for tonight."

"Look, sweetheart. Some of the crew, Carpus, Lucas, and Zenas, have already set up tables for you outside the stable." Speaking to the three men Jake said, "Are ya hungry, fellas? Let's unload the groceries Hannah has brought us. And let's chow down!"

Jake and Hannah settled into their hotel room in downtown Caesarea for the evening. It was a cozy little room, with red curtains and a view of the ocean. It was a pleasant oasis from the drone of activity at the race track. They decided to spend their quiet moments during the evening in prayer. With all the hub-bub of the frantic day, they both felt the real need to draw close to their Lord and spend time with Him. They also invited their Christian brother, Alexander, to visit with them, to join them in prayer for a few minutes.

"This has been quite an exhilarating day," Alexander remarked. "Not only do the horses need to get accustomed to this new race environment, but I do, too. My excitement level has peaked out!"

"Well, I know this is all new to you," Jake said, "but it's not like you haven't done simulated races back at headquarters. When Nathan raced with you on our practice track in Samaria, he showed you all the tricks of driving a chariot that he knew. And Jonathan, one of the trainers, also showed you the skills in handling the chariot in competition."

"I know," Alexander stated, "but it's a little different when they were racing me in the other chariot and not trying to wreck me. I realize my competitors will not be so kind to me."

"I think they taught you enough tricks that you'll be able to avoid trouble," Jake remarked. "Plus the fact that they showed you some winning moves in heavy traffic; that could be exactly the maneuverers you'll need in a pinch."

"Like the maneuver they showed me to set up my opponent going into the turns, so I can slip under him and accelerate out ahead."

"Right, and how they showed you to put the chariot into a boardslide and get through the corners faster," Jake encouraged.

"Yes, they showed me those moves and more. And the new wheels that are different diameters on each side, really help in the cornering of the chariot. Your design idea really works!"

"That's our trade secret," Jake stated quietly. "We don't want any of the other teams to catch on to it. The difference in wheel circumferences is so slight, no one should be able to catch on to our secret weapon. And there is nothing in the rule book that says anything about wheel size. The rules basically say 'run what ya brung' in wheels."

Alexander leaned forward. "If there's one thing I've learned in this business, we need every legal edge we can get."

Hannah interrupted. "A-hem. Well, let me jump right into the middle of all your 'man talk'. It's about something far more important than 'bench racing'. I learned something on the trip over here with Octavius and Linus. They both have received Christ and surrendered their lives to Him."

Both men stared at her in surprise. "Wow, that *is* great news!" they both exclaimed together.

"When did this happen?" Jake asked.

"After Diotrephes had his team meeting, where both of you explained the Good News of Jesus' salvation from sin, both Octavius and Linus realized their need of a Savior. And they told me that a few days later they yielded themselves to Christ. That means all three of the race team owners are now Christians! And they also told me that several of the other guys on the team are contemplating giving their lives to Jesus! I was so happy to hear that news, I nearly cried." Hannah stopped short and put her hands out in an abrupt "stop signal". "Nearly cried, I said. Nearly. I didn't want to start crying in front of grown men who are my bosses."

"I think they would have understood," Jake said. "But, wow! That is great news! Jesus in moving right through into the midst of our team, speaking to hearts."

"It is so neat to watch the Lord's intervention in saving and loving people," Alexander remarked. "My time here as a slave truly has not been for naught. Even though I had no other Christian friends to talk to before you came here, Jesus was always here with me. He constantly revealed His presence to me and stood beside me. I witnessed to my teammates. And now, I have many more new Christian friends! This is so perfect!"

Hannah spoke up. "Fellas, it is so obvious that God is hovering over all of us with His presence," she said folding her hands in front of her in a prayer-like gesture. "These past few weeks the Lord has been inspiring me to write a poem about His great love for us. I've brought it with me. Can I read it to you both?"

"Absolutely," Jake said. "I love to hear your poetry."

"Please, Ms. Hannah. I want to hear it," Alexander stated in an almost yearning manner.

She pulled out a flimsy, yellow piece of papyrus from her knapsack. "I've called this poem, <u>That's Why God Sent His Son</u>. Here goes …

"When you love somebody,
You will go to all extremes,
To show the one you love,
Just how much they really mean.

That's why God sent His Son,
To show how much He cares,
And I know He really loves me,
'Cause He gave His Son, my sins to bear.

So on the cross of Calvary,
He bled and died for all my sin,
So one day I would learn to love Him,
And have God's new life within.

That's why God sent His Son,
To show how much He cares,
And I know He really loves me,
'Cause He gave His Son, my sins to bear.

Blessed be the God and Father,
Of our Lord, our Lord Jesus Christ,
Who has given, us new hope,
With His gift, of eternal life.

Now I have, all His possessions,
His faith, His love, His grace, His power,

His unmatched peace, His gentle kindness,
His mercy, and His strength each hour.

That's why God sent His Son,
To show how much He cares,
And I know He really loves me,
'Cause He gave His Son, my sins to bear."

Hannah paused after reading the poem. She put the flimsy piece of yellow papyrus down on the tiny table in the room. "That little scrap of papyrus was all I could find to write on. Well, what do you think?" she asked, her voice rising in anticipation.

"Angel, wow! That poem you wrote truly is angelic," Jake stated in profound admiration. "You turned that little piece of papyrus into a heavenly message for all of us."

Alexander sat in awe. "Those words are God's words to me," he said placing his hands on the sides of his face. "Your words are so right. When a person does love someone, they will go to all extremes to prove to that person that they really care about them. God did that. He went to the ultimate extreme to prove His love for us. He sent Jesus to die in our place and take away the sin of all the world. Thank you, Ms. Hannah. All those promises God has given to us, which you mentioned, I will carry with me forever. I'll carry them into the race tomorrow!"

Jake hesitated thoughtfully. "This whole blessed conversation this evening and then this wonderful poem about Jesus – my heart is full!" he exclaimed. "Let's pray. We have so much to pray about. We need to pray for Alexander and for his safety in the race tomorrow."

"Please pray for God's wisdom in the race tomorrow," Alexander said. "I'll really need His wisdom in the midst of all those flying chariots."

"We will do that and we can also thank the Lord for all the blessings to our team He has revealed to us today," Jake said.

Prayer that evening was sweet. Loving the Lord Jesus seemed to come so easy and natural that night.

19

THE GRAND JUDEAN CHARIOT RACES AT CAESAREA

A ction! Finally!

The organizers of The Grand Judean Chariot Races at Caesarea announced that they would allow one day of race practice for all participants, prior to the actual race events. With over fifty entrants, the race track would be far too crowded to be safe. So, the large field of contestants was divided into five practice groups of approximately ten each. Every team needed to get their horses accustomed to the track and stadium environment and the teams needed to get their equipment limbered up.

Alexander and Caleb ventured out onto the track early in the morning before race practice began. Jake watched them rambling around on the track surface and at times stomping on the sandy dirt. They walked the entire length of the 950 foot seaside West Seaside Straightaway, kicked around the dirt of the racing surface at the far south end of the track and headed back toward Jake.

"Well, how does the racing surface look?" Jake asked them.

"It has rained here not long ago," Caleb observed. "The rain packed down this sandy soil on the track. Because of that, today the track is really hard, almost as hard as stone. The chariot should run really well on this hard surface."

"But one thing we will have to watch is how the track surface holds up," Alexander stated, looking back at the race track and sweeping his hand in that direction. "If the track surface gets really chewed up from all the races during the whole race meet, we will have to change our strategy."

"Right, with the track being really hard right now," Caleb said, "we'll start out using the smaller set of wheels. But as the track conditions deteriorate due to the many races, we will have to change over to the larger set of wheels."

"Sounds like a plan," Jake said, as the three men headed back to the paddock stable complex.

Nathan and his crew of trainers had already hitched up the four primary horses to the chariot, in the new, radical "four up" hitch. During practice testing back in Samaria, the team confirmed the "four-up" hitch to be far superior to the conventional four-wide hitch. The new setup, with all the horsepower pulling from the center of the lightweight chariot, proved to be very potent. Unbelievably potent!

For the first time, Jake caught a glimpse of Alexander in his full racing regalia. Alexander dressed, head to toe, totally in black. Thin red piping ran around all the edges of his uniform, making his whole outfit pop. He wore a shiny black leather helmet, trimmed in red, especially crafted by Caleb. The driver was outfitted with a black breastplate, for protection in a crash. He wore a shimmering black, thigh-length tunic, with a short, flowing black cape. His black shoes laced halfway up the calves of his legs. And a glossy black belt adorned the whole outfit. Lucas, the artist who had painted the tribute to the city of Samaria on the dashboard of the chariot, had also painted a black diamond, edged in red, on the front of Alexander's breastplate.

"Man, you are one sharp looking dude!" Jake exclaimed as he ran his eyes up and down the menacing-looking uniform of his driver. "You actually look a little scary!"

"That's part of the plan," Alexander laughed. "It is a great looking uniform, isn't it!"

"You look like a fierce warrior, charging into battle."

"And it may be a real battle out there on the track," Alexander stated., with a hardened glint in his eye.

The Black Diamond Team had to wait until the second practice session. The horses eagerly pranced in anticipation of doing what they truly loved – running fast! A racing official came by and announced that all the second practice group would be unleashed in just a few minutes. The official stopped when he came to the Black Diamond chariot.

"Very interesting hitch you boys have come up with," the official stated, looking over the 'four up' hitch closely. "Never seen anything like this before. But as far as I can tell, it's a legal hitch. Very creative. Very innovative. But legal, as far as I understand the rulebook."

The racing official moved on down the line of contestants, who were scheduled for the second practice round. In a moment, the official walked back up the line of chariots and announced, "Almost time for your practice session! Mount up!"

Alexander mounted his chariot. Trooper, Rascal, Thunder, and Swifty all understood that command! Their ears pricked up. They sensed the excitement. Their muscles tensed. It was time to GO! In just a few seconds, Alexander would be flying around the race track!

Diotrephes stepped up beside his driver and looked up into Alexander's excited eyes. "Go out there and take a few easy laps, just to get the feel for the track. And then when you're ready, turn the boys loose!"

Suddenly, one of the head officials ran up to Alexander screaming and shouting and frantically waving his arms. "Stop! Hold it! Stay right where you are!" He grabbed the reins of the lead horse, Trooper, and the official yelled, "You're not going anywhere! Get off your chariot!"

Diotrephes glared at the head official. "What's the problem, sir?" he asked. "We've only got a limited time for practice and we need to be out on the track now."

The head official smugly strode up to Diotrephes. "You're not going anywhere. We have a rival team that has registered a protest against your team. They are protesting your use of this very strange way you have hitched your horses. It is not at all conventional or acceptable. The protesting team claims you will have an unfair advantage over all the other teams, with this unorthodox hitch of yours. Frankly, to me, it looks a little bizarre."

"May I ask who has filed this protest?" The Captain asked.

"Gladly. The protest has been filed by a man named Dominic and he has filed the protest on behalf of the Blue Team," the head official declared unemotionally.

"Our good ol' friend Dominic strikes again!" Caleb chided.

The head official continued. "This man, Dominic, complained to the officiating judges that he had seen your team practicing with this unauthorized hitch before your team even arrived here in Caesarea. I'm sorry but we cannot allow this unorthodox hitch to participate in our races."

"But we just had a different official tell us that the rulebook allowed our hitch," Diotrephes stated. "He told us we are legal according to his understanding of the rulebook."

"Well, I'm overruling what that official told you! I will not allow this contraption!" the head official huffed loudly.

"Can you show me in the rulebook that this hitch is illegal?" The Captain argued.

"Listen, I don't have to show you any rulebook!" the head official blew up. "I am the head official! What I allow, I allow! What I disallow, I disallow! Is that plain?"

"Then I will also file a protest, against your biased officiating," The Captain stated matter-of-factly.

The head official sighed and bowed his head in resignation. He then lowered his voice. "Listen, sir, I have been placed in a tight spot, caught between a rock and a hard place," he said in a much softer tone. "The rich benefactor who is sponsoring these races does not want controversy or arguments to spoil his races. This sponsor has invested a fortune in this racing meet. I asked him about this protest and he firmly told me, in no uncertain terms, to quell any ballyhoo or uproar during his races. He wants absolutely no bad press connected with his race meet. As I said, he has put up a fortune of his own money to sponsor these events and he wants everything to flow smooth as silk. So, please have a heart! Work with me, man. Help me out and just accept the protest with grace."

Diotrephes smiled and edged a little closer to the head official. "Why didn't you tell me in the first place that you were in a tight," he said quietly. "Of course, I'll agree to the protest. After all, the sponsor is paying for all this and providing the prize money, so of course I'll agree. I'm just grateful to the sponsor for pouring his money into this event. We all should be grateful."

"Thank you, so much," the head official said gratefully. "You've got another hitch, don't you?"

"Yep, we'll swap over and jump into this practice session," The Captain said.

"No, the second session is already on the track," the head official stated. "There is too little time left in this session. Take your time and get your new setup hitched like you like it. I'll make sure that there is room for you in one of the next practice sessions."

Then the head official squinted his eyes and surveyed Diotrephes a little closer. "Aren't you the team owner who won last year's big race?" he blurted out.

"Yeah, that's me. And this is us!" The Captain beamed, spreading his arms out over the rest of the team standing nearby. "We won that Black Diamond Trophy that Caesar provided as a grand prize last year."

"Well, you know what this year's grand prize is," the head official stated. "It's called The Golden Cup of Caesar. It's a magnificent gold cup from Caesar's own personal collection."

Diotrephes edged a little closer to the official. "Rumor has it that Tiberius Caesar will be here to personally present the Cup as the grand prize," he said quietly. "Any truth to that rumor?"

"Nope. Not gonna happen," the official said. "Tiberius has too many other problems in the Empire to deal with to take time out to come here to Judea. But it's a great rumor though, huh," he laughed. "That rumor alone will bring in a lot more spectators than ever before!"

The team busied themselves swapping the harnessing arrangement over to the four abreast hitch. Once again the horses were hitched side-by-side with Trooper taking his leadership position on the inside, Rascal next, Thunder next, and Swifty on the outside. Alexander realized 'the boys' had practiced so much in the "four up" hitch that they would have to readjust their running positions. But he also knew his stallions were pretty smart and they would readapt quickly to their new assignments.

The head official directed Alexander to line up with the third practice group. Then the official walked up and down the line of competitors and announced, "All of you in this third practice session will be going out on the track in a few minutes! So, drivers, mount up!"

Anxious from the first delay, Alexander nearly leaped onto his chariot, nervous to get going. The horses heard the command to 'mount up' and they fully understood it was time for them to go! The Black Diamond Team gathered around the chariot, yelling encouragement to their driver. The Captain again instructed Alexander, "Just remember what I told you earlier. Easy laps at first. Then turn 'em loose!"

Octavius ran up to the conversation, out of breath. "Listen, I've been watching the last practice session. The track condition is deteriorating. The earlier practice groups have chewed up the track pretty bad. The dirt is starting to dry out. Just thought you should know."

The Captain looked Alexander square in the eye. "This is good! We need to know how well we can do on a heavy track! Orders are still the same! Slow laps! Then go at my signal!"

As was the standard practice of Roman charioteers, Alexander wrapped the reins around his waist. He drove the team by holding the reins with his left hand. In a sheath fastened to his belt, he carried a short dagger to cut through the reins, if he was thrown off the chariot. But unlike other chariot drivers, Alexander carried no whip. "My 'boys' listen and obey me. They love to please. I don't need to whip them." That allowed his right hand to hold the reins if it was required.

"Third session!" the head official yelled. "Go!" and he spun his right hand over his head to signal all competitors to 'wind 'em up and turn -em loose!'

Alexander flicked the reins and 'his boys' took off. Out onto the dirt track, The Black Diamond chariot surged in a mighty rush. All the horses were so anxious to run that Alexander had to rein in his stallions somewhat to follow The Captains orders. "Easy boys!" Alexander called to his horses. "Take it easy! Trooper slow up! Everybody stay in line."

The four steeds obeyed and settled into a trot. Some of the other ten chariots in the third practice session immediately blasted out into full blown competition speeds. Dust flew everywhere. But Alexander stayed content to turn slow laps, staying out of the way on the outside, getting the feel of the dirt under his wheels, letting his horses get warmed up.

With the pack of charging chariots clattering around the race track, the noise was deafening. Pounding hoofs, rattling chariots, drivers yelling commands to their steeds, combined into a loud, chaotic blur of thundering sound. The earth shook! The air boiled into spinning clouds of churning dirt. Metal on metal clanged as competitors' wheels banged together at speed! The sharp crack of whips snapped through the rolling racket.

After four slow laps riding the perimeter of the track, Alexander glanced over at Diotrephes, standing in the north turn. The Captain then raised his hand and swirled his hand around and around in circles above his head. That was the 'GO' signal.

Alexander then unleashed pent up fury the likes of which no one at the Caesarean Hippodrome had seen all day! The Black Diamond horses launched into a blaze of speed, kicking up clods of dirt and clouds of dust. A slight breeze blew in from the west, from the ocean, which helped dissipate the dust. Alexander charged into the south turn and purposely slid his chariot through the turn.

'Right now this track is perfect for broad sliding through the turns,' Alexander thought to himself. *'I like this track. It's a lot like our practice track at headquarters.'*

The horses and chariot rocketed down the main straightaway. "Come on, Trooper! Let's go Swifty! Go, Rascal! Run, Thunder, big fella!" Alexander encouraged 'his boys'.

The horses and driver blended into one flowing unit. Around and around they surged, lap after lap. The Black Diamond driver was now oblivious to the chaotic noise of the track. He was totally absorbed in the job at hand. Alexander practiced running beside other chariots. Then he practiced negotiating the turns in the midst of other chariots filling the track ahead. He experimented at drifting out of the turns, making a wide arc, to help maintain his speed. He tested his skill at the 'slide job', sliding up under a competitor in a turn and then drifting out in front to take the position.

After several laps, Alexander slowed and took some breather laps around the outside perimeter of the track. "Take a breather, boys!" Alexander called to his steeds. "Easy, big fellas. We'll trot a little bit for now!"

The horses snorted and flicked their heads as they trotted. They protested. They wanted to go!

"Patience, boys!" the charioteer called to his horses. "You're doing just fine!"

In a few more laps, Alexander yelled, "Heeyaw!" And the pent up fury erupted once again.

For the next several minutes, Alexander and his stallions learned a lot of valuable lessons about each other, about the track, and about running in a track filled with churning chariots and thundering horses.

At the close of the practice session, Alexander pulled into the runoff area and dismounted his chariot. He immediately ran to his horses and began to love on them. "Good job, Trooper! Rascal, you're such a good boy! Thunder, you're my man! Swifty, you're great!" The steeds breathed hard after galloping for about ten minutes but their eyes said it all – they loved every minute of their performance on the track! And they wanted more!

"You boys gave all you could for me! I love you guys!" Alexander affectionately repeated to them, rubbing each one on the nose and patting their necks.

Jake run up to Alexander. "Wow, man! You looked really good out there!"

"We both know where my strength comes from; the Lord" the driver smiled. "But that, my friend, was really fun! A real blast!"

Just then, the fourth practice session competitors rolled out onto the track. An ominous blue chariot slithered past with Scorpio, dressed in dazzling, satiny blue, aboard. The Blue Team driver glared at Alexander and all the Black Diamond Team members as he rolled past. Then he snapped his whip in their direction over their heads. "Yours' is comin'," he snarled as he rumbled by and rolled out onto the practice track.

20

THE BATTLE FOR THE
GOLDEN CUP OF CAESAR

Two days of fantastic racing! Lots of spine-chilling action! Thrills and spills! The betting customers loved it! Twelve races the first day produced twelve elated winners! One of those winners was Alexander and the Black Diamond Racing Team in Race 3. Another race winner was Scorpio and his formidable Blue Team in a hotly contested and controversial Race 8.

The second day of racing dawned bright and clear. Not a cloud in the sky. As the bright yellow sun rose higher in the morning sky, a cool, steady breeze began to waft in from the Mediterranean Sea. The Caesarean Hippodrome looked resplendent in the brilliant yellow sunshine. Spectators began arriving early. Exhilaration filled the air. This was the biggest day of the year on the local racing calendar and the excited fans flooded into the venue to watch the spectacle. The noisy crowd rapidly filled the 5,000 seat stone grandstand to overflowing. Soon it became standing room only in the packed stadium.

Behind the grandstands, there were numerous amenities for the race fans. All sorts of festival foods, their wonderful fragrant aromas drifting over the stadium, tantalizing everyone in the arena. There were local wineries providing much sought after libations. Souvenir booths carried paraphernalia of your favorite driver or team. Groups of people gathered to talk racing or just to chit-chat. And, of course, there were the ever present gambling facilities. A spectator could buy a beverage, purchase a bite to eat, buy a souvenir, and place a wager all in one trip behind the grandstands. A day at the races was a highly anticipated delightful experience and typically turned out to be an exhilarating, memorable affair.

The honored sponsor of this magnificent two-day event arrived and took his seat in the special, reserved celebrity box, situated in the center of the main straightaway grandstands. This special celebrity grandstand had a colorful red cover made of the finest linen, with golden tassels adorning the edges of the cover all the way around. The honored sponsor of the racing events was a local government official, named Antoninus Pius. When he arrived in his place of honor, the throngs of people cheered wildly for their wealthy, benevolent patron. He alone was responsible for this wonderful time of merriment and thrills!

Antoninus Pius could easily be identified in the midst of the crowd by his distinctive regal toga that he wore. His beautiful soft, cream-colored robe had a strikingly bold purple boarder. He wore his robe in a confident, dignified manner, with the long fold thrown over his left shoulder. Antoninus Pius waved to the crowd, laughing and smiling to all the race fans. Truly his enthusiasm and pride in sponsoring this scintillating event, radiated from his joyful expression.

On this second day of races, twelve more contests were to be run, with the additional special feature race at the end of the daily racing card, the race for The Golden Cup of Caesar. Because of the additional special race, today the racing program had a different purpose. These races were not just for the betting customers. Not just for the delirious race fans. Not just for personal riches and glory of the participants. These races were known as 'heat races' and the outcome of these races determined which teams participated in the final race for The Golden Cup of Caesar.

There had been several crashes during the first day of competition. Numerous chariots had been destroyed in these crashes but thankfully none of the drivers had been seriously injured. One of those crashes left a dubious cloud over that particular wreck, when Scorpio cut sharply over and slammed wheels with the chariot of the White Team. The open wheel of the White Team chariot rode up over Scorpios' wheel, lifting it up into the air and rolling the White Team chariot over. Scorpio cruised on to win that race.

Due to the many crashes from the first day, the field of competitors had been thinned out. Only forty of the original fifty-five entrants were left to compete on the second day. Now the field had to be narrowed down even more to twelve contestants for the final, feature race for The Golden Cup of Caesar. To accomplish this elimination of teams, the series of 'heat races' was set up by the race organizers to achieve the final twelve.

"Okay, Caleb, explain to me one more time how this elimination process is supposed to work," Jake asked.

"Okay. Let me enlighten you, one more time," Caleb laughed. He started drawing in the dirt of the paddock with a stick. "Four races will be contested with all forty teams competing in these races. Each race will line up and start ten chariots. Only the winner from each of those four races advances to the feature race.

"So, after the first four races, there are now thirty-six teams remaining, vying for a position in the big race. These remaining thirty-six teams will compete in four more races, with nine chariots in each race. Only the winner from each of these four races will advance to the feature race.

"Now, there are thirty-two teams left. These remaining thirty-two contesting teams compete in the last four races on the normal racing program., with eight chariots in each race. Only the winner of each of these four races advances to the feature race. Clear as mud?"

"Clear as mud!"

The second day of racing was filled with electrifying speed and excitement. The 'heat races' provided all the thrills that they were advertised to deliver! Close wheel-to-wheel battles. Daring moves and passes for positions. Slipping and sliding in the turns to gain an advantage. With prize money on the line, in addition to advancing to the feature event, some drivers were using cut-throat tactics to win. A few chariots crashed and were destroyed in the on-track chaos. The wrecks thinned out the field of competitors even more.

Through the 'heat race' regiment, the final field of twelve competitors was set for the glorious feature race. Alexander survived and won his 'heat race' in strong fashion. Scorpio also won his 'heat race' in an equally stunning manner.

The feature race field was now set. The final race set at seven laps. Twelve combatants. Seven laps of all-out combat to declare the ultimate victory.

After the last 'heat race', all twelve teams were allotted one half hour for final preparations for the big race – the race for The Golden Cup of Caesar. Jake and Caleb did a final check of all the leather straps on the harnesses, bridles, and reins. Nathan and his helpers pampered the horses, watering them, brushing and currying them, making them as magnificent looking as possible. Reuben and Levi had already changed over to the larger diameter set of wheels, since the race track had become extremely chewed up and 'heavy'. Ezra did a once-over check of the chariot chassis to be sure there were no fractures or stress cracks in the frame. Carpus and Zenas washed down the black, Black Diamond chariot, scrubbing it clean of track dust and dirt. The chariot now sparkled!

Jake and Caleb found Diotrephes and Alexander lingering off to the side, watching the preparations.

"Captain, I think we are ready to race," Jake stated to both of them. "Alex, you've got the best chariot in the contest. And you've got the best team of horses. The competition still has not figured out our different wheel size arrangement. Use that advantage to your advantage."

"I definitely have more confidence in the turns," Alexander said quietly. "Keep praying for God's wisdom today."

Linus and Octavius ran up and joined the group. "We have just come from trackside and the grounds crew has just completed watering down the track. It was fascinating to watch. There must have been fifty men and boys out on the track with buckets of water, dousing the track surface to help control the dust. They've got to keep the paying customers happy and not all covered in grit!"

"That is good information to know," Alexander stated. "It's a lot easier to race if I can see where I'm going!"

Suddenly, Jonathan ran into the group, out of breath. "Listen everybody! I had to go to the officials paddock just now to ask them a question and as I passed Stable 44, I overheard Dominic telling Scorpio to use his whip on his opponents. He especially told him to use his whip on Alexander."

The whole group of men stood stone-faced. "That's exactly what I would have expected from Scorpio," Diotrephes stated grimly. "Now we know for sure what he will do." Turning to Alexander, he said calmly, "You'll have to anticipate Scorpio's attacks. Watch out for his whip. He nearly kills his horses with his whip. He won't hesitate to use it on you. Try to stay away from his whip hand."

"Sir, no whip of Scorpio's is going to stop me," Alexander stated, his mouth set firm.

Word from the racing officials came to the twelve teams starting in the special feature race to line up for a celebratory parade lap around the track to salute all the cheering race fans in the stands.

Alexander mounted up. The Black Diamond driver looked magnificent and powerful in his totally black driving uniform. He grinned a very wide grin, as he stood like a conqueror on his platform, poised for battle. He wedged his feet into the two special stirrups Caleb had designed and mounted to the floor of the chariot. These stirrups would keep Alexander from flying out of the chariot during the bumps and gyrations throughout the race.

"This is it!" Diotrephes exclaimed to his driver. "Remember, seven laps. Watch the lap counter at each end of the spina. Watch the streamers on the meta columns at each end of the spina, to keep track of the wind coming off the sea. God be with you! Have a safe race!"

The rest of The Black Diamond Team yelled encouragement to Alexander, as their driver began to roll out onto the track. The rest of the field began to move out, as well.

Scorpio rumbled past to take his number one starting position at the head of the parade line. He yelled at Alexander as he rolled by, "I'm going to grab this race by the throat! I'll grab you by the throat if you try to take it from me!"

Scorpio rolled on by to the head of the parade line. "The Demon Driver" yelled a parting shot back to the whole Black Diamond team, "Don't get between me and the finish line! I will get my revenge!"

The rest of the field of competitors formed a long, single-file parade line following Scorpio.

Up ahead of the line of competitors, rode a Roman military unit of mounted soldiers on horseback. Next came men on horses displaying acrobatic skills, pleasing the crowd enormously. Behind them marched a myriad of brightly clad men carrying flamboyant banners and waving colorful flags.

The crowd cheered enthusiastically as the parade circled the track. And as the prancing four-abreast horses pulling their dazzling chariots and drivers into view, the throng shouted and applauded wildly for their favorite teams. The dazzling colors of all the chariot teams lined up, blended into a beautiful array of splendor. The bright red, gold, yellow, and orange. The stunning blue, green, and purple. The brilliant white. The distinguished black. All the teams paraded in this grandiose moment before the heated battle began. There was lots of money riding on this race. And the race fans let it be known who their favorite teams were that their money was riding on. And who the rivals were. The crowd began to chant the names of their favorite drivers – and sling insults at the 'evil' opponents! The noise from the cheering throng in the stadium became deafening!

As Alexander slowly paraded down the front straightaway during the celebratory procession, he glanced over at the large crowd of over 5,000. It was a sea of people. Everyone in the grandstands was standing, cheering, and waving their hands frantically, yelling to the drivers, celebrating the anticipated pitched battle on the track. Alexander caught sight of Antoninus Pius, the prestigious sponsor of this spectacular race. He stood in his place of honor, in a dignified pose, waving to the drivers with a large red cloth in his hand. That red cloth would be the flag he would use to start the race. The gorgeous, sparkling Golden Cup of Caesar rested on a low podium right in front of Antoninus Pius.

The celebratory parade lap concluded after one circuit of the track, at the starting gates located at the north end of the track. Jake and Caleb had been assigned by The Captain to help load the Black Diamond chariot into Number 9 starting box. All the teams had drawn lots to determine their starting positions. Diotrephes had drawn Number 9, a starting box far to the left, facing the track. Alexander knew, because of his far left starting position, that he would have to drive hard to his right at the start to get lined up for the first straightaway, The seaside West Straight. Alexander gently tugged on the reins to get his horses to back up into the starting box. The driver and horses had grown accustomed to the starting procedure, after participating in the earlier races. But now the pressure was really on. This race was no cheap money dash! This was the big race! For the largest payday of the year and the most prestigious prize of the year - The Golden Cup of Caesar! This race carried the tremendous weight of the Emperor's approval and authentication for the winning team.

Scorpio and the Blue Team had drawn starting gate Number 1, all the way to the right. This gate was the best starting position, since Scorpio had a straight shot out of the box onto the first straightaway. The Red Team had two entries and had drawn Gate 2 and Gate 5. The White Team had repaired their crashed chariot and had drawn Gate 3. The Green Team had two entries and had drawn Gate 4 and Gate 6. The Gold team had drawn Gate 7. The Purple Team had drawn Gate 11. The Orange Team had drawn Gate 12. The Yellow Team had two entries and had drawn Gate 8 and Gate 10. That positioned the Black Diamond Team, in Gate 9, squarely between the two Yellow Team chariots.

Alexander realized the possible tight bottleneck he would be in at the start. He was flanked by the two Yellow Team chariots, one on either side of him. At the start, they might try to put the squeeze on him out of the gate. His strategy was to watch the starting flag closely and try to anticipate the opening of his starting gate.

"Go get 'em, Alex!" Jake yelled to his driver above the din of the crowd noise. "Remember! Seven laps! Watch the lap counter on the spina! You're the best! And you've got the Lord ridin' with ya, too!"

"Bring back the Cup!" Caleb yelled. "Watch out for Scorpio!"

Alexander bent down and softly said to Jake, "You see the pinch I'm in, between these two Yellow Team mates. You can see the starting flag better than me from where you'll be near the back of the starting box. Give me a signal when it's about to drop."

Jake stared at his driver. "How 'bout this?" he stated and then he clapped his hands together loudly.

Alexander smiled, nodded his head, and gave Jake the thumbs up. Then he turned his focus toward the starting gate right in front of him.

Jake and Caleb backed away from the chariot toward the back of the starting box, so they would be out of the way.

Jake could see the celebrity box with Antoninus Pius standing up, far down the track at the midway point on the main straightaway. Jake watched as Antoninus Pius raised the red cloth to start the race. In the prearranged signal, Jake clapped his hands together, letting Alexander know the starting flag was up in the air. Alexander tensed, anticipating the start.

A second later, Antoninus Pius dropped the red cloth and the starting gates all flew open! Twelve tightly coiled chariots sprung out of their starting boxes in one blinding blur!

That fraction of a second anticipation by Alexander proved to be the fractions of inches he needed to launch onto the track slightly ahead of the two Yellow Team chariots. The Yellow Team did try the squeeze play on him but Alexander was just far enough ahead for them that their play did not slow him down.

The start was wild! Chariots everywhere! Drivers slicing and swerving in and out among their competitors, trying for a good position on the eighty foot wide straightaway. 950 feet of race track stretched out before them. All the drivers knew the pack had to funnel down into the tight left turn ahead of them. Scorpio and The Red Team drag raced down the long West Straightaway at breakneck speed, vying for the lead. Directly behind them the White and Gold Teams fought it out for third and fourth. Alexander had already stormed past several competitors and settled into fifth position as the swirling tornado of men and horses charged toward the first turn.

The pack careened into the tight left-hander, full blast. Scorpio dove hard into the first turn under the Red Team chariot. He thundered out of the turn, slinging dirt and easing ahead by a horse length. The Red Team driver fought back on the outside coming out of the turn, as the field of chariots fanned out all across the main straightaway, right in front of the packed grandstands. The fans cheered wildly, yelling encouragement to their favorite drivers, as the pack flashed by.

Alexander slipped out into the middle of the main straight to avoid a wildly fishtailing Gold Team chariot and he charged past into fourth place.

Lap 2.

Up ahead Scorpio still fought hard with the Red Team driver, side-by-side. As the leaders completed the first lap, the entire pack charged down the long 950 foot straightaway is one mass rush. The next turn loomed ahead. Scorpio cut down close to the edge of the spina barrier in the next turn and held the inside advantage over the Red Team. This time Scorpio had so much exit momentum out of the turn that he quickly surged ahead of the Red Team. Scorpio and the Blue Team now firmly held command of the lead!

Alexander trailed the third place White Team and the Black Diamond driver pressed the accelerator. "Let's go!" he yelled to his horses. He flicked the reins so they danced on the backs of his steeds. And the boys got the message. The Black Diamond chariot leaped forward. Alexander hung on. As he and his team thundered down the back straightaway, his chariot came alongside the White Team. Alexander could feel the breeze blowing in from the ocean and a wind gust suddenly caught him and pushed him over toward the White Team. To avoid banging into his opponent, Alexander tugged on the reins, turning his stallions away from the other chariot. When he swerved, he lost momentum and dropped back slightly as the pack of competitors pounded into the south turn.

Swinging out of the turn and accelerating down the main straightaway again, the churning field of competitors crisscrossed each other's paths, attempting to break the momentum of the drivers behind them. There were some very near misses, as one or two chariots nearly clipped the team of horses of their opponents. The cheering fans loved it! And they wildly screamed for more action!

Alexander now was trapped behind the White Team driver, who had slid up directly in front of him. He slowed slightly, so his team of horses didn't run up the back of the White Team driver. One of the Yellow Team drivers took advantage of Alexander's loss of momentum and slipped in beside the Black Diamond driver on the inside. Now Alex really was boxed in.

Lap 3.

As the thundering herd crossed the line to complete lap 2, Scorpio still held the top spot for the Blue Team. The Red Team driver still dogged Scorpio, nipping at his heels. As the leaders neared the north turn again, the Red Team driver swung wide to his right, hoping to dive under Scorpio in the approaching left turn. Scorpio caught a glimpse of the Red Team maneuver and he cut to his right to block the move. As the pair of leaders entered the north turn, Scorpio suddenly cut hard back to his left and glided into the left turn, leaving the Red Team driver caught out on the far outside.

The White Team took advantage of the mistake by the Red Team and attacked the inside, taking over second place. Alexander and the Yellow Team driver trailed close behind and they both followed the White Team into the hole vacated by the Red Team.

Up ahead, Alexander could see Scorpio whipping his team of horses mercilessly. Scorpio drove like a wild man, possessed with fighting off all challengers. Scorpio kept glancing back over his shoulder watching his charging competition. For a moment, Alexander locked eyes with the madman and realized Scorpio purposely had fixed his attention on the Black Diamond driver.

Down the long 950 foot West Straightaway next to the sea shore, plunged the swirling, thundering torrent of chariots. Alexander could hear drivers behind him yelling and screaming at each other and at their teams of horses. The clattering of the chariots and the pounding of the hoofs and the yelling of the drivers thundered like the deafening roar of a giant waterfall smashing on the rocks below. The contestants again had fanned out all across the wide straight. But up ahead, the narrow funnel of the south turn beckoned them all to crush back together into a tight group to negotiate the hairpin.

Scorpio charged into the south turn at blinding speed with the lead. But he "over cooked it" and came in too hot into the tight turn. His outward momentum caused him to drift out from the spina in an overly wide arc. As he tried to pull his chariot back toward the center divider, he scrubbed off speed and the White Team driver shot into the gaping hole along the inside. The White Team chariot grabbed the lead, with Scorpio 'hung out to dry' on the outside. Alexander and the Yellow Team driver sucked right in behind the new leader and passed Scorpio, as well.

The entire pack of chariots charged valiantly down the long grandstand straight. Again they spread out attempting wild passes and desperate moves on each other. Drivers attacked for position all through the field. Whips cracking. Fans screaming. The roar of battling chariots splitting the air.

Down the straight, Scorpio attempted a bold move. From his far outside fourth position, he dived in a slicing, suicidal cut, right across the track toward the inside. He was attempting to slam into Alexander, broadside, in an effort to take out the Black Diamond driver. But Scorpio timed his diving move poorly and he completely missed the collision. Instead, Scorpio nearly slammed into the side of the spina. Just in time he collected his gyrating chariot and fell in behind Alexander.

Lap 4.

The field completed lap 3 and funneled into the north turn again. The White Team led the charge with Alexander and the Yellow Team driver nipping at the leader's heels. Alexander, on the outside, saw his chance to take second place. He setup the Yellow Team driver for the 'over and under' move. Alexander swung out wide just before the turn, knowing that the Yellow Team driver had to enter the turn in a tight arc. As the two drivers barreled into the turn, Alexander cut down toward the inside and behind his opponent. The Yellow Team driver had to take a wider arc out of the turn and Alexander slid up under his rival, barely grazing the spina barrier. Alexander glided into second place.

Now Alexander set sail for the lead. "Come on, Trooper, you big boy! Go, Rascal! Go, Thunder! Gittup, Swifty!" Alexander hollered to his team. "Show 'em what ya got!"

Alexander trailed the White Team down the long backstretch by the sea. He was content to ride along for the moment to study his opponent up ahead. In the next turn, he got the information he needed.

Alexander noticed that the White Team driver was not taking the turns close to the spina. Instead, he tended to stay several yards away from the center barrier as he negotiated the sharp curve. As the two competitors thundered down the long main straightaway, to complete lap 4, Alexander sized up his opponent.

Lap 5.

The White Team driver charged into the north turn. Alexander charged in behind him, but cut down deeper, riding Jake's wheels, toward the central barrier. As the pair drifted out of the turn onto the backstretch, the Black Diamond driver slid up in front of the White Team, in the classic 'slid job', preventing his opponent from gaining any acceleration out of the turn. Now, Alexander grabbed the lead!

"Good boys!" Alexander yelled to his team. "Go! Go!"

Behind him, the Black Diamond driver could hear Scorpio screaming viciously at his competitors. He could hear the crack of Scorpio's whip, even above the rumble of the careening chariots. Then there came the horrible, audible clang of banging wheels and then the sickening sound of a chariot slamming into the side of the spina.

Alexander continued to race into the next curve – the south turn. He could hear the clattering charge of the rest of the pack chasing him as he slid through the turn and drifted out onto the long front stretch once more. The crowd in the grandstands was standing and yelling and pointing toward the backstretch.

Alexander feared what might have happened behind him, but the race plunged on.

The Black Diamond chariot crossed the line in first place to lead lap 5. Two laps to go!

Lap 6.

Alexander glanced over his shoulder. Scorpio was right there! His horses were breathing down Alexander's neck!

The dueling pair charged into the north turn once again, dirt flying from their wheels. Scorpio slid up alongside on the outside. Side-by-side they thundered through the turn. Scorpio lurched toward Alexander from the outside, trying to pinch him into the stone spina. Alexander refused to give ground and they banged wheels. Together they pounded out of the corner onto the backstretch. Up ahead, Alexander saw the reason for the crash he had heard on the previous lap. The White Team's mangled and twisted chariot was being dragged off to the side. It had made heavy contact with the side of the spina. The driver and horses all appeared to be okay, standing along the outside wall. Alexander knew the only person who could have caused the wreck was the driver closest to the crash – Scorpio. And now the Black Diamond driver was locked in a life-and-death battle with that same Scorpio, his menacing rival.

The wreck site along the inside spina barrier had been cleared of all wreckage. So, the track was wide open as Alexander and Scorpio charged headlong down the stretch and into the south turn. With Scorpio on the outside, pressing inward toward Alexander, the curve seemed to compress into the size of a needle's eye. Alexander knew Scorpio would not give him space to get through the turn, so he cut hard to the left and, miraculously, the chariot turned on a pinpoint around the end of the spina. *Jake's wheels!'* he thought to himself. His exit speed out of the corner outmatched Scorpio's. Drifting out of the turn onto the main stretch, Alexander had a length lead on Scorpio! The delirious grandstand crowd cheered in a frenzied roar.

The entire field of racers was still tightly packed. Dust began to boil up behind the racers in a cloud as the track began to dry out. They were all chasing Alexander and Scorpio. The pack charged hard down the long main straight once more, as to screaming grandstand mob went bonkers.

Alexander crossed the line to lead lap 6! One lap to go!

Lap 7. The charge to the finish line!

Again Scorpio clawed his way back toward the front. He made a desperate move to the outside as the Black Diamond chariot and the Blue chariot raced head to head. Up ahead the north turn loomed like the gaping mouth of a devouring beast. It seemed impossible for both

Alexander and Scorpio to enter that turn and come out on the other side alive!

Both drivers plunged aggressively for the corner at spectacular speed. They both slid into the corner, dirt and dust slinging from their wheels. Alexander's special wheels stuck like glue and he turned into the corner with authority. Scorpio slipped out just a little, giving the Black Diamond driver the edge.

Down the long, seaside backstretch, Scorpio managed to again pull up alongside, whipping his horses mercilessly. He then turned loose his final weapon. He lashed at Alexander's face with his whip! He missed. Lashed again! Hit Alexander's arm! Lashed again! The whip bounced off Alexander's helmet! Alexander glanced over at Scorpio. Scorpio's face was a fiery red, twisted, hideous, ferocious mass. Scorpio savagely slung the whip again. Missed again. His gyrations caused his chariot to swerve and slam wheels with Alexander. Down the long backstretch, Scorpio repeatedly, purposely swerved and banged wheels with the Black Diamond chariot until the final turn loomed just ahead.

It was obvious that Scorpio intended to wreck Alexander. He was so intent on wrecking Alexander that as the pair barreled into the final turn, Scorpio didn't realize his chariot had dropped back a slight fraction. When he attempted to bang wheels with Alexander in the middle of the turn, his wheel ran up over the Black Diamond's wheel and launched Scorpio and his chariot high into the air. His chariot rolled over in mid-flight and crashed hard. The chariot harness attachment twisted and snapped, releasing the horses. Scorpio's body flipped through the air. He landed hard in a distorted heap in the dirt, as the other drivers behind him frantically tried to avoid the prone figure laying on the track.

Alexander slid on through the last corner and drifted out onto the main straightaway. Behind him, Scorpio's chariot cartwheeled and tumbled into a tangled mess. His horses ran free. The pack still close behind chased Alexander, with the Yellow Team driver in hot pursuit. "Gimme all ya got," Alexander cried to his team of valiant stallions, flicking the reins.

The final gallop to the finish line seemed to stretch out forever.

Alexander could see the finish line at the celebrity box seats in the grandstands, but it looked like it was ten miles away. His team of horses dug hard with enormous power in the final charge for the victory.

To the roar of the crowd, Alexander crossed the finish line in first place – the victor! The winner of The Golden Cup of Caesar special race!

"Praise, God!" Alexander shouted as he crossed the finish line, his right hand held high in both praise and triumph.

As the Black Diamond driver allowed his mighty steeds to slow down, he praised them. "Good job, boys!" he sang to them. "Trooper, Rascal, Thunder, Swifty, great work! You're my boys! Take it easy, now! You have proven you're the best! The best!"

As Alexander slowed, the other drivers behind him slowed and came along side and offered their congratulations. The Yellow Team had finished in second place. The Gold Team made a late charge through the chaotic last turn mess, passing two chariots to finish in third place. As the other drivers turned off the track to the paddock area, Alexander took a victory lap, waving to all the cheering fans along the outside of the track. His team of stallions sensed that they had beaten all the other horses and, for them, it was a proud moment of satisfaction. This victory lap was quite exhilarating!

As the cool down lap progressed toward the scene of the big crash in the final turn, Alexander could see track attendants helping Scorpio to his feet. The Blue Team driver appeared to be alright, just a little shaken up. He was limping a little.

Alexander slowly rolled passed Scorpio. He glanced over at his arch rival, trying to express a concern for the man. In return, Scorpio spit in Alexander's direction and yelled something unintelligible. He turned away in angry, frustrated defeat.

The Black Diamond driver turned one final time onto the main stretch at reduced speed, still waving to the cheering, delirious crowd. Trooper, Rascal, Thunder, and Swifty sensed the adoration from the giant throng, too, and began prancing, even though they were exhausted and winded. Winning is always fun – even for horses!

Up ahead, the track suddenly had become clogged with humanity as the triumphant Black Diamond driver approached the victory area.

21

CELEBRATION!

The Black Diamond chariot slowly rolled up in front of the honored celebrity box seats and stopped. Jake and Caleb met the team on the track and held the horses as Alexander dismounted. The rest of the team members ran up and collected around their horses and chariot. Their driver stepped over toward the ecstatic crowd and faced the celebrity stand. He waved to them. Then Alexander removed his shiney black leather helmet, in respect for the honored sponsor of the race, Antoninus Pius. Antoninus Pius already was standing to congratulate the winner. He had a huge smile on his face and he held up his hands to silence the crowd.

"All hail to the winner, Alexander of the Black Diamond Team!" Antoninus Pius declared to the crowd. A mighty cheer erupted throughout the packed stadium. Chants of "Alex! Alex! Alex!' rippled through the crowd. As the noise subsided, Antoninus Pius declared, "All hail to the Black Diamond Team, winner of The Golden Cup of Caesar!" More cheers thundered from the thousands of voices in attendance. "And credit also must be given to the valiant stallions who won the race! The team of horses led by the lead horse, Trooper!" Antoninus Pius announced. Again, shouts of praise shot through the crowd, in admiration for the magnificent courage of the intrepid stallions.

Antoninus Pius again raised his arms seeking to quiet the massive throng. "Resting in front of me on this podium is the prestigious Golden Cup of Caesar. This Cup has been donated by our esteemed excellency, Emperor Tiberius Caesar. It is a gift from his own treasures presented to us here in Judea, a gift to show his benevolence and goodwill to all of his subjects in our province. We must remember to always pledge our gratitude to our great Emperor."

Antoninus Pius stepped over to the podium. Then he spoke loudly so all could hear.

"And now, Alexander, please step forward to accept The Golden Cup of Caesar! You are the victor! You have proven to be the best of the best!"

There was a narrow opening in the five and a half foot high retaining wall which separated the racing surface from the crowded grandstand. Aligned with this opening was an ascending set of steps which rose up to the celebrity viewing box, where Antoninus Pius stood waiting. Upon seeing the important celebrity waiting for him, Alexander began to nervously climb the steps. It was the first time all day he had been nervous. This element was not his realm. He was a slave. Not a superstar. But this place was where the Lord had miraculously positioned him, for this moment. He shook off the uneasiness and confidently stopped right in front of Antoninus Pius. Then he bowed politely.

"You have executed a superb performance today, young man. A marvelous accomplishment," the honored patron stated. "I have witnessed many races this past two days but never have I seen such a combat on the track! There were battles all over this race track between all the competitors. But, young man, your excellent performance today stands out from all the rest! I will long remember your courage and bravery you displayed in the heat of battle! Your stunning victory is the crowning jewel to this whole two day extravaganza!'

Then stepping toward Alexander, the benevolent event sponsor stated, "Please bow the knee."

Alexander knelt down on one knee and bowed his head. Antoninus Pius took a wreath made of wild olive leaves and branches and placed it on Alexander's head as a victor's crown. "To the victor!" Antoninus Pius shouted and raised both hands to confirm his crowning of the winner.

"Now, please rise," the honored sponsor stated to the winner. Then Antoninus Pius turned to the podium and lifted up The Golden Cup of Caesar for all the crowd to see. "I now present this trophy of victory to Alexander and the Black Diamond Racing Team as the winner of this year's contest. To the victors, I present The Golden Cup of Caesar."

The crowd burst into delirious cheers as Antoninus Pius handed the glittering gold trophy to Alexander. The winning driver held the sparkling gold cup up high above his head and turned toward the crowd for all to view. The cheers continued unabated, rolling through the stadium throng for several minutes.

As Jake watched Alexander, the huge grin on his driver's face proved that all the struggle to get to this moment was worth all the effort. To the victor *did* come the glory of triumph! As the crowd quieted, Alexander spoke to the faithful race fans who surrounded him.

"I want to praise my God today!" Alexander shouted. "God has protected me today! God gave all of us a safe race! We drivers are all still alive and uninjured! Even those involved in crashes have walked away to race another day! Also, God protected all the horses today, which I am very thankful for! This has been a blessed day! A miraculous day! A day to long remember! And I will always thank my God and praise my God for allowing me to win today! Praise the name of the Lord!"

Once again the crowd erupted into a frenzy of excited praise. The cheering continued for several minutes. Then Antoninus Pius raised his hands one last time to get the attention of the people.

"I am so pleased with the outcome of this two day event, that I hereby announce, that I am going to sponsor this event again at this time next year." Again the crowd burst into applause and cheers. "I am already making plans to do this all over again next year. So, I wish all of you a safe trip home! We will see you all next year!"

After the trophy presentation, Alexander descended the grandstand steps to the track level. With a big smile on his face, he presented The Golden Cup of Caesar to Diotrephes and the other team owners. The crowd continued to applaud.

"Climb up there," The Captain said pointing to the chariot. "You are the victor. Ride like the conquering warrior that you are!"

Alexander mounted up. Diotrephes rested the gold trophy next to his driver on the chariot floor, steadying it with his hand. Nathan and his horse handlers took charge of the horses and began the victory promenade to the paddock area. The horses were breathing heavily from running for about fifteen minutes in completing the seven lap race. They were extremely lathered up. As Jake released the bridle he had been holding at the finish line, he knew the beautiful stallions would very soon be well taken care of. Nathan would love on them and praise them. The four horses would feel the admiration that was undeniably due to them.

The Black Diamond Team walked together slowly down the track toward the paddock area on the north end of the stadium. Team members continued waving to the ecstatic throng. And the crowd waved and yelled congratulations back to them.

As the team entered Stable 51, they found an honored place for the gold cup on a work bench. Then they all stepped back and stood, admiring the breathtaking prize they had just won.

At this point, Nathan and his crew led the horses away for a very welcomed cool-down walk in the paddock.

Alexander sat down and breathed a heavy sigh of relief. He looked over at the winner's Cup. Then he turned his attention to the Black Diamond men. "That was some race. guys!" he stated, breathing another sigh as he laid his black leather helmet on the bench next to the golden trophy. He picked up a white cloth from the workbench and wiped the dirt and sweat from his face. "You guys are the best. We couldn't have won today, if you fellows hadn't given me the best equipment on the planet. This was a team effort."

"Well, team effort or not, you're the one who put your life on the line and made it all happen," The Captain said. "All race long you had to face Scorpio's killer instinct, his whip, and his attempts to annihilate you."

"We need to pray for that man," Alexander said. "Him and Dominic, both."

"Agreed," Diotrephes stated softly.

"But you know what? I could not have won today without 'my boys'!" Alexander stated. "They were like four powerhouses, digging hard all race long. They proved they all have the fighting heart – the heart of champions."

"I'm sure Nathan will give the horses an extra special treat tonight!" The Captain laughed. "They deserve it! Those big fellas are a part of all of us. 'The boys', as Alexander calls them, are very special."

Everybody agreed and began to applaud.

Nathan couldn't have timed his entrance into the 51 Stable any better, for at that moment he led the four victorious steeds in the stable doors.

"Here come the conquering champions!" someone yelled, as the team saw the horses enter.

Everyone on the Black Diamond Team began to applause and cheer. The four stallions pricked up their ears, as they all came to attention and felt the human praise being lavished upon them. It was a proud moment for them. Alexander stood up and applauded and cheered along with the rest of the crew. "What a team! What a team!" he shouted. "Thank you, boys!"

Nathan then led the four horses into their stalls and his horse trainers got to work rubbing down the horses and caring for them. And, as was predicted, Nathan did have a special treat waiting for each of "the boys".

About that time, Hannah hurried in the stable doors. She found Jake and ran over to him.

"Jake, that was the most thrilling thing I have ever seen!" she exclaimed. "I found a seat in the grandstand at the south end of the track. What an unbelievable experience! From my seat I could see the chariots as they raced through the south turn. Then I could see them racing all the way down that long stretch in front of the main grandstand. Wow! I still can't believe I saw what I saw today!"

"You had a really great view of the race, honey," Jake laughed. "And lots of excitement! I'm really glad you were able to find a seat to see the race. There wasn't much room left in those crowded stands."

"It was great fun!" Hannah bubbled. "But that last lap of the race!

Wow! And then on that last turn of the race! Oh, my! When Scorpio's chariot flipped up into the air, I was petrified! He flew one way. His chariot flipped and cartwheeled another way, right toward me in the grandstands! His horses broke free and started running along with the rest of the chariots. Thankfully his chariot tumbled only a few times and then stopped. And I can report, Scorpio is alright."

"Well, I'm sorry I couldn't sit with you today," he stated. "But I was kinda busy!"

"Oh, that's okay," Hannah said wistfully. "I was able to sit with The Captain's wife. We had great fun. And we talked about the Lord Jesus, too. I think Diotrephes must have been talking to her about Jesus after he surrendered his life to Christ. She and I had a good talk. And I think both he and she have patched things up. All in all, I think I had a very encouraging and thrilling day!"

"It sounds like the Lord Jesus has been everywhere today."

As the Black Diamond Team basked in the glow of victory, Diotrephes summoned the whole team to gather around.

"Listen up everybody," The Captain announced. "I have a big, very important announcement to make to everybody on our team. As you all know, we acquired our new driver, Alexander, at the beginning of this racing season. We paid the price on the slave market to purchase Alexander, because we had come to learn that he was an excellent horseman and horse groomer. Alexander is a slave. We all know that fact. And it is for that reason I have gathered you all around for this proclamation."

Then turning to Alexander, who was standing in the middle of the group, Diotrephes said to him, "Alexander, you are a faithful man. You have shown yourself to be a selfless servant. I have the greatest admiration for you. You are a credit to this team and, might I say, a benefit to the world at large. Because of these qualities, the owners of this team have come to a decision. We realized that you have proven to be a man worthy of your freedom. Worthy to make your own choices in life. Therefore, we, the owners of the Black Diamond Team, are cancelling your debt to us and extending to you your freedom as a legitimate free man in Roman society! Congratulations, free man!"

Alexander jerked stiff, completely stunned. The entire team was shocked. No one had expected this striking gift to be bestowed upon Alexander, especially so close after his scintillating victory on the race track. Jake looked at Hannah, his eyes wide in surprise, a big smile crossed his lips, and his eyebrows arching high on his forehead. Hannah placed one hand up to her mouth in disbelief and grabbed her husband's hand with the other.

Diotrephes spoke to the whole team. "After my experience of repentance and surrendering my life to Christ, I no longer could continue my former practice of owning a slave. After all, Jesus has set me free from the slavery of sin and now I am truly free! Octavius and Linus, who also have become Christians, likewise agreed that setting Alexander free is the right thing to do. In fact, Alexander is a Christian. How could three Christian team owners, who have been freed from the slavery of sin by the Lord Jesus, continue to own a slave! We could not! Alexander is our brother in Christ! And I know that many of you on the team have likewise become Christians! Truly this day has been a fantastic day of blessings!"

Alexander stood speechless. He looked at Diotrephes with gratefulness radiating from his expression. In a swell of emotions, Alexander bowed his head and began to cry in happiness. At length, he finally was able to speak.

"I don't know what to say, accept … thank you," he spoke, his voice choking. Wiping tears away he smiled and said, "Something wonderful has happened to this team. We have always been a great group of guys who are bonded together because of our love of racing and our one vision to win races. But something much deeper has merged us together. It's Christ. Many of us on this team have become Christians. And it is the Christian ideas and teachings that has created a new freshness to our team. A new purpose. We've all felt it. Even those of you who are still considering becoming Christians, I am sure, have felt the difference Christianity has created in the midst of our team."

Caleb spoke up. "I know what you mean. I only recently surrendered my life to Christ and my whole attitude toward life has changed. I know Jesus has promised me eternal life. That fact brightens my every moment of life every day!"

"So, what will you do with your new found freedom?" asked Octavius.

Alexander thought for a moment. "Wow! This is all new to me! A real shock! I do know I want to continue driving for the Black Diamond Team, if you'll have me. This sport is my first love. It is a dangerous sport. But I love the competition. And I love the horses and being around horses. I want to continue living around these wonderful animals. I've always loved horses, even from the time I was a little boy, hanging around the few horses my father owned, as a tradesman.

"But now, as a freed man, there is one final action I know I must do. There is one part of my past life I must bring to a close. That is, I must travel back to Jerusalem and tell Pastor James, my Christian mentor, that I have discovered Jesus Christ's mission for me in life. Through some very strange twists and turns in my life, I have found a means of ministering for Christ through racing."

"Alright," said Diotrephes. "I know that is something you must do. I will go with you to confirm to James that we have released you from being a slave and that you are now a free man!"

"Well," Jake remarked, "Hannah and I must also accompany you back to Jerusalem. There is some unfinished business I must finalize with James, as well. The Jerusalem church's prayers have been answered. But maybe not in the way they thought."

"Well, Alexander, we are going to allow you make that trip to Jerusalem," Diotrephes smiled, "just as long as you come back! But first let's all celebrate your great victory today in winning The Golden Cup of Caesar special race! This is a day of fantastic accomplishment. Alexander is the celebrated winner! And this calls for a day of festivity in honor of his winning the race and also for him being set free!"

The entire team applauded. As the hubbub subsided, the team began to disperse and head back into the city of Caesarea. Team owners, Octavius and Linus, hefted the beautiful gold cup trophy and led the precession into the city.

Jake and Hannah lingered for a moment in the stable, watching the

Black Diamond Racing Team as they left, happily talking and joking with each other.

Suddenly, like a flash of lighting revelation, Jake looked at his wife and said with amazement written on his face. "Now, I finally get it!" he exclaimed

"Get what?"

"I think the Lord has just helped me put all the pieces together about this mystery."

"What mystery?"

"The mystery of The Black Diamond," Jake said with a glint in his eye. "Hannah, I think I have just realized what the mystery of The Black Diamond is. It's the mystery of how God used The Black Diamond to draw all these people into a saving knowledge of Jesus Christ. It was no accident. God put this all together. He planned it out to the smallest and final detail. It's a mystery story God wrote!

"The Lord, in His infinite wisdom, brought Alexander here to Samaria as a slave. Then He directed us here in search of him. God immediately guided us to the Black Diamond Racing Team, which then led us straight to Alexander. And because of The Black Diamond itself and our recovery of it when it was stolen, Diotrephes gained a lasting trust in us. His trust in us allowed us to share Christ with him and then to all the guys on the team. And salvation fell on the team! It is obvious! What Satan meant for evil to Alexander, God meant it for good. And now we see God's salvation spreading out into many people's lives!"

Hannah burst out in laughter, "God used The Black Diamond for His perfect plan! It's the stuff that hope and eternal life are made of!"

And she was right!

ADDENDUM

That's Why God Sent His Son
By Donald Craig Miller

When you love somebody,
You will go to all extremes,
To show the one you love,
Just how much they really mean.

That's why God sent His Son,
To show how much He cares,
And I know He really loves me,
'Cause He gave His Son, my sins to bear.

So on the cross of Calvary,
He bled and died for all my sin,
So one day I would learn to love Him,
And have God's new life within.

That's why God sent His Son,
To show how much He cares,
And I know He really loves me,
'Cause He gave His Son, my sins to bear.

Blessed be the God and Father,
Of our Lord, our Lord Jesus Christ,
Who has given, us new hope,
With His gift, of eternal life.

Now I have, all His possessions,
His faith, His love, His grace, His power,
His unmatched peace, His gentle kindness,
His mercy, and His strength each hour.

That's why God sent His Son,
To show how much He cares,
And I know He really loves me,
'Cause He gave His Son, my sins to bear.

ABOUT THE AUTHOR

Donald Craig Miller has been writing Christian papers for local churches and newsletters for 50 years. His Christian writing was a result of attending a Billy Graham writing school in Minneap-olis in 1971. This experience encouraged him to develop his already growing desire to write and redirect his desire toward glorifying the Lord Jesus Christ in his writings. Through the coopera-tion of pastors, he has been able to write for church newsletters and bulletin inserts for churches in the Dayton, Ohio area and more recently in the Macon and Warner Robins, Georgia area.

Donald Craig Miller also has been a Bible teacher for over 50 years, teaching in Sunday School and church settings, in home Bible studies, and as a lay preacher. He found Christ through The Navigators while stationed at Kadena AFB in Okinawa. Not long after accepting Christ, Mr. Miller realized that God had gifted him with the gift of teaching. From then on his great desire has been to dig scriptural truth from the Bible and pass it on to other Christians, much like Ezra of the Old Testament. Based on these years of teaching, the life of Christ has especially come alive for Mr. Miller. His desire is to translate his passion for the life of Christ into the lives of his readers. In his first book, Trailing the Bloody Footprints, Mr. Miller's desire was to awaken a new, fresh love for Jesus Christ using the novel approach of seeing Jesus through the eyes of a first century detective, Jake Jezreel. In his sequel, Terror Outside The Door (The Persecution of Jesus Christ), Mr. Miller continues the story through the eyes of the same first century detective. The reader is launched into the early church's desperate fight for survival, as the religious leaders attack, attempting to destroy Christianity.

In The Mystery of the Black Diamond, Mr. Miller portrays his first century detective as a man, growing in his faith, who is trying every day to live for the Lord Jesus. Mr. Miller's desire is for the reader to find a place of affinity with the detective as he struggles with everyday choices and in his learning to grow in his love for Jesus.

Lightning Source UK Ltd.
Milton Keynes UK
UKHW011834040621
384966UK00007B/714/J